MIND Games

LOSING IS NOT AN OPTION...

DIONNE ELLISON

To my parents
(Mary & Harvey)
I love and miss you dearly.

To my son Noah,
you make me very proud,
I love being your mom!

Chapter

1

The windshield wipers were going crazy, making that notorious, nerve-racking, scraping sound. The rain was coming down in buckets and visibility was poor. Parris was gripping the steering wheel so hard, her knuckles were aching. Between the tears and the rain, she could barely see three feet in front of the car. Fighting her emotions like a boxer with his belt on the line, Parris replayed what had taken place over and over again in her head. How could he do this to her? This wasn't the way it was supposed to turn out, she thought. Looking back, there were signs, but like most women, she ignored them or let's just say they were stored in her memory bank for recall on demand. She did everything she could not to appear insecure and God forbid she acted anything like the last women he was involved with. She knew you had to pick and choose your battles in relationships. After what had just taken place, all of her efforts to make things work between them were mute. None of it mattered anymore. The tears continued to run down her face as she thought about the mysterious phone calls, business trips and late hours at the office. She felt like a fool.

The anonymous package had arrived at her door just in time. She was unsure if the nameless person sent the package to hurt her or save her from making the biggest mistake of her life. Either way, she was crushed. She could not imagine who the sender was and right now, she didn't care. All she knew was that he could no longer deny it because now she had proof. She hated herself for not acting sooner, before all the wedding plans were confirmed. This time she should have listened to that little voice inside that told her something was not right. Some people say a woman always knows when her man is cheating, but this time, Parris was simply unsure or maybe just naive. She took pride in the fact that she did not bitch and nag her man, nor did she make it a habit of accusing him of things she could not prove. It was a waste of time and energy because a man will always instinctively maintain his innocence -- deny, deny, deny. Her mother told her a long time ago that if you bitch, you will get ditched. She wanted to trust her man and to some degree she did, maybe that was her mistake. Everyone says that communication and trust are the keys to a good relationship and she thought that's what they had, until now.

Parris knew that couples went through their share of trials and tribulations occasionally; she just didn't think it would ever happen to her, at least not like this, and certainly not with Victor. She was always very picky when it came to the men in her life, almost too picky. That's why her dates were so few and far between. But when she met Victor, he was different. He was everything she ever wanted in a man and more; he was handsome, successful and smart and let's not forget the fact that he was a great lover. She had only been in one other serious relationship before him and maybe that's why she didn't see it coming.

She always thought her father was the ideal man, husband and father figure. Parris thought Coleman Reed was every little girl's prince charming. He was handsome, distinguished, smart and funny too. As far as she was concerned, the man she decided to spend the rest of her life with would have to be pretty damn close to Coleman Reed's twin. Victor Baxter was that twin or so she thought, because now he was looking more like the evil stepbrother.

They met a little over a year ago at a mutual friend's party. Sean Edwards was Victor's childhood friend and Parris' new co-worker. Parris had just started working for a large insurance company downtown. This was the dream job she had been working and waiting for. All of her networking had finally paid off. The Director of Human Resources position practically dropped into her lap, like most things in Parris's life. She was a stranger to rejection and that sometimes made her feel vulnerable. Fortunately, her exceptional interpersonal and communication skills had a way of smothering those insecurities when they occasionally tried to resurface.

After a month on the job, Sean started taking an interest in her. She had seen it coming and was bracing herself, hoping he would take it like a man when she turned him down. First the subtle nods and waves in the hallway or on the elevator, then it escalated to small talk about the weather in the break room. Her corner office was directly across from the break room which gave him an excuse to pass by several times day. She could tell he was intimidated, because he still couldn't muster up the nerve to formally introduce himself. So, one morning Parris decided to put him out of his misery and break the ice. She got up from her desk, adjusted her skirt and headed towards the break room.

"Hi, I'm Parris Reed." she said extending her hand.

"Sean Edwards, would you like to have dinner tonight?"

Completely caught off guard, Parris spilled some coffee on the counter as she poured it into her mug that read; *Geminis are twice as nice*!

"Excuse me?" She said reaching for a paper towel.

"I said, I'm Sean Edwards and this coffee's just right." He said with a nervous smile.

That's when she noticed his front teeth needed some work.

"It's not as good as Dunkin Donuts, but it serves the purpose. Nice to meet you Sean Edwards." She said taking a sip before she walked out the room.

"Congratulations on your new position!"

"Thank you." She said not bothering to turn around.

The phone rang as soon as she sat down at her desk. She pressed the speaker button to answer it.

"Parris Reed."

"Good morning Pumpkin, how's the new job going?"

"Hey Mom, I'm sorry I didn't get a chance to call you back the other night, I've just been so busy trying to get settled."

"That's okay, you just treat your mother any ole kinda way." The sweet voice said with a chuckle.

Parris picked up the receiver and took another sip of her coffee, ignoring the last comment.

"How's Daddy?" she asked as she logged onto her laptop.

"He's fine; he's out playing golf as usual. Are you still coming for dinner on Sunday?" her mother asked.

"Yes, I might even go to church with you."

"Well, praise the Lord!"

"Oh, would you stop; you make it sound like I'm a heathen. Just because I don't go *every* Sunday like you do, doesn't mean I'm going to hell!"

Before her mother could respond, another phone line started ringing.

"Ma, I've gotta go, oh and by the way, the job is great. I'll see you on Sunday. Love you."

"I love you too Pumpkin."

This new job kept her busy. It was only eleven-thirty and Parris had already finished two meetings and a conference call that she thought would never end. Her predecessor was terribly unorganized and left behind a big mess. Parris hated disorder, this was one of her many pet-peeves. She insisted everything had its place and should be returned there when not in use. The first meeting was to restore order and set the precedence for her staff of three. An older woman, named Gladys Slater; a young mother of two, named Maria Torres, who was her secretary and a recent college grad named Paul Pruett. The meeting ran smoothly, Parris was direct, but friendly. They were very receptive and things looked like they were going to work out fine.

By noon, Parris' stomach was growling, so she started looking over a few lunch menus. That's when Sean popped his head in her office.

"Hi Parris, do you have plans for lunch?"

Parris looked up and smiled, but didn't answer right away.

"It is Parris, right?"

"Yes, and as a matter of fact, I don't have plans."

"Would you like to grab a bite?"

"Sure, I'll meet you by the elevators in five minutes. I just need to use the ladies room."

"Great!" he said exposing those crooked teeth again.

Center City Philadelphia was full of folks hustling to and fro at lunch time. Landmarks like the "Love" statue and the "Clothes Pin" were near City Hall and made for prime people-watching spots. As they walked down Chestnut Street, Sean suggested Chinese, Parris agreed. Their conversation was general and impersonal for the first thirty-minutes. Parris was very conscience not to give him the wrong impression. He wasn't her type and even if he was, she was convinced that inter-office affairs always ended in disaster. The fact that his teeth were crooked and he waited too long in between haircuts, made it easy for her to keep things friendly. Her best friend always tells her that she's too superficial, but Parris explained to her friend that she just wants someone who takes as much pride in his appearance as she does, simple as that. He wasn't an ugly guy, just average. Average height and weight, but appeared to be in good physical condition. His caramel skin matched his caramel eyes that were actually kind of nice. Maybe, if he kept his hair cut and got braces, better yet, Invisaline, he wouldn't be half bad Parris thought to herself. During the next half hour, Sean decided to test the waters and get a little more personal.

"Are you originally from Philly?" he asked.

"I was born here, but raised in Jersey."

"Oh yeah, what part?

"Cherry Hill."

"It's nice out there. I have a buddy that lives out there."

"How about you? Are you a Philly native?"

"Born and raised. I love this city."

There was a comfortable silence for a minute or two while they finished their meals. The waitress asked if they needed anything else. They both replied and she started clearing the table.

"Do you have plans on Saturday night?" Sean asked with some hesitation.

"I'm not sure, why?" she said curious to see if he had the balls to ask her out again.

"Well, I'm having a little party, no big deal, just some friends and family. I thought you might like to come."

"Thanks for the invite, but I..."

"Look Parris, before you start making up excuses, relax. It's just a friendly invitation, no pressure. You seem like a nice person who has their shit together and I like surrounding myself with positive people."

"What time?" She replied, relieved that she didn't have to go through her let-him-down-easy speech.

"What time what?"

"What time's the party silly?"

"Any time after eight." He replied.

"Cool, I'll be there. Send me an email with the directions when we get back to the office."

"Will do. Thanks Parris for joining me. I really enjoyed your company."

"Me too."

Sean insisted on paying, and then they headed back to the office. As soon as Parris got to her desk, Maria handed her a stack of messages and some file folders.

"Brian Williams says he needs those 401k updates as soon as possible and Catherine wants to meet around three." Maria rattled off.

"Okay. Can you print a copy of the updates and I'll take it with me to the staff meeting. Thanks Maria."

"Sure, no problem. Oh, Parris, my youngest is sick and has a doctor's appointment at four-thirty today. Do you mind if I leave early? I'm sorry? I know its last minute, but it was the only time they could fit me in."

"Sure Maria. Do what you have to do. I believe family comes first. I hope he's okay."

"Me too. He has a terrible cough that won't go away." She said looking concerned.

"In that case you should definitely let a doctor take a look at him." She replied sorting through the pink slips.

"Do you have any children?"

"No, not yet, I want at least one, but I've gotta get a husband first."

"Hey, I've got one, they're overrated." Maria replied as she walked back to her desk.

She had twelve new emails, the first of which was Sean's with the directions. She smiled to herself reflecting on their conversation at lunch. She thought Sean seemed like a nice guy, as she gazed out of her twenty-eighth floor window. Unfortunately, being nice doesn't always get you dinner and a movie, but it might get you a lunch date. It's a shame our society is so focused on looks, she thought feeling guilty.

The sound of the stack of files hitting the desk snapped her back to reality.

"The meeting's in Room 215." Maria said. "You should be all set. I'm going to head out in about twenty minutes. I'll see you tomorrow."

"Okay, thanks, have a good night. I'm going to head up to the meeting right now."

She did a quick lipstick check, quickly refreshed it, grabbed her portfolio and the copies and headed for the meeting.

Chapter

2

The week was moving slow and the weekend seemed like it would never come. By three o'clock on Friday afternoon, Parris was ready to relax and have some fun. She was finally getting settled at work and feeling good. She called her best friend Shelly and arranged to meet after work for some drinks. With Sean's permission, she invited Shelly to go with her on Saturday to the party. She was actually excited about having something different to do for a change.

Shelly was going to meet her at The Swag on Walnut Street. The place was packed with a professional after-work crowd trying to unwind from a long week. Parris arrived a little early; tardiness was another one of her pet-peeves. She decided to order a drink and an appetizer while she waited. Within ten minutes, three men approached her either inviting themselves to join her or asking her to join them, all of which she found unappealing for one reason or another. Parris could never understand why some men, especially the not so attractive ones, couldn't read a woman's body language and take a hint. Maybe we should all carry a sign that says, "I'M NOT INTERESTED. DON'T GO AWAY MAD, JUST GO AWAY!"

When Shelly walked through the door, damn near every head turned. She was looking sharp, as usual. She was slim, short and sassy. If you looked up the word 'sex-kitten' in the dictionary, there was a picture of Shelly. Cat eyes, high cheek bones and perfect teeth combined with her fit and curvy body made her the envy of women and the lusty fantasy of most men. Showing enough leg and cleavage to make both L'eggs and Wonder Bra proud, Shelly made her way over to Parris' table.

"Hey girl, what's up?"

"You know, same ole, same ole. What took you so damn long, every Jimmy-Crack-Corn in here has asked for your seat."

"You always did attract the corny guys." Shelly said with a chuckle.

"That's because all of the fly guys where in a trance from staring at your boobs!"

"Don't hate. Just go get surgery like everyone else who's not naturally endowed."

"Girl, you know I'm scared of the knife. Besides I like my small breasts." Parris replied fixing her blouse.

"So do the corny guys."

They both laughed and Shelly got the waitress' attention and ordered two glasses of Chardonnay. For the next two hours, they sipped several glasses of wine, laughed and caught up with each others lives. They met in college and have been the best of friends ever since. Parris is a great talker and Shelly is a great listener. Parris is tall, Shelly is short. Parris has brown skin, Shelly's is light. The one big difference between them that wasn't so obvious was their taste in men. Shelly likes the fly-guys, while Parris went for the more conservative, professional types. There was never any concern about falling for the same guy, which is key, if two women are going to hang out together.

Three years ago, when Shelly's mother died of cancer, Parris was there to help pull her through. They were very close and Shelly was devastated. She didn't leave the house for two weeks after the funeral and Parris was the only person she would talk to. Since then, their friendship has been stronger than ever.

"So, what does what's his name look like?" Shelly asked while she was making eyes at some guy at the bar.

"Who, Sean? Girl, please, he's N.Y.T." (Not Your Type)

"Well, I hope his party isn't gonna be more of the same, because there's nothing worse than wasting a Saturday night."

"Amen to that!" Parris replied saluting her glass. "Hopefully he has some cute friends."

Just as Parris was about to take another bite of her buffalo wing, a brother with dreds walked up to the table and asked if he could buy them both a drink. Before Parris could finish chewing, Shelly had accepted, ordered and invited him to sit down.

"So, how are you ladies this evening?" Rasta man asked, clearly directing his question to Shelly's breasts.

"Fine now, I'm Shelly and this is my friend Parris."

"I'm Kyle, nice to meet you."

"Likewise."

Since Parris didn't have to worry about holding a conversation, she continued to get her grub on. Right on time, the waitress brought over two Cosmopolitans and a Heineken. Parris took a sip and thanked Kyle for the drinks. Shelly was flashing those pearly whites putting Kyle in a trance, so Parris took the opportunity to use the ladies room. She didn't realize how buzzed she was until she tried to squat over the toilet and almost lost her balance.

"Oh shit! It's time for me to go."

Back at the table, Kyle and Shelly were exchanging numbers.

"Parris are you ready to go?" Shelly asked.

"Whenever you are?"

"Aw, you're not gonna leave me now are you beautiful?" Kyle asked looking genuinely disappointed.

"Yes, I am, but you've got the digits, so I'm sure I'll be seeing you again soon." Shelly said as she stood up and grabbed her purse.

"It was nice meeting you Kyle." Parris said following behind Shelly.

When they got outside, the air was warm and even though it was after midnight, folks were still coming in.

"He's a cutie Shell."

"Yeah well, we'll see if he's got a program to go with those good looks."

Parris confirmed what time Shelly should be at her house tomorrow night. She was notorious for being late and did not care who she kept waiting.

"If you're not at my house by eight-fifteen, I'm leaving without you, I mean it."

"Don't worry, I'll be on time, I promise. And you're not leaving anybody, especially me, so stop talkin' trash."

"Okay, we'll see."

They hugged and headed in opposite directions to their cars. When Parris crossed the bridge into Jersey, traffic was still heavy on Rt.42 with everyone heading for the Atlantic City and Wildwood for the weekend. She popped in her Maxwell CD to make the slow ride home more pleasurable. His smooth, sexy voice, along with her buzz, made her wish there was a handsome hunk with a glass of wine and candlelight waiting for her when she got home.

To her dismay, no hunk, no wine and no candlelight. Just a hot, stuffy house nicely decorated. She immediately kicked off her pumps and took off her suit jacket as she flipping through the mail.

"Bills, junk mail and more bills. What else is new?"

She grabbed a bottle of spring water from the refrigerator and headed for the bathroom. The bathroom was Parris' favorite room in the house, her get-away-from-it-all. This was the one place she could spend hours, so when she was looking for a townhouse, there were two things she could not live without, a large bathroom with a Jacuzzi and a garage. She had to pay a little more to have the Jacuzzi installed, but it was well worth it.

Just as she was ready to step into the tub, the phone rang.

"Damn it!" she ran naked into the bedroom to pick up.

"Hello!" She said sounding annoyed.

"Cool, I'm home too. Bye." Shelly said and hung up.

"She is so crazy." Parris said looking at the dead phone.

She returned to the bathroom, this time bringing the cordless with her. The wall behind the large whirlpool tub was completely mirrored. Parris liked to get the full view of her body, this way she could take note of what needed to be toned up. Her mother taught her how to enhance her best features and tone down the others. She was 5'9" and 150 pounds with a decent figure. Her sense of style, accompanied by her soft features made her easy on the eyes. Her dark almond shaped eyes and smooth chocolate skin were an enchanting combination. She had hips and a butt like her mother and small breasts like the women on her father's side of the family. Overall, she thought she looked pretty damn good for twenty-nine.

"Twenty-nine, good job, no kids and you still don't have a man. What is your problem girl?" She said to her reflection.

When she finished her bubble bath, she put on a wife-beater and some shorts. It was still about 75 degrees outside and about 85 in the house. Parris couldn't sleep with the air on; it made her sinuses congested, so ceiling fans were in every room. Her buzz was wearing off, but she took some aspirin anyway to avoid a headache in the morning.

Every Saturday morning, Parris had a routine that was rarely broken. Walk three miles on the treadmill, clean the house and do the laundry. Her house was decorated in a contemporary style. The furniture was black leather, with silver and red accents. Several pieces of artwork that had been purchased from different cities covered the walls. Parris enjoyed bringing home souvenirs from vacation that she could decorate with.

Saturday afternoon was spent on the pamper treatment; manicure, pedicure and a facial at the salon. She decided she would even get her eyebrows waxed since she had a party to go to later. It was almost six o'clock by the time she got out of the salon. She figured she better check on Shelly and make sure she was going to be on time. Careful not to mess up her nails, she grabbed her cell phone from her handbag.

"Hey Shell, what are you doing?

"I'm in the mall trying to find something to wear tonight, but I'm not having any luck."

"How 'bout you?"

"I just left the salon and I'm stopping by the supermarket to pick up a few things. You need anything?"

"No thanks. What are you wearing?"

"I think I'm gonna wear the new sundress I got from Lord & Taylor's. I hope he doesn't have the air conditioner blasting because it's a halter and I don't want to be cold."

"What color is the… Oh my God, (whispering) Parris, if you could see this big-ass woman in these tiny-ass shorts, you would die! Now, she knows she's in violation."

"Stop talking about people and look for something to wear."

"I am. I am!" She replied giggling.

"And you better be on time Shelly!"

"Good-bye Parris!"

Her queen size bed was completely covered with almost every piece of clothing she owned. Shoes were all over the floor, sandals, mules, flats, and heels; you name it, it was out in every color you could image. Parris, like most women, thought you could never have too many shoes.

The phone rang as she was trying on the new sundress for the second time, this time with different shoes.

"Hello."

"Hi Pumpkin, you busy, you sound busy?" her mother asked.

"Kind of, Shelly and I are going to a party a co-worker of my mine is having and I can't figure out what to wear."

"Is the co-worker a man?"

"Yeah, why?"

"Then put on a dress." Her mother insisted.

"Oh Ma, he's not my type and besides we work together and you know I can't be bothered with that kind of drama. You remember what happened to Linda, right?"

"Yes, but Linda had issues before she even got involved with that man. Just put on a dress, a nice bright sundress or something. Lord knows it's hot enough and if I have another hot flash on top of this heat, I'm gonna hurt somebody."

"Don't you have the air on?" Parris asked trying on another pair of sandals.

"Yes chile, but it doesn't help. These flashes feel like your on fire! That air conditioner don't mean a thing!" she said sucking her teeth. "So, are there going to be some eligible men at this party?"

"I hope so." Parris replied.

"Me too, so put on a dress and a high heel. You never know, one of his guests might be your type."

"You're right. The sundress it is." She said whirling around in the mirror.

Her mother continued to chit-chat about her day and update her on all the activities going on at the church. Meanwhile, Parris was trying on different accessories to go with the dress.

"Alright, you go ahead and get ready. Your Aunt Mary just walked in with her crazy self. And hang all those clothes up before you leave. I know that room's a mess!"

"Yes mother. Tell Aunt Mary I said hello."

"I will, you and Shelly be careful and have fun. And Parris, the man don't have to be perfect because there ain't no such thing."

"I know Ma; I'm not looking for perfection, just Mr. Right. Give Daddy a kiss and I'll talk to you later."

Parris threw the phone on the bed and quickly began hanging up the other outfits like her mother said. She was amazed how much mother's opinion and values still influenced her. The shoes would have to wait, no time she thought glancing at the clock. The dress was a little wrinkled, so she plugged in the iron. The phone rang again.

"What are you wearing Parris?"

"The sundress. What are you wearing?"

"It's between this denim mini dress or my black capris. Which one? Is this thing dressy or what?"

"I'm not sure, but Mommy says go with the dress."

"Cool. Mommy's always right. See ya in about twenty minutes."

She quickly ran the iron over the ice blue dress and started accessorizing. Silver and platinum were her favorites. The larger the hoops the better, accompanied by an anklet and a toe ring, finished off with a pair of pewter mules. Her hair was short and freshly done, so it didn't require much fuss. The style was similar to Toni Braxton's when she first came on the scene. Her skin was flawless and only required the accents of a little eyeliner and mascara. Lipstick and perfume completed the look and she was ready to go.

It was 8:10pm and Shelly had five minutes. Parris made sure she had the directions, her keys and lipstick. Now all she had to do is wait and try not to start sweating. 8:22pm Shelly pulled up in the driveway. Parris opened the door with purse and keys in hand.

"Only seven minutes late. That dress is really pretty P, the color looks really good on you."

"Thanks, your hoochie momma dress looks good too." She joked.

"Very funny. Don't knock it, till you try it."

"Do I need a bra? I feel a little self-conscious with this halter."

"Girl please, those itty-bitty's don't need to be all cooped up. You look great! You see I've got my girls out for a good cause." Shelly said grabbing her breasts."

"You are so wild. Let's go tramp."

"Yes, lets, because I'm about to melt in here. Parris, you really need to turn on the air. Damn!"

Chapter

4

Sean lives in a section of Philly called Mt. Airy. This was one of the few neighborhoods left in the city where most folks kept their property up and there were single homes with yards. You could hear music from the street and it looked like some of his guests were outside in the backyard. When Parris rang the doorbell, a friendly looking, heavy-set sister with a blonde weave opened the door.

"Hi, come on in, Sean's out back. I'm Pam, let me know if you need anything!" she said sounding like the perfect hostess.

"Hi, I'm Parris and this is my friend Shelly."

The living room was full of people, some were playing cards others were watching music videos. Everyone was eating and drinking and clearly enjoying themselves. More folks were in the kitchen, two older women were preparing food. A thin gray haired woman was shucking corn on the cob and introduced herself as Sean's mother. It was obvious that he had told her about Parris because she knew who exactly who she was.

"You must be Parris and you're just as pretty as he described."

"Thank you. This is my best friend Shelly."

"Pleased to meet you both, I'm Sean's mother Bertha, but you can call me Bert; this is my sister Cassie and her daughter Anita."

Each of them was preparing a different dish. Cassie was cutting up onions to mix into the potato salad and Anita was seasoning the chicken.

"Sean is outside quein', go on out and have a good time baby. Whatever you want to drink is down in the basement, my other son Darryl is playing bartender. The food will be ready shortly. Don't be shy, go on now!" Bert insisted.

As soon as they stepped out onto the patio, all heads turned in their direction. The backyard was decorated with multi-colored Christmas lights and tiny tea candles. It was a beautiful summer night and there was a full moon. The atmosphere was warm and mellow. There was an even mixture of men and women for a change. Usually, there are too many women and not enough men or vice versa. This was obviously an adults-only party because there wasn't one child running around the house or yard. Sean was in front of the grill "queing", as his mother put it and talking to three other guys. As soon as he saw Parris, he signaled for them to come over.

"I don't know P, looks like we might have some prospects by the grill." Shelly whispered.

"Let's wait until they turn around before we get happy. I feel overdressed; I should have put on my jeans." She whispered back.

"I don't, you gotta look your best at all times, because…

"You never know!" they both said in unison.

As they approached the grill, Sean was grinning from ear to ear and obviously surprised that Parris had come.

"Hey Parris, glad you could make it. How were my directions? Did you have a problem finding it?" he said giving her a hug.

"No, not at all. The directions were perfect and even if they weren't, you can hear the music all the way down the street. Sean, this is Shelly, Shelly, this is Sean."

"Hi. I hope you know what you're doing on that grill." Shelly teased.

"Don't worry baby, I've got it all under control. I'm a master when it comes to grillin'."

One of the three men thought Sean was taking way to long to introduce, so he took it upon himself.

"Hello ladies. I'm Tim."

"Hi, I'm Parris and this is Shelly."

"Hello." Shelly replied looking in the other direction.

The other two men were sort of off to the side, busy laughing about something and didn't appear interested in making acquaintances, but bold-ass Shelly insisted.

"Sean, aren't you going to introduce us to the rest of your friends?" she said loud enough for them to hear.

"Oh yeah, my bad. Yo! Vic, Kev, stop being so rude and introduce yourselves to the ladies."

When he turned around, it was like the music had stopped and everything was in slow motion. If this scene had been video taped, the replay would show Parris frozen with her mouth open and drooling. The man standing before her was truly a vision to behold. He was around 6'2", and whatever he weighed, it was just right; he had broad shoulders and a six o'clock shadow. His skin was a smooth light-brown complexion with dark eyes and long lashes. His haircut was fresh and cut close. He had on a pair of tan linen pants and a crisp, white linen shirt hanging loosely over his muscular shoulders. His sandals were brown and didn't expose too much toe. Parris wasn't positive, but she swore he looked just like Mr. Right.

For the first time in the history of their friendship, both Parris and Shelly were awestruck by the same man. The one named Kevin was the first to speak and break their spell.

"My apologies ladies, I'm Kevin and this is my buddy Victor."

Both Parris and Shelly acknowledged Kevin with smiles and nods, but never took their eyes off of this gorgeous man who went by the name of Victor.

"How are you this evening?" Victor answered in smooth baritone voice, with his dreamy eyes focusing on Parris.

"Just fine, now." Shelly quickly answered.

"Can I get you ladies something to drink?" Kevin asked.

"That would be nice." Parris answered never taking her eyes off of Victor.

"Come on, I'll show you to the bar." Kevin said as he gently grabbed Shelly's arm.

"P, what do you want?" Shelly asked sounding reluctant to leave present company.

"Whatever you get is fine." She replied, relieved that Kevin didn't grab her arm.

"P?" Victor asked.

"It's short for Parris. Parris Reed." She said extending her right hand.

"It's pleasure to meet you Parris Reed." He answered shaking her hand, but not letting go.

"Alright Vic, before you start your "Mac Daddy" routine, go tell Mom I'm ready for the chicken." Sean said sounding a little jealous.

Sean was turning over the steaks as flames flooded the grill. Parris was thankful for the interruption; she needed a minute to get herself together. She also got to check out the rear view as he strolled into the kitchen. His back side was just as nice as the front.

"I'm really glad you came. For a minute I didn't think you would show."

Parris didn't respond. She was still looking at the door waiting for Victor to come back out.

"Parris. Hello, earth to Parris."

"Oh, I'm sorry Sean, what did you say?"

"I said, you look very nice tonight."

"Thanks. I'm sorry I was a little distracted by your friend."

"Who? Victor?" Sean replied unenthused. "He's a pro when it comes to getting all the attention."

"A pro? What's his deal? And please don't tell me he's married or gay!"

"No, he's divorced and definitely not gay. He's the friend I was telling you about who lives in Cherry Hill."

"Well then what's wrong with him?"

"Nothing's wrong with him and I guess he just hasn't found the right woman. Why do women always think something's gotta be wrong?"

"Because it's usually true, there's always something wrong." She insisted. "I believe that when a man reaches a certain age and his maturity and financial status have reached a certain level, it's inevitable that he will want a woman to share his life with. When he doesn't, something is wrong."

"Maybe, maybe not. He could just be waiting for the right woman to come along." Sean replied.

Shelly, Kevin and Victor all returned at the same time. Shelly had what looked like two Vodka & tonics in hand, while the guys had beers.

"Man, where's the chicken?" Sean asked Victor.

"Ma Bert said she'd bring it out when it was ready." Victor replied.

Parris noticed he had dimples. Whatever was wrong with this man must be mental, because everything on the outside was flawless and he was looking more and more like Mr. Right.

Chapter

5

Sean definitely knew how to throw a party. Sean was truly a grill master, his mom was a good cook and even his drunk brother Darryl was pouring drinks like a pro. The mosquitoes were taking over the backyard, so Sean suggested they eat down in the basement where it was much cooler. The room was decorated with a 70's theme; bean-bags and red lights brought back memories for everyone.

Kevin and Shelly seemed to be hitting it off; he was catering to her every need. He was nice looking and a little more conservative than she preferred, but she seemed to be enjoying his company and conversation. Sometimes a woman needs to experiment with the unfamiliar for a balance. Little did he know that once he started this pamper treatment, Shelly wasn't going to let him off the hook. Not only did he refresh her drink, he fixed her plate to top it off. Needless to say, Shelly was having a good time.

Meanwhile, Parris, Victor and Sean were sitting at the bar eating and talking about their jobs. She found out that Victor was an entertainment lawyer. He told several interesting stories about his clients, some of which were well known, from Hip-Hop artists to Broadway performers. He commuted to New York daily and did not seem to mind. Parris admired him for his dedication and it was clear he was very passionate about his work. When Sean's mom called him to come upstairs, he reluctantly excused himself and Victor took the opportunity to get to know more about Parris.

"Do you live here in Philly?"

"No, Jersey and I was told we're practically neighbors."

"Really?"

"Yes, I live in Voorhees."

"You're kidding. Sean always gives me a hard time about Jersey, but it's clean and quite. And that's just what I need after a day of dealing with New Yorkers."

"I bet. How do you do it everyday? I don't think I have the patience for that kind of commute."

"It's not that bad once you get used to it. I take the train because driving is completely out of the question. On the train, I get a chance to go over my cases without interruption. I stay up there some times if I have to work late. How about you? How do you like the new job?" he asked.

"So far, so good. My staff appears to be competent; I have a great view from my office and the money's good. No complaints here, at least not yet."

"I heard that. I'm glad someone else likes their job besides me." He said with a smile. Then he glanced at his watch.

"I know this might sound rushed, but I have to leave and I would really like to see you again. Would that be possible?" he asked.

Parris was wondering if this man was crazy or stupid. He didn't really think she would say no, did he? Rushed? What rush? She was wondering what took him so long.

"I would like that very much." She said in a sexy tone.

She grabbed one of her business cards from her purse and wrote down her home and cell phone numbers, this way he couldn't lie and say he couldn't reach her. He took the card and put it in his shirt pocket without even looking at it. Then without saying a word, he stood up and took her hand in his. He guided her to her feet, so they were facing each other. The smell of his cologne made Parris want to wrap her arms and legs around him and never let go.

"Until next time." He whispered in her ear as he pressed his hard chest against her breasts as they hugged.

"Until next time." She replied as they separated.

"Oh and by the way, the dress is awesome." He said, then winked his eye and headed for the stairs.

Parris felt like she was on top of the world. Some mothers really do know best she thought to herself. She found herself staring at the stairs and basking in his lingering scent. It wasn't until a husky man sitting in the corner let out a hardy laugh that Parris snapped out of her daze. She didn't even notice that Shelly and Kevin must have gone upstairs too. She took a deep breath and went upstairs find out where everyone had disappeared to.

They were all was sitting around the dining room table playing the board game Taboo. Shelly absolutely loved that game. It was her turn and she was so animated and funny as she tried to describe the word "picnic" without saying the other words on her card. She was having a great night too and Parris knew that their ride home would be full of laughs as they filled each other in on the details. When Shelly saw Parris, she motioned for her to play along.

"No thanks, I'm okay." Parris said motioning back for her to join her outside.

The buzzer when off before anyone on Shelly's team guessed the word.

"Damn, yall stink!" She said laughing and then excused herself from the game and grabbed Parris' arm as they walked towards the backyard.

"Girl, please tell me he got your number before he left."

"Yes."

"My girl! So was his conversation as good as his looks?"

"Better. He's an attorney with a firm in New York."

"Jackpot! We can save the juicy stuff for the car." She said laughing.

"How about Kevin, Queen of Sheba? Did he go to the bathroom for you too? Damn, I've never seen a man's nose so wide open after an introduction." She teased.

"I told you, don't knock the hoochie-momma gear 'til you try it!" She teased back.

"Are you ready to go?" Parris asked.

"Whenever you are, but let's have one more drink for the sistahs who know how to work it!"

They ended up staying another hour, Shelly begged Parris to play one round of Taboo. When Parris' team won, Shelly was ready to go. Sean and Kevin walked them to the car.

"Sean, thanks for inviting me, I had a ball." Parris said.

"I'm really glad you came. We'll have to do it again soon." He replied.

"Your mother is sweet; she knew exactly who I was."

"She didn't embarrass you, did she?"

"No, not at all. It was cute. Make sure you tell her I said the food was delicious!" Parris said unlocking the car doors.

Shelly and Kevin were saying their good-byes on the other side of the car. He kissed her on the lips before she got into the car. Parris gave

Sean a quick hug and got in too. Sean stood in the middle of the street and watched the car disappear.

"It looks like there was a love connection between you guys. Am I right?" Parris asked opening the sunroof.

"Can't you put the air on?" Shelly asked ignoring her question.

"No. It's a beautiful, warm summer night."

"It's a hot and sticky summer night P, something must be wrong with your body temperature."

"Oh, so you're gonna ignore me? I thought we were gonna talk about the juicy stuff in the car."

Shelly started laughing.

"What? What's so funny?"

"Nothing." She replied still giggling.

"Come on Shell, tell me!"

"Okay." She paused. "Did you notice that Kevin and I disappeared for a while?"

"Kind of, why? Where'd you go?"

Shelly was silent.

"No!" Parris shouted. "Shell, you didn't, did you?"

"Well, um, not quite, but we were damn close!" She said laughing again.

"Girl, you are too much! I can't believe you were in Sean's house making out with some dude you just met." She said shaking her head in disbelief.

"P, we knew each other for two hours before any of that went down, so technically..."

"Don't even try it Shell, technically my ass! I ain't mad at you. I haven't been with a man in so long it's a shame."

"How long has it been?"

"Almost ten months." Parris hated to admit.

"Damn P! You really need to get some. I really hope Victor calls, because that is ridiculous!"

Parris spent the rest of the ride home thinking about Victor. She didn't want to admit it, but she really hoped he called too. She even said a little prayer to the man upstairs for backup.

Chapter

6

Bethany Baptist church was filling up quickly, but Helen Reed was saving a seat for her daughter, regardless of how many folks showed up and asked to sit. Coleman Reed just shook his head as he watched his wife tell them, one after another, that the seat was being saved. Parris finally arrived twenty minutes late, just as Reverend Williams was about to begin the sermon. Coleman gave is famous wink and nod as his daughter took her seat.

"What took you so long?" Helen whispered.

"I woke up late, sorry." She said giving her a kiss on the cheek.

Not only did Parris wake up late, but she had a pounding headache. That cheap Vodka will do it every time she thought. After about twenty minutes into the sermon, Parris' thoughts drifted to Victor. The recollection their conversation and the way his dimples appeared when he smiled made her smile too. She was wondering if he was a good kisser, when her mother nudged her to get the bible from the back of the pew. She needed Jesus and she knew it, fantasizing about a man in church, so she asked for forgiveness and tried to concentrate on the sermon.

During the ride to her parents, her cell phone rang. Butterflies immediately started to flutter in her stomach. She hoped it was Victor, but the caller ID read Shelly's number.

"Hey, do you have a headache? Because I do from that cheap-ass Vodka." Shelly said with an attitude.

"I do too. I woke up late and didn't hear a word Reverend Williams said. Did Kevin call you yet?"

"You know he did, we're meeting for dinner tonight at Christine's. How 'bout you?"

"No, not yet. Mommy's cooking, so I'm on my way over there now." Parris replied trying not to sound too disappointed.

"Don't worry, he will." Shelly said like she knew something.

"Well, I'm not going to get all excited about it. If he does, he does, and if he doesn't, he doesn't. No biggie. You know those Joe-Look-Good brothers are always trouble any way."

"Didn't you just leave church? Stop sounding so negative. Give the man a chance before you start doubting."

"Whatever." Parris replied.

"Tell your folks I said hello and I'll talk to you later P. Bye."

"Bye Shell."

Her parents owned a beautiful, four bedroom house in Marlton, New Jersey, about fifteen minutes from Parris. The sight of it made her remember running around the yard and catching lightening bugs with her younger sister, Kenya. She wondered if she was coming for dinner too. The "girls", as her father would say, were like night and day. Kenya was wild and irresponsible, the total opposite of Parris. There was a five year age difference and her parents were obviously tired of parenting by the time Kenya came along because she got away with things Parris couldn't even imagine doing when she was her age. At twenty-four, she surprisingly graduated from college and was now working in the mall at Nordstrom's department store. She was more worried about looking good and partying than a career. Parris was convinced that Kenya was waiting for her prince charming to ride up on a white horse and carry her away so she could live happily ever after.

Parris pulled up right behind her father's SUV in the driveway. It was hot and humid, so she thought she might take a swim before dinner. Helen insisted they keep some clothes in their old rooms; it made her feel like they never really left.

As soon as she stepped through the door, she could smell the roast beef cooking. The aroma was scrumptious. Her mother always put something in the oven on low, before they left for church so that the house would be filled with flavor when they returned. Helen kicked off her shoes and put on her apron. She never changed out of her church clothes until she got the rest her dinner started. Parris followed her footsteps and asked how she could help.

"You can start grating the cheese for the macaroni." She said.

"Okay. Have you heard from Kenya?"

"She called the other day, rambling on about some guy she met. I don't understand her sometimes. She goes from one thing to another. Now, she's tired of Nordstrom's and wants to take some more classes." She said as she started cleaning the collard greens.

"She really needs to slow down and get herself together." Parris replied. "I hope you and Daddy aren't planning to finance more classes for her."

"I'm not, but I can't answer for your father. That's his baby you know."

"Don't remind me." Parris said rolling her eyes.

Before they could say another word, Coleman walked into the kitchen; they both shot him a look. He walked over to the stainless steel refrigerator and got a shiny red apple.

"What? What did I do now?" he asked innocently after taking a bite.

"Nothing." They both replied.

"Go on back and enjoy the game or whatever you were watching, dinner will be ready shortly." Helen said.

Dinner was delicious and the roast beef, collard greens, macaroni and cheese, sweet potatoes and homemade biscuits, had Parris feeling like a stuffed pig. She would have to walk five miles on the treadmill to get these pounds off. As she began clearing the table, Kenya walked through the front door, late as usual.

"Hey yall!" she said loudly as she entered the kitchen.

"Hi baby!" her father replied giving her a great big hug and kiss.

"Hi, you just missed dinner Kenya. Let me fix you a plate." Her mother answered.

"Everything smells good. Thanks Mom." She replied. "And you can put some extra sweet potatoes on there."

"Hey P."

"Hello, Kenya. How are you?"

"I'm cool. How about you? How's the new job?" Kenya replied as she kicked off her sandals and sat down at the table.

"I like it, so far so good."

"You just ought to like it! I mean, who wouldn't like a job with a big office and six figures?" She said getting a bottle of water from the fridge.

"You could be making six figures too, if you put that expensive education Daddy paid for to good use. But, no, you'd rather run the streets."

"Look Parris, don't start! Kenya said rolling her eyes. "I'm not in the mood for one of your lectures!"

Parris shook her head, "That's your problem Kenya! You're not in the mood for anything but a party."

"Why don't you shut up and mind your business for a change?" Kenya snapped back.

"Girls, please! Not today, it's Sunday." Helen protested as she placed the dinner plate in front of her daughter.

"She started it." Kenya said under her breath. "Thank you Mommy."

"You need to grow up." Parris replied.

Once the kitchen was clean, Parris and her mother went outside on the deck and sat by the pool. Kenya and her father remained inside, playing chess. They loved challenging each other, they even bet money sometimes. Kenya was a better player and won most of the time, it was just one of the clever ways she managed to get some money out of her father without actually asking.

The sun was beginning to set and it was starting to cool off some. The sky was a beautiful array of orange, pink and blue, Parris closed her eyes as she reclined in the lounge chair.

"What are you thinking about over there?" her mother asked curiously.

"Nothing." She lied.

"How was the party last night?"

"Fun. We had a good time."

Helen chuckled, "You met someone didn't you?"

"How'd you know?" she said opening her eyes.

"Cause you were grinning in church for no reason and I know it wasn't Reverend's sermon that you found so amusing." Helen teased.

"I was not!" Parris quickly protested. "Was I?"

"Yes, you were and it was clear you weren't paying attention either."

"Now, that part your right about and I did meet someone and he is just… I can't even put it into words."

"He's that fine, huh?"

"You have no idea!"

Helen chuckled again. "Oh, yes I do. That's how I felt when I met your father. I was all messed up chile, I couldn't eat or sleep. Your father put a spell on me that I still haven't been able to shake after all these years."

"Well, as you can see, I didn't have a problem eating!" she said rubbing her stomach.

They both laughed and Parris got up and sat at the end of her mother's lounge chair.

"Well now, what's his name?" Helen asked.

"Victor."

"Where's he from?

"Originally, I don't know, but he lives in Cherry Hill. We're practically neighbors Ma. I can't believe I haven't run into him in the supermarket or something."

"What does he do?"

"He's a lawyer and he commutes to New York everyday."

"You're kidding. That must be tough. He isn't married is he? Any kids?" Helen was getting excited.

"No, he's divorced and he didn't mention any kids, but I'll have to verify that one."

"Oh, Pumpkin, looks like you might have hit the jackpot!" she teased.

"Mom, you sound like Shelly. Let's not get too excited, he's gotta call first."

"Did you wear a dress?

"Yes, and he even complimented me. He said my dress was awesome." She said grinning.

"Oh, yeah girl, he'll call, don't you worry yourself about it." Helen insisted.

"Let's hope you're as right about this, as you were about the dress."

"Oh, I am." Helen replied confidently.

Chapter

7

When the alarm went off Monday morning, Parris opened her eyes wishing she could sleep just one more hour. The voice on the radio was giving a forecast of possible thunderstorms today, one more reason to stay in bed. She went to the bathroom only discover that her period had arrived. She always thought it was funny how the cramps didn't start until she saw the evidence. She hoped a nice, hot shower would brighten her mood.

Even though she felt like jeans, she decided to put on a grey pants suit, when she remembered the presentation she had to give today. The company had just switched and made some major changes to their medical benefits and she was presenting the specs to upper management. The shower did little for her mood or her cramps, so she took two extra-strength Tylenols with a glass of orange juice.

While putting on her makeup, she discovered a pimple on her otherwise clear forehead, one more thing to dampen her day. She glanced at the clock and knew she'd better get a move on, or else she would be late. It was amazing how ten minutes, give or take, could offset the flow of traffic. She put on her shoes and emptied the contents of her purse into her black Coach bag. Her closets were mirrored, so she took one last glance and headed out the door. "This is as good as it's gonna get today folks." She said grabbing her keys.

Sean was holding the elevator door as she hurried on. They were alone.

"Good morning Parris."

"Hi Sean. What time did everyone leave the other night?"

"About one-thirty, but I didn't get to bed until after three. It was crazy."

"Why, what happened?"

"Drama. My cousin Cheryl came over, right after you left, all upset and crying. Her and her old man are going through it. She caught him cheating with their neighbor."

"That's a shame."

"She's like my little sister, so I couldn't brush her off. She must have cried for an hour."

"Poor thing." Parris sympathized.

"No, the neighbor is who you should feel sorry for because she whooped that girl's ass. Then she tried to fight her man, she was ready to kill him too. Cheryl does not play; the neighbor had to call the cops. That's when she left and came over my house."

"Get outta here, Sean!"

"I'm serious, the way she was talking; I wouldn't be surprised if she tried to hurt him again." Sean said holding the elevator open again when they reached the twenty-eighth floor.

"No one is worth all that. And I'm definitely not going to jail over a man." She replied heading towards her office.

"Yeah, some folks loose their minds when they fall in love. Are you available for lunch? I want to hear your version of Victor's Mac-Daddy story." He said following her.

"Sean, don't tell me he's playing games." She whispered as she passed by Maria's desk.

"Good Morning!" she said with a smile. "How's your son?"

"The doctor gave me a prescription and he sounds a lot better. Thanks for asking." Maria replied.

Sean followed Parris into her office.

"Victor's a real cool brother. I've known him since junior high school. Did you get the digits?"

"He got mine, I didn't get his." she said putting her handbag in the desk drawer.

"Did he call?"

"No, Mac-Daddy didn't call, at least not yet. Now, get out of my office so I can get some work done. I'll call you about lunch once I check my schedule."

The morning was moving at a snail's pace. It was only ten o'clock and Parris was hungry and still had cramps. She called Paul into her office to put together the some pamphlets.

"Hi Parris, you called? Paul asked.

"Yes, Paul, we need to have twenty-five dental pamphlets ready for my presentation this afternoon. Can you get with Gladys and make sure they're ready please?"

"No problem."

"Thanks Paul. How was your weekend?" she asked.

"Great! I went with friends down the shore and partied." He said grinning.

"How about yours?"

"It was nice. I had dinner with my family."

"Cool. I'll have those ready for you by lunch." He said as he left her office.

When she returned from the break room with coffee in hand, the phone started ringing. She didn't like to answer the phone on the first ring, she thought it made you appear anxious or worse, not busy, so she let it ring again.

"Parris Reed."

"P, you got a minute?" Shelly asked with excitement.

"Sure, what's up? How was dinner?"

"Nice. Kevin is really nice, the dinner was good too. He's kinda corny, but I'm trying to work with him."

"Good for you. Corny? How?" Parris said as she looked through some papers in her inbox.

"Corny like, he had on an ensemble with matching shirt and pants."

"Oooooo, that's bad."

"Exactly and he's into jazz, which is cool, but you know I like a little hip-hop now and then."

"His clothes and taste in music you can tweak. What does he do?" Parris replied opening a piece of mail.

"He's a plumber. Has his own business, makes good money. Oh, and he has a daughter that's six, so I'll have to do the step-mom thing."

"Oh, looking that far ahead are we?"

"Who knows, I'm just talking. He's gotta get some new gear first, I've got an image to maintain, you know." She said laughing. "We're going shopping this weekend for sure."

"Well, at least he sounds like he's got some potential. More than I can say for Joe-Look-Good."

"He didn't call yet?"

"No." Parris replied as she slammed the desk drawer shut.

"He will."

"Why does everyone keep saying that?"

"Because I've got a good feeling, that's all." Shelly replied.

"Whatever."

"Look P, I've gotta get some work done. I just wanted to say Hi"

"Me too. Bye."

When lunchtime came around, she didn't have time to go out, so she had Maria pick her up a grilled chicken Caesar salad. She sent Sean a quick email to let him know she was unavailable, and then went over the outline for the presentation while she ate at her desk. Paul brought in the pamphlets and sat them on her desk. She checked each one to make sure they were correct. She couldn't afford to screw up her first presentation to upper management. She knew the material well, so she wasn't worried about what she was going to say. The cramps had almost subsided, but she took two more Tylenols just to make sure.

She checked her watch and there was ten minutes until show time, so she went to the ladies room to freshen up her makeup. When she entered the conference room, there were twenty-five VPs, directors and managers seated at the table. They were all men and all white except for one, John Jenkins was African-American. He was bald and kind of hefty; he looked like an ex-football player or something. They hadn't officially met, but he gave a reassuring nod just as she was about to begin.

An hour later, her presentation was concluded with applause. She was shocked. She knew her presentation was thorough, but she had no idea it was that good and they would respond so favorably. The president, Harvey Brennan, a very uptight and serious looking man, stood and congratulated her.

"Well done Parris, I think I speak for everyone when I say that you have simplified and clarified many of the questions and concerns we had about the new benefits. Great job. Thank you." He said managing to smile a little.

"Thank you, Mr. Brennan. If you gentlemen have any specific questions, please feel free to call me. I will be glad to answer them."

When Parris got back to her office, Maria, Paul and Gladys were all anxiously waiting the verdict.

"So, how'd it go?" Gladys asked.

"Great! They loved it. Thank you all for your help."

"Way to go Parris!" Paul said.

She sat at her desk, feeling drained but happy. Sean popped his head in her office, right as she went to reach for the phone to retrieve her messages.

"Maria told me you were presenting to the big boys, how did it go?"

"Very well, thanks for asking. Sorry about lunch, but I had to make sure I had my shit together."

"No problem, maybe later on in the week. I'll be out tomorrow and Wednesday."

"Sure."

"Alright, I'll check you out later. I have a staff meeting at three."

"See ya Sean."

She gazed at the blinking message light on the phone and said quick prayer before she picked up the receiver and dialed voice mail.

> *"Hello, Parris it's Victor. I'm sorry I missed you. I'm in*
> *court all day and I just got a break. I'll try to call you*
> *back later. I hope you're having a wonderful day. Bye."*

"I am now." She said with a smile. "Damn! Why didn't he leave a number?" Just for GP, she played the message again. His voice was smooth and confident. "Everyone was right, he finally called."

Chapter

8

Three days passed and still no call back from Victor. Parris was almost convinced he wasn't going to call again, she didn't know why he even bothered to call the first time. Today, people have a thousand different ways to communicate, so there was no excuse. He had her home, work and cell numbers and all of them were working. All day she had contemplated asking Sean for his number, but decided against it. When she got home from work, even though she had a busy day, she still felt anxious, so she decided to work off some of the nervous energy and hopefully some cellulite at the same time. She quickly changed out of her dress and threw on some sweats. Thursday night was her TV night, Will & Grace, Scrubs, Law & Order and then ER, so she started walking on the treadmill while Will and Grace was on. Karen was her favorite character, that woman is a trip. After four miles, she was still uptight, so she called Shelly to vent.

"Hey girl, what's up?"

"Oh hey P, what's wrong, you never call me on your TV night."

"Nothing, I'm just sitting here trying to decide if I should ask Sean for Victor's number."

"No, he called you once, he'll call you again. He's probably busy, don't sweat the brother."

"Don't even try it Shell, ain't nobody that damn busy!"

"Yes, they are because I'm that busy right now. Remember the guy Kyle, with the dreds we met at the Swag?"

"Yeah." Parris replied taking a sip of water.

"Well, he went to get some wine and when he gets back, we're gonna get busy!" she said laughing.

"What about Kevin?"

"What about him? I'm not married. I've gotta keep my options open. Besides, until I see how well the plumber lays his pipe, I'm still dating!"

"You are so crazy! Go ahead girl, get your groove on. I'm glad somebody is."

"Alright, I'll talk to you later."

She hung up the phone and decided that the only TLC she was going to get was from her whirlpool. There were bubbles, candles and a glass of wine; she even invited Maxwell to the party via CD. She relaxed in the warm water and allowed Calgon to take her away. Her body told her it had been too long since she had a date. Bobby was probably the only man she had met that she seriously considered marrying. He was smart, handsome, and fun to be around and the sex was always an adventure. He loved kids and treated her like a queen. They dated for a year, until he got a job offer in California. The thought of moving away from her family was not appealing and the earthquakes didn't help the situation. He begged her to come with him, but she was in between jobs and just not ready to make such a major move. In the beginning, he called once or twice, but after a while the calls stopped. She had heard from his brother that he was doing very well. He was running his own division and well into six figures. The last time they talked, he had just brought a new Benz and was trying his hand at investing in the stock market. She often wondered how things would have turned out if she had gone with him. She was sure they would be married by now and probably have a child on the way. Bobby loved kids; he used to take his nephew everywhere. Sometimes people would mistake little Curtis for their child. Her mother really liked him and encouraged her to go. Kenya called her a "damn fool" and Shelly was behind whatever decision she made, as long as she was happy. But it was her father who told her to follow her own dreams, not someone else's and it was his words of wisdom that helped her make the decision to stay.

"Coulda, shoulda, woulda." She said to the bubbles surrounding her.

Between the treadmill, whirlpool and the wine, she was exhausted. By the time she was ready for bed, the news was on and she was hungry. Too lazy to cook, she got some vanilla ice cream instead.

"Way to go P, ice cream after a workout." She said to herself.

"Whatever." She said adding another scoop.

After the news went off, she stood in front of the closet looking for something to wear to work tomorrow. It was Friday and they allowed employees to dress down. She pulled out her favorite jeans and figured she would decide on a shirt, depending on the weather. She hadn't gotten on her knees in a while, so she knelt beside her bed and said her prayers. Once she laid down, she closed her eyes and tried to remember exactly what Victor looked like. It had been a week and like her excitement, his image was fading.

Chapter

9

The next day was going to be hot and humid again, so she put on a sleeve-less white blouse with her jeans. She carried a black blazer with her just in case management surprised her with a meeting. Her hair was in desperate need of a wash, blow-dry and cut and she was glad she had changed her appointment to right after work.

Traffic was heavy for a Friday, usually everyone was headed down the shore on Friday, but today cars were creeping across the Ben Franklin Bridge into the city. Power99 played thirty minutes of old-school jams on Friday mornings, so Parris had the music pumping in the car. She was singing along to Frankie Beverly's "Before I Let Go", when her cell phone rang. The music was so loud, she missed the call and didn't notice there was a message left until she got all the way to the office.

"Damn, damn, damn it! I can't believe I missed him again."

This time the message was more specific and left Parris grinning for about twenty minutes.

> *"Hi Parris, its Victor. You're a hard woman to catch*
> *up to. I'm on the train thinking about you and I know*
> *you've called me every name in the book, but I'd like to*
> *make it up to you. I've got tickets for a midnight cruise*
> *in Baltimore tonight. Sorry for the short notice.*
> *Call me if you're down.*
> *609-555-4445 Peace."*

She was so excited; she didn't know who to call first, Shelly or her mother. Shelly was going to be more fun, so she hit the speed dial button.

"Hey, Shell, guess what."

"What?"

"He called and this time left his number."

"See, I told you. What did he say?"

"He was on the train thinking about me and he has some tickets for a midnight cruise in Baltimore tonight and asked if I wanted to go."

"I know you said yes."

"He left a message remember? I have to call him back."

"Oh yeah, that's right."

"Thank God, I've got a hair appointment after work or else I'd have to get a rain check."

"Oh no you wouldn't, you'd put on a damn hat!"

"Your right, I'd wear a wig if I had to." she said looking into the little mirror she kept in her desk. "How did it go with Rasta man last night?"

"Girl, his body is all that, six pack, tight ass and everything. A little quick on the draw, but foreplay made up for it. Overall, he's cool and I'll probably see him again."

"What should I wear tonight?"

"Call him and see what he's wearing. This way… hold on P, Okay Karen thanks, just leave it on my desk. Sorry P, she don't have anything to say until I get on the phone. I think she does that shit on purpose."

"That's alright, I'll call you back. Bye."

Still too excited to concentrate on work, she decided to get some coffee and stop by Sean's office. He was on the phone, but gave her the signal to wait. A minute later he hung up.

"He called didn't he?" he said sounding a little disappointed.

"Yes, how did you know?" she said surprised.

"One, because you're grinning like a Cheshire cat and two because you never stop by my office."

"Very good, you're very perceptive Sean."

"I know. So did he say why his sorry ass took so long to call?"

"No, well kind of, but who cares, he invited me to join him on a midnight cruise in Baltimore."

"That sounds cool, are you going?"

"I'm thinking about it."

"Who are you kidding? You know damn well you're going."

"You're right!" she said laughing. "Look Sean, the real reason I came down here was to make sure he wasn't some psycho or something. I don't want to go all the way down Baltimore and you never hear from me again. The next thing you know my face is on the back of a milk carton. You hear about that kind of stuff happening everyday, men killing their wives or girlfriends and nobody knows who, when or where it happened."

"Parris you sound like a crazy, paranoid woman right now. I told you, I only hang around folks that have their shit together. Vic's a good guy and as usual, a lucky one too."

"You're right Sean, my bad."

"I've got a report to finish, so…"

"Oh, okay, I'll talk to you later." She said. "Have a good weekend."

"Yeah, you too." he replied.

Chapter

10

Parris got back to her office, returned a few emails and made a couple of business calls. It was almost noon and she knew she had better call him back soon so that final arrangements could be worked out. Standing at her office window, she could see the new football stadium in the distance and airplanes descending into the airport. Things were taking a turn once again for the better, new job and possibly a new man. She took a deep breath, picked up the phone and dialed his number. She decided to close the door for some privacy. He picked up on the fourth ring.

"This is Vic."

"Hi Victor, its Parris." She hoped she didn't sound nervous.

"I see you got my message. How are you?" he sounded distracted.

"I'm fine, how are you? You sound busy; did I catch you at a bad time?"

"Not really, I'm just trying to tie up some loose ends before I leave. I'm planning an evening out on the town with this beautiful woman I met last week."

"Oh really? She must be very special and probably pretty too."

"She is and don't forget sexy."

"Aren't you a lucky man."

"I don't believe in luck, its fate. Some things are just meant to be." He said confidently.

"You sound mighty confident for someone who hasn't even had a first date."

"Let me ask you a question. Do you think you got that job because you were lucky or because it was meant for you to have it?"

"Honestly, I think it was a little of both."

"I don't. I think you were in the right place, at the right time, with the right skills. If any of those three factors had been out of whack, you'd still be job hunting and since they were not, you got the job, therefore, giving you another example of what I like to call fate. Just like me meeting this special woman I was telling you about. The right place, at the right time."

"Well counselor, I think you've made your case. Now, what time would fate have me ready tonight?"

"Cute, very cute." He said with a chuckle.

"I figured I'd pick you up around seven. Hopefully traffic won't be backed up on the drive down and then we could have dinner at the Harbor and hang out until midnight."

"That sounds like a plan. Do you want to take down my address, you have a pen?"

"No, I don't have one, just give it to me."

"Are you sure?"

"Yes."

"Alright now, I don't want to hear you got lost and I believe in being on time."

"So do I. What's the address?"

"2205 Jessup Street, right off of Main Street. It's the third townhouse on the right."

"Got it. 2205 Jessup, third house on the right. I'm gonna throw on a pair of jeans, I want to be comfortable."

"Okay, I'll do the same."

"Cool. I've gotta go, but until next time." He said in that same sexy baritone voice.

"Until next time." she replied.

Parris hung up the phone grinning from ear to ear. The rest of the afternoon flew by, she felt like she was floating on a cloud. When she opened her door, Maria handed her two messages, one was requesting a report that was due on Monday, so she got started on it right away. Nothing was going to dampen her mood for the evening she had ahead of her.

She left around 4:15pm to see if the salon could fit her in for a manicure and pedicure too. The receptionist told her it wouldn't be a problem if she could come right now. When she left the office, the sun was shining and huge, white puffy clouds were scattered across the sky. You could tell by the number of people on the street that they had the same idea and left work early too. The old street preacher was out on his corner as usual, reciting scripture and all the buses were packed. She called Shelly as she walked down Chestnut Street to the salon. She got her voicemail.

"Hey Shell, I'm on my way to the salon. Victor's going to pick me up at seven. I'll call you when I get home. Bye."

An hour and ten minutes later, she was looking like a model on the cover of Vogue magazine, at least from the neck up. Bruce worked his magic on her hair and Mei-Lin gave her a French manicure and pedicure that was flawless. All she had to do now is figure out what to wear with her jeans. She decided to stop in a new fashion boutique called, LaChic, in hopes of finding a cute top. One might think this would be a simple task, but not for a woman on a date with a man like Victor. Parris was determined to look her best and was sparing no expense.

"Everything has to be just right, right hair, right clothes, right shoes, right man." She told the young girl who was very eager to make a sale.

"How about this?" the salesgirl asked holding up a plain white peasant top. "What about a tube top, we have a cute one with sequins."

Parris shook her head negatively and asked if they had anything cute in black.

"Black? Umm, you know what? I've got something I know you're just gonna love!"

Parris looked at the price tag and wished she had left home without her American Express card. Although she had to admit, it was gorgeous. Hundreds of tiny black pearl beads covered the halter. The salesgirl did a wonderful job of justifying the purchase by mentioning that it was a one of a kind and handcrafted in India. She sealed the deal by suggesting a cute cropped sweater to match, should the temperature drop. The store owner would be proud. Two hundred and fifty dollars later, Parris was happy and on her way home to get dressed.

There were two messages on the answering machine. She grabbed a bottle of water and started the bath before she listened to the messages. Undressing down to her bra and panties, she pressed play.

> *"Hi Pumpkin, it's me, Mom. Do you think you could*
> *ride with me to Cowtown tomorrow? I want to pick up a*
> *few things. Your father doesn't feel like the long ride. Of*
> *course, He would if there were some golf balls involved.*
> *Anyway, let me know.*
> *Thanks. Bye"*

Beep.

> *Parris, its Bobby. I just flew in for a few days, but I'm*
> *moving back to Jersey. I'm at my brother's. Give me a*
> *call, I'd love to see you. Maybe we can hang out like old*
> *times.*
> *Call me 335-555-5258.*

Parris stood staring at the answering machine in disbelief. Bobby was back. She glanced at the clock, it was 6:27. She only had thirty minutes to get ready and no time for reminiscing.

After two years of suffering through a man drought, now at this very minute, it was raining men, old and new.

Chapter

11

Parris was pacing and very nervous. It was 6:57 and she couldn't keep still. She watered her plants and checked her hair in the mirror. She closed the blinds and checked the mirror again. Hair and makeup were perfect and her faded boot-cut jeans and new beaded top looked hot. She was stylish and comfortable, except for the butterflies fluttering around in her stomach. She felt like a high school girl waiting for her prom date.

She turned on the TV to kill the silence. 6:59, she checked her breath and popped a peppermint Tic Tac for backup. At 7:01, a black, shiny BMW 745i with tinted windows pulled up in her driveway. Parris peeked through the blinds, "Ma, you are right again. Jackpot!"

Victor had on pair of faded jeans and a light blue long sleeved shirt; it looked like it was made of rayon or silk the way it laid against his chest and flowed in the warm breeze. Parris backed away from the window as he approached the door. As soon as the doorbell rang, so did the telephone. For a second, she didn't know which one to answer first. She quickly opened the door, and then hurried into the kitchen to get the phone.

"Hey, come on in, I've just gotta get the phone."

From the kitchen, Parris answered and watched him as he boldly scoped out her living quarters.

"Hello." She said impatiently.

"How's my Pumpkin Pie?"

"Oh, hey, what's up?" she said trying to sound casual.

"You baby! Did you get my message?"

Victor sat down sofa watching her as she spoke. "Damn, he looks good." She said to herself.

"Yes, yes I did. Um, can I call you back? I'm on my way out the door."

"Sure. You think we can get together tomorrow or something?"

"I'll let you know. I've got the number; it's still on the machine. Alright, I'll call you back." She said and then hung up the phone.

Victor was still staring, making her feel slightly uncomfortable. For a split-second, the look on his face kind of freaked her out, but as soon as he spoke, it passed.

"Are you ready?"

"I'm sorry, yes. Just let me get my purse."

He got up from the sofa and walked to the door. Parris turned on the light over the stove, grabbed her handbag and met him at the door.

"You look great." He said.

"Thanks, so do you."

"You should bring a jacket in case it gets cool on the boat." He said as if he had known her for years.

"Good idea." She said and making note of his thoughtfulness.

She went back into the bedroom and got the overpriced sweater, she couldn't believe she had almost forgotten it. When she came back into the living room, he was gone. She turned on the porch light, stepped outside and locked the front door. He was standing by the car, holding the passenger door open. She made another mental note, he's a gentlemen.

The two hour drive down to Baltimore was filled with interesting stories about his job, family and aspirations. Parris found it fascinating to find a man, with so much accomplished, still setting goals for himself. He was thirty-two, divorced, no children and a very successful lawyer about to make partner. Marriage to his college sweetheart lasted a little over a year and the divorce was nasty. With the exception a divorce decree, his resume was near perfect, so far. His father was deceased and his younger brother and mother lived in Miami. He made sure he mentioned that the three most important things in his life right now are his job, his mother and his car. Parris got the impression he was a momma's boy and hoped that wouldn't be come an issue later down the road. She once dated a guy who couldn't take a dump without asking his mother first and she was more than happy to tell him exactly how to do it. Needless to say, that lasted two weeks.

Parris gave him the run down on her family and her likes and dislikes; she even told him about her pet-peeves, many of which she was happy to find out they had in common. He was a steak and potatoes man and allergic to shellfish. His favorite color is black, zodiac sign was Taurus, born May 12th.

She knew that meant he was stubborn, but other than that, it was hard to find something wrong with him. His spirituality seemed to be intact and he was very comfortable talking about it. He went to church, admittedly not as often as he should, but he believed in prayer and acknowledged his blessings. This was a biggie for Parris because Bobby didn't go to church, except for holidays and even then he complained. Victor's taste in music was also impressive. Parris perused his CD collection and found music from every genre. Classical, rock, R&B, rap and even a few gospel.

When they arrived, he parked his pride and joy in a spot that was furthest away from the elevator. He opened the car door and held her hand as they walked. When they reached the street, his cell phone rang; he looked at the number and turned the phone off.

"We will have none of that this evening. I am officially off the clock. What do you feel like eating?" he asked.

"Anything, but Italian."

"Cool, there's a place a friend told me about that has a little bit of everything and it's supposed to be really good."

The night air was warm with a light breeze and you could smell the salty water in the harbor. The moon and stars were out; picture perfect. The harbor was crowded with plenty of things to do and sights to see. There was a blues band playing on the pavilion, so they stopped to listen for few minutes. When they reached the restaurant, there was a fifteen minute wait, so they sat at the bar and ordered drinks. He remembered what she drank and ordered for the both of them. The mental notes were racking up: good memory.

"So, tell me, why is it that a beautiful woman like yourself is still single? I'm surprised you've never been married."

"I was close once, but our timing was off."

"How so? If you don't mind me asking."

"No, not at all. It's pretty simple. He was offered a job in L.A. and I wasn't ready to make the move." She said sipping her Grey Goose and tonic.

"So you weren't really in love?" He asked more like a statement then a question.

"Of course, I was *really* in love. Why would you say that Victor? Better yet, how would you know? She said with an attitude.

"Because I can't imagine letting someone I truly loved, get away over a dispute in our physical location." He said matter-of-factly.

Parris was offended, but could clearly identify with his point of view.

"You seem to be trivializing picking up your entire life and moving it clear across the country. Don't you think?"

"Absolutely not. If this is the person I'm planning to spend the rest of my life with, have a family, etc., then, my entire life, as you put it, is *with* that person and if that means we have to move, then so be it."

"Well, I disagree. My life can't be packed in a suitcase and moved at will."

"That's because you haven't *really* been in love. And even though I don't know you very well, I think that if you were in love with the right person, you would do a lot of things that would surprise you."

On that note, Parris excused herself and went to the ladies room. It was rare she found herself at a loss for words, but Victor had done a fine job of leaving her speechless. She didn't know whether she should be pissed or happy she didn't go with Bobby? Maybe, Victor was right; she really wasn't in love with him after all.

"Who the fuck does he think he is?" she said squatting over the toilet. "He doesn't even know me, how the hell does he know if I was in love."

When she returned, the waitress showed her to their table, Victor was already seated. They ordered and enjoyed their dinner with much lighter topics of conversation. Parris was grateful.

Around 11:30, they headed towards the end of the harbor to board the boat. They found a spot on the upper deck in the corner away from the crowd. She was just about to comment on how beautiful the moon looked when he placed his hand under her chin, tilted her head and kissed her passionately on the lips.

"I've been waiting all night to do that." He said as their lips slowly parted.

Chapter

12

The rest of the evening was full of laughter and light kisses. The DJ was jamming and everyone was dancing on the lower deck. When a slow song came on, Victor asked her to dance and she gladly accepted. Their bodies moved together slowly and Parris felt safe in his arms. Unfortunately, the DJ only played one slow song and it was back to fast stuff, so they danced a few fast ones and then returned to the upper deck. He ordered a bottle of wine. Victor talked about his childhood and friendship with Sean. They met freshman year in high school. Sean was a quiet, average student who kept mostly to himself. Victor was a star athlete and honor student. Victor convinced Sean to try out for the basketball, that's when they became good friends.

They sat under the moonlight exchanging stories and finished the bottle in no time. This was hands down, the best first date Parris ever had.

When he excused himself to use the bathroom, Parris took the opportunity to freshen the lipstick that had been kissed away. Victor returned with an older gentleman named Kenneth Franklin. Kenneth was a senior partner at the firm. He was tall and slender and looked to be in his mid-to-late fifties. His salt and pepper hair and beard reminded her of Ed Bradley from 60 Minutes.

"Parris, this is my mentor and very good friend Ken."

"Pleased to meet you." She said extending her hand.

"The pleasure is all mine." He replied kissing the back of her hand.

"Where's Toni?" Victor asked

"Around here somewhere. She's probably downstairs dancing if I know her. That woman loves to dance." He said with a chuckle. "It's a beautiful evening for a boat ride. Are you enjoying yourself Parris?" Kenneth asked.

"Very much so, thanks." She said smiling at Victor.

"Are you guys staying over?"

They both looked at each other unsure how to answer. Victor placed his arm around her shoulder.

"We haven't decided yet?" Victor replied.

"Well, if you do, the Hyatt on the Harbor has a great view from any room and they serve a mean breakfast."

"Thanks, we'll keep that in mind." Parris replied.

"Alright Vic, I'll leave you kids alone. Toni's probably looking for me by now."

He shook hands with Victor and then disappeared down to the lower deck.

"That's my man. Ken's a cool brother. He's like a father to me."

"He seems very nice. Is Toni his wife?"

"Yeah, you'll like her. She's like a black Martha Stewart. Their house looks like something out of a Good Housekeeping magazine. She cooks, sews, bakes; she does everything." He said shaking head.

"I wish I had some of her energy."

"You and me both." Victor replied. "They've been married thirty-six years. Can you believe it?"

"Wow, that's great. My parents are working on their thirtieth this year."

"See, that's what I'm talking about. I hope one day I can say the same. I want to get old and gray together. It's sad, because all of my friends are either separated, divorced or pretending to be happy living the single life." He said.

"Mine too. But, marriage is hard these days."

"Agreed." Victor solemnly replied.

It was 2:20 in the morning and the boat was due back at the dock in ten minutes. Parris suggested they make their way downstairs so they could be one of the first to get off.

When they reached the car, Victor asked if she wanted to go home or spend the night.

"I don't know; what do you want to do? Do you feel like driving?"

"I'm okay, unless, you want to stay." He said paying the parking attendant.

"Kenneth did make that breakfast sound tempting, but I think we better head home."

"Once again, I agree."

Parris really wanted to stay and make love until sunrise, but the 'good' girl in her, told her to do the right thing and take her horny ass home. Her feelings for Victor were strong and she did not want to jeopardize the chances of having a real relationship by appearing easy. Parris felt that men were all the same and no matter how unattractive or handsome they were, when it came to sex, they were all greedy. The key was to always keep them wanting more, men are natural hunters and a little chase is always good.

When they finally arrived at her door, he kissed her one last time and before he could say it, she said it for him. She gently placed her index finger over his soft lips and whispered. "I know, until next time."

Chapter

13

Even though she only got four and a half hours of sleep, Parris had more energy than a two year old. She was up early and eager to start her routine. She had already put in three miles on the treadmill and it was only nine o'clock. She was about to clean the bathroom when the doorbell rang. She went to the bedroom window to see who it was, she wasn't expecting any company. She hoped it wasn't a Jehovah's Witness again, it wasn't, just Shelly.

"How was it? Come on, tell me, and don't leave anything out!" She said as she walked through the door.

"What are you doing up so early?"

"I came to see you, now give up the dirt!" She said looking in the refrigerator for something to drink. "Oh good, you've got orange juice."

"There's some cranberry juice in there too."

"Well?"

"Well what?"

"Stop playing P and tell me what happened!" Shelly said, sitting down at the counter and making herself comfortable, like she was getting ready to see a good movie.

"It was…" Parris said as she spun around on her tippy toes. "It was the best first date I've ever had!"

"Girl, I knew he had to have his shit together looking that good."

"He picked me up seven o'clock on the dot and oh, Shell, wait, guess who's in town?"

"Who?"

"Bobby."

"Stop lying!"

"I wish. He called while Victor was here." She said taking a seat across from her.

"What did you say?"

"I just told him I was on my way out the door and I'd call him tomorrow and of course, he wants to see me."

"Sounds like you've got your hands full. Finish the story about Victor first; we can talk about Bobby's ass later."

"Um, dinner was nice. I met a partner and friend of his at the firm, an older guy named Kenneth. He was handsome and very distinguished looking."

"I know you didn't give him any, but did you at least get a kiss or two?"

"Yes, I got several kisses and no, I didn't give up the panties, but I wanted to. We even thought about staying the night, but we agreed it would be better to come home."

"Better for who? You are good P, I don't know if I could've resisted."

"Shelly I really like him and I don't want to mess this up. Did I tell you he drives a 745i?" she asked nonchalantly.

"Okay, okay, go Vic! Damn, fine as hell, great job, nice car. How lucky can you get?" Shelly replied.

"Victor doesn't believe in luck. It's fate."

"Well, whatever it is, where can I get some?"

"What do you have planned for today?" Parris asked.

"I have a hair appointment at twelve-thirty. After that I'm free, how about you?"

"Mommy wants me to take her to the flea market, but I don't feel like it. I'm gonna try to get lazy-ass Kenya to do it. Oh, and I have to call Bobby back."

"Call him now, so I can say hello." She said walking into the living room turning on the television.

Parris listened to the message again, this time writing down the number. Shelly was dancing in front of the TV to a new Usher video. She dialed the number and waited for someone to pick up.

"Hi Curtis? It's Parris, is your brother there?"

"Hey Parris, what's up? How ya been?"

"I'm good Curt, how 'bout you?"

"I'm getting old and fat, but other than that, I'm great. Hold on, he's right here."

"Hey Baby, how are you?"

"I'm fine Bobby, so did I hear your message correctly? Are you really moving back to Jersey?"

"Yup. My company is opening an office in New York, so I'm here for about a week to make sure things go smoothly. They needed someone to run the northeast division and I volunteered. I'll probably move back within the month, if I can find a place to live that soon."

"That shouldn't be very hard. I'm sure you'll be able to find a condo or something."

"Nah, I want a house. I was hoping maybe you would go house-hunting with me today."

Parris could not believe her ears. The man she wanted to marry two years ago, left her behind and now he's back and wants to just pick up where they left off. Shelly finished her J-Lo routine and walked over to grab the phone.

"Hey Bobby, what's up? Long time no hear! I heard you were moving back this way."

Parris walked over to the kitchen sink and stared out the window. What did all this mean? Did he really expect her to help him pick out a house, then what? The bigger concern was did she still have feelings for him? All these questions raced threw her mind and she didn't want to consider the answers.

Chapter

14

Parris reluctantly agreed to go look at houses and was able to bribe Kenya into chauffeuring their mother around. After she finished cleaning, she jumped in the shower and thought about how much fun she had last night. Victor made her feel alive, safe and sexy all at the same time. She wanted to call and thank him for such a lovely evening, but got his voicemail.

"Hello Victor, its Parris. I just wanted to thank you for last night, I had a great time. I hope we can do it again soon. Bye."

She threw on a pair of shorts, sneakers and a tank top because she had a feeling they would be doing a lot of walking. She called her mother while she waited for Bobby to arrive.

"Hey Ma, if you still want to go to Cowtown, Kenya said she would take you. Is that alright?"

"Sure baby, that's fine as long as she doesn't get all impatient and start rushing me."

"You know she will." Parris teased.

"I know it, pain in my behind, but it's better than your father complaining. He's worse than a child."

"I had a date with Victor last night."

"Oh yeah, how did it go?"

"Mom, it was the best date I've ever had. We drove down to the Baltimore Harbor and took a midnight cruise. The stars were out and we just talked and laughed the whole time. I had a lot of fun, I really like him."

"It sounds like it. When do we get to meet him?"

"Soon I hope. Guess who's moving back to the east coast?"

"Not Bobby?" Helen asked in disbelief.

"Yes Bobby! Can you believe it? He's on his way over here now, we're going, I mean, *he's* going house hunting and he asked me to tag along."

"Well, what are you going to do?"

"What do you mean? I'm just helping him look for a house Ma, no more, no less. It's been two long years, we've been over." She said not sounding too convinced.

"If you say so. Well, tell him I said hello and I'd love to see him before he leaves."

"I will, have fun with Kenya." She said sarcastically.

"Very funny P."

Bobby was thirty minutes late and Parris was getting pissed. After all, she was doing him a favor and now he had the nerve to be late. When he finally got there, Parris had an attitude. She opened the door and started right in on him.

"What took you so long? Do you know what time it is?"

"Well, hello to you too. The realtor made a mistake with the time and I had to print some information off the web. I saw a few new houses that I liked and I wanted to check them out too."

"Well, you could have called." Parris said rolling her eyes.

"Can I get a hug now, or are you gonna bite my head off." He asked extending his arms.

"No, I'm not gonna bite off your head." She said as she gave him a hug. "Same ole Bobby."

When they released, they both took a quick second to look each other up and down. He was just as fine as she remembered, those hazel eyes were hypnotic. She use to loved running her fingers through his dark, wavy hair after they made love. He was a real ladies man and knew exactly what to say to get what he wanted.

"You still look good Parris."

"Thanks, so do you. Are you ready?" she said grabbing her backpack.

"Yeah, let's go." He said watching her walk by.

Parris knew he was looking at her ass, so she put an extra bounce in her step to remind him of what he was missing.

They weren't in the car five minutes before he started reminiscing about old times. They agreed they had some good times together, traveling, concerts and picnics in the middle of the week just because.

After looking at three very similar houses, Parris was bored. Two years ago, she would have been ecstatic, now all she could think about was Victor and the home they might purchase one day. At one point, Bobby was rambling on about the yard and she didn't hear a word he said. She kept checking her cell phone to make sure she didn't miss his call. She thought he would have noticed her lack of interest, but apparently he was in "Bobby-Land" right now. He promised they would head home after they saw one more house. Parris couldn't wait because right now, this was turning out to be almost as boring as walking around Cowtown with her mother.

"So, what do you think? You like this one?" he paused waiting for her to respond. "I do. It has a huge master bath just like you like." He asked.

"It's very nice." She said admiring the faucet. "But, it doesn't really matter what I think Bobby, you've got to live here."

"Well, I was hoping we could try again and the house would be *ours*." He said.

Parris laughed. "You're kidding right?"

"No, I'm very serious."

She continued to laugh, but he failed to see the humor.

"P, what is so funny?" he was clearly annoyed now. "Damn it, would you stop laughing. I'm serious. I miss you and not taking you with me was the worse decision I've ever made."

"Then why did it take you two years to tell me?"

"Because I knew you wouldn't change your mind and, honestly, I didn't know how. All I know is that I want us to try again."

Parris turned away and started slowly circling the empty room. This was the second time in two days she was at a loss. Now, she wished she had just said no to his invitation, because then she wouldn't be standing in the living room of this beautiful four-bedroom home with marble countertops, stainless steel appliances and an in-ground swimming pool, listening to him talk about getting back together.

"Parris, we talked about having children, a dog, everything. Back then it was just a dream for me, because I wasn't making any money. But, now things are different and my dream can become our reality. Don't you still want that?"

"Of course I do Bobby; we used to talk for hours about it."

"Well, it's not too late. We can still have it all." He said walking over and standing in front of her. "I understand if you need a little time to think about it, but I've given this a lot of thought and I'm sure now that this is what I want. I want you. I love you Parris and I always have." He said and then kissed her. His kiss was as sweet as she once remembered.

Parris wanted to push him away and run out the door, but his touch brought back feelings that took her months to get over. They kissed and held each other for a minute, until the real estate agent walked in.

"Oh, pardon me." The middle-aged white woman said looking embarrassed.

"No, that's okay. We really like this one." Bobby said smiling at Parris.

"I'm sorry; I didn't mean to interrupt. If you too feel this is your house, we can get the paperwork started, shall I?" She replied.

"What do you think P?" Bobby asked.

"I think I've made a mistake and I need to get outta here." Parris said walking quickly past the woman and out the door.

Bobby followed behind her and got in the car. Before they pulled off, Bobby reached across the center console of his car and grabbed her hand. Parris was staring out the window with a blank look on her face.

"Parris, are you okay?"

She did not answer.

"P, answer me baby, please."

Parris looked at him and said, "Bobby, what do you want from me? Do you think that kiss back there is going to magically make everything better and we can just pick up where we left off? Two years have passed! Two damn years! I was devastated when you left."

"I'm sorry, I know." He replied.

"No Bobby, you don't know! So stop saying that! As a matter of fact, you don't have a clue. Do you know how many times I prayed that something would happen and you would come back?" She said snatching her hand away.

"I'm so sorry, just let me make it up to you. Parris, here's our chance; all you have to do is say yes. I love you."

Parris laughed. "Do you know what you sound like right now?"

"I sound like a man who wants to get his woman back, that's what the hell I sound like." He replied with an attitude. "But you insist on being so damn stubborn!"

"Me? Okay, now I know you're not trying to turn this shit around and put the blame on me!"

"Well, what else do you want me to do? Beg? Cause I tried that remember? Begging doesn't work with you."

"You are un-fucking-believable! You've gotta a lot of nerve flying in town after two years talking some, I still love you shit! You obviously don't know what love is. You left *me*, remember?"

"Only because *you* didn't want to come!" he yelled back.

"What about me Bobby, what about my career? What about what I wanted, my dreams? You said, to hell with what I want! It was all about you!"

"I had to go. I would have been a fool to pass up an opportunity to make this kind of money!"

"You know what, just take me home. I don't want to hear the opportunity and money speech again." She said rolling her eyes.

"Fine. Some shit just doesn't change, does it?" he said as they pulled off. The twenty-five minute ride back to her house was spent in complete silence, no radio, no nothing, just silence. Parris was furious that she allowed this to happen. She should have seen it coming. He was right, some things just don't change and are better off left alone. Bobby still looked good, but was still selfish and that made him very unattractive.

When they pulled into her driveway, he put the car in park and ran his hands through his hair looking frustrated. Parris didn't hesitate to grab her backpack and open the door.

"Wait P."

"What Bobby."

"Can't we work this out?"

"It will never work." She replied.

"Why not? See, here you go thinking all negative again."

"I'm not being negative, just honest."

"Honest? You mean to tell me that deep down inside, you don't still have feelings for me? You *really* don't love me anymore? Wait, before you answer, think about it and think long and hard because this opportunity won't come around again."

Parris took a long look at the man she once thought was the best thing since sliced bread and couldn't believe how wrong she had been. "Bobby, deep down inside, I think you were a fool for leaving me two years ago and I think you're an even bigger fool for coming back, because if you think I want your selfish, smug-ass back, then you are dreaming and you're even dumber than you look and sound right now!" She said and then got out and slammed car door.

Chapter

15

Once inside, Parris stood leaning against the door. She relieved and finally felt free. She finally got to say all the things that she was afraid to say, or feared would hurt his feelings and shatter his fragile ego. She kicked off her sneakers and went to check her messages. She could see through the blinds that he was still sitting out there, but she didn't care, he could sit there all night. To her surprise, there were three messages on her answering machine.

> *(beep)*
> *"It's Vic, I got your message and I feel the same. I've got a few files to go over, but after that I'm free. What are you doing later? Call me."*
> *(beep)*
> *"You owe me big time P! Mommy has been looking for shit with ladybugs on it for two hours and all we see are cows and pigs! She's trippin'. Bye!"*
> *(beep)*
> *"Hey it's me. Ken and I are getting together tonight and wanted to know if you and Victor would like to join us? Call me."*

Parris was delighted at the thought of having plans two nights in a row, especially with Victor. This was definitely going to be a weekend to remember. The fiasco with Bobby soon dissipated and she was able to concentrate on planning the evening ahead. She was starving, so she went into the kitchen to make a salad. She called Shelly from the phone in the kitchen. Stretching the cord as far as it would go, she dialed her number and started rinsing off the lettuce.

"Hello Shell, can you hear me? Shell, what's wrong with your phone?"

"Nothing's wrong with my phone, that's *your* phone." Shelly protested.

"Yeah, you're right, it must the cord. Anyway, what's up for tonight?"

"You tell me. Ken and I were just going to grab something to eat and maybe go get drinks somewhere."

"That sounds like a plan. I'll call Victor and see what the deal is. I'll call you back."

"Oh P, wait, how'd it go with Bobby?"

"Girl, I had to cuss that fool out."

"Get out! Why? He's trippin' right?"

"Trippin' is putting it lightly, he's on a damn sabbatical." Parris said laughing. "He actually thought that if we went and looked at some houses together, that would rekindle the fire and we could just pick up where we left off. Can you believe the audacity Shell?"

"Yes. You know how these men are. Some of them just think we're here for decoration or something, they don't think women have a brain and they damn sure don't want you to use it."

"Wait, he had the nerve to say some shit like, you better think long and hard cause you ain't gonna get another opportunity to be with me again."

"Okay P, no he didn't!"

"Oh, yes he did."

"Did you slap the shit out of him?"

"No, but I shoulda." Parris said laughing. "It doesn't matter because I don't think he'll be calling me ever again."

"Good. Well, let me go and I'll call you back when I find out the deal for tonight."

Parris hung up and finished making her salad, adding cucumbers, shredded cheddar cheese and croutons to top it off. She didn't care for tomatoes, so she left them out. She poured an excessive amount of Catalina French dressing on top, grabbed a fork and knife and headed for the bedroom. The cordless phone had much better reception. She sat on her bed Indian-style and dialed his number.

"Hi Victor, it's Parris."

"Hey what's happening? Did you get my message?"

"Yes, that's why I'm calling. Well, actually that's not true, I would have called you back regardless of whether you called me. As a matter of fact, I would have started stalking you if you didn't call." she teased.

"Stalk on baby." He said laughing.

"Don't tempt me. Ken and Shelly are getting together later for dinner and drinks. Do you want to join them?"

"That sounds cool, but I really want you all to myself."

"You can have me all to yourself if you want."

"No, no, it's cool, I'll wait."

"You're a smart man. I've heard good things come to those who wait."

"I hope you heard right."

"I'll tell Shelly we'll meet them. What time?"

"Let's say around eight, eight-thirty."

"I'll be ready when you get here." She replied.

She gobbled down the salad and opened her closets to begin the complicated task of deciding what to wear. She called Shelly back to tell her what time, when call-waiting beeped in.

"Hello."

"Parris, can I borrow your black rhinestone belt? I'm going to the club tonight and it goes perfect with my black jeans."

"Yes, Kenya. Come get it before eight, I'm going out too."

"What! Call the paramedics! P is going out two nights in a row, what's gonna happen?" She teased.

"Oh, shut up Kenya!"

"Are you going out with Victor again? Mommy told me you really dig him."

"Yes, he's very nice and fine too girl. Oops! I forgot Shelly's on the other line. Let me go. Don't forget, come before eight Kenya." She said then clicked back over.

"Hello, Shell?"

"I'm still here." She said sounding annoyed.

"So, where do you want to meet?"

"How about the Red Rose Lounge? This way we can have dinner and hang out there for while. Victor's going to pick me up between eight and eight-thirty."

"That's sounds good, I haven't been there in a while."

"Me either. See ya later."

Parris ran her bath and continued to scope out the closet. It was still warm outside, but not as humid, so she decided on a short black dress. Simple, but sexy. She didn't stay in the tub long, fearing she would sweat out her hair. It was still looking good from last night. She put on a black Victoria's Secret thong and decided to go bra-less again. She slipped the dress over her head and fixed her hair. She added silver hoops and a thin silver choker necklace. The black mules hurt her feet, but went perfect with the dress; she would have to endure a little pain for the sake of beauty once again. It was seven fifty-five when Kenya rang the doorbell.

"Go on Miss Thang! You look nice P." She said walking quickly through the door.

"Thanks. The belt is on my bed."

"No bra, I'm impressed." She said as she walked into the bedroom. "You must be taking tips from Shelly!" she yelled.

Parris ignored her and finished putting on her makeup in the bathroom. Kenya followed right behind, standing in the doorway like she used to do when they were kids. She always loved watching Parris get dressed; sometimes she even helped her pick out her clothes. She actually had a great sense of style and fashion, it was a shame she didn't seriously pursue it.

"So what did Mommy get?" she said applying her mascara.

"Nothing! All that walking and she didn't buy a damn thing. No wonder Daddy doesn't like to go shopping with her."

"I really think she just likes looking, she probably has no intention of buying anything." Parris replied.

"Well, she can look on somebody else's time. I'm not doing that shit no more."

"That's your mother Kenya." She said applying her lip liner.

"So, she's yours too. You take her." She said rolling her eyes.

"You are such a trip." Parris replied shaking her head.

"Alright I'm out, cause you're getting ready to start preaching and I'm not trying to hear it." She said leaving the bathroom.

"Wait Kenya, seriously, what's up with the job, school, or whatever?"

"Do you really want to know or are you just going to judge me?"

"Yes, I really want to know and I promise I won't judge." Parris replied putting lotion on her legs.

"Well, to be honest P, I really don't know what I want to do. But I ran into this photographer on South Street last week and he gave me his card. He said I should really consider modeling. I have the height and God knows I look better than most of those anorexic chicks in those magazines."

"I agree with you on the anorexic part, but don't you think you're a little too old to begin modeling? Most of your competition will be an average of sixteen or seventeen years old."

"See, there you go. I knew you couldn't resist." She said sucking her teeth.

"Okay, I'm sorry, but I'm just trying to be realistic and unless that photographer works for an agency in New York or something, you're gonna have to pound the streets looking for a gig. And all that partying has got to stop. Are you ready for all that?"

Kenya stood in the door way looking down at the floor.

"No." she admitted.

"That's what I thought. Just sit down and really think about what you like to do, because that's really important. Once you figure that out, that's half the battle."

"I like to party, you know, planning and coordinating, stuff like that!"

"Okay, that's a start. Maybe you can look into Event Planning. You'd be great at that."

"Yeah, that sounds like a plan. I could definitely handle that."

"See, now all you have to do is follow it through. Just because you run into some obstacles, or stuff doesn't go your way, you can't quit. You hear me? And if you need any help, just let me know."

"Thanks P."

Parris could tell that her sister was excited about the idea of planning parties and getting paid to do it. She just hoped she could stick with it long enough to get her first check. The doorbell rang and before Parris could take a step, Kenya flew out to answer it.

"I'll get it!" Kenya yelled running to the front door.

"Hi. I'm Victor, you must be Kenya."

"Yes you are, I mean, yes I am. Come on in." She said surprised at how handsome he was.

When he walked past her, she also noticed how good he smelled. He sat down on the sofa and patiently waited.

"Where are you guys headed tonight?" Kenya asked him.

"I'm not sure, your sister was supposed to work all that out." He replied showing his dimples.

"You should go to the Red Rose Lounge. It's nice there and the foods good. I'll go check and see what's keeping P."

Parris was spraying perfume and putting on her watch. Kenya ran in the room and shut the door.

"Girl, he is fine!"

"Told you." She said confidently.

"No, I mean really fine. Where did you find him and does he have a brother?" she whispered.

"At a co-worker's party and yes, he does."

"Well, hook a sistah up!"

"Shhhh! Come on, I'm ready." She said turning off the light.

Kenya grabbed the belt and walked into the living room with Parris. Victor had turned on the television and was watching CNN. Parris walked over and gave him a peck on the lips.

"Hello handsome."

"Hello beautiful."

"Okay, you guys are sickening. I'm leaving. It was nice meeting you Victor. Bye P, have a good time." she said and then left.

"We're going to meet Ken and Shelly at the Red Rose Lounge, is that okay?"

"That's fine. Is it on 12th or 13th street?"

"I think it's on 13th. You ready?" she said turning off the TV and closing the blinds.

"I'm ready, but first come here."

"What?" she said innocently.

"Just come here." He insisted.

Parris walked over to the sofa where he was standing and looked him in the eye. He put his hands around her waist and pulled her close to him. First, he kissed her neck, and then slowly ran his tongue along the edge of her left ear. She caught a chill of pure delight from his touch. She wrapped her arms around his neck and kissed him. He slowly glided his hand down her right thigh and up again, raising her dress up to the top of her hip and stopped. Parris reluctantly slide his hand and dress back down and gently kissed him again.

"We better go." She said not wanting him to stop.

"You're right, we better."

Chapter

16

The Red Rose Lounge was packed and Parris was thankful that Shelly had made reservations. She and Ken were already seated when they arrived. Parris saw a woman from the office sitting at the bar, looking like she needed to call a cab. A jazz band was on stage sounding really good. They were playing a Grover Washington tune and had everyone grooving.

When they reached the table, Parris couldn't help but notice two vases with a dozen, picture-perfect red roses in each. One vase was in front of Shelly, who was grinning and pointing at the other, that was obviously hers. Victor pulled out her chair and she took her seat in front of the crystal vase.

"Aren't they gorgeous P?" Shelly beamed.

"Beautiful. Thank you." Parris said looking at Ken.

"I can't take credit for this one, it was Vic's idea."

Parris turned to him and smiled, "Thank you Victor."

"You're welcome, any time." Victor said winking his eye at her.

Parris loved it when he winked; it reminded her of her father. He was such a gentlemen; opening car doors, pulling out chairs and even walking on the side closest to the curb when they walked down the street. She knew something had to be wrong with this man; she just didn't know what and hoped she never found out.

Ken called the waiter over and ordered a bottle of champagne.

"What are we celebrating?" Shelly asked.

"Yeah, what's the occasion?" Parris said.

"We're going to celebrate the possibilities of love." Ken replied giving Shelly a kiss on the lips.

"I'll drink to that." Victor added.

Parris and Shelly smiled at each other and tapped each others knees under the table like school girls. They ordered their meals and continued to enjoy the band while they ate. Shelly ordered strawberry cheese cake and Parris chose carrot cake for dessert. Ken was allergic to strawberries, so he missed out. Victor shared her carrot cake and ate most of it.

They finished the bottle of Moet, ordered more drinks and talked about various topics, from current events to religion. Ken and Shelly were having a ball debating about President Clinton and how different things would have gone down if he were a black man. Parris and Victor were very amused by their playful banter. Victor excused himself to use the men's room, laughing at Ken's last comment.

"Ken man, you know damn well, if *you* were president, you would have been making booty-calls too!" He said before he walked away.

"Not if I was the First Lady." Shelly said laughing. "I know how to take care of my man."

At least ten minutes had passed and Victor had not returned. Parris tried not to look concerned, but it was very crowded and she could not see the restrooms from their table.

"I wonder what's taking Victor so long." she said.

"Let the man handle his business P, he'll be back. Although, he has been gone a long time, he must be taking a dump." Shelly replied matter-of-factly.

Parris and Ken both looked at Shelly and shook their heads. When another five minutes passed, Parris decided to go look for her man. There were too many desperate looking, single women there for her to act like there was no cause for concern.

When she turned the corner that lead to the restrooms, she saw Victor talking to a young woman. She was brown skinned with long hair and Pamela Anderson breasts. Her blouse was too small and her skirt was way too short. Parris tried to act normal as she approached them. Victor's back was to her, but the young woman could tell from the look on her face that she might be treading on dangerous territory. Victor turned around to see what had caught the young woman's attention.

"Hey Parris, I'm sorry, I'll be right there." He said touching her hand.

"Okay." She replied.

Annoyed and feeling a little awkward, Parris continued walking and went into the ladies room. She walked up to the sink, looked in the mirror and exhaled.

"Breathe Parris breathe, he's just talking." She said under her breath while fixing her hair, and then she went into a stall.

"He could have at least introduced us." She mumbled flushing the toilet.

There were two young females in the bathroom talking very loud and she couldn't help listening, while she washed her hands.

"Did you see that fine brother talking to that hoochie!"

"Yeah, lucky bitch. I'd like to get me some of that!"

Parris continued to wash her hands as they walked out. They didn't notice that she had turned on the hot water and when she stuck her hand under the faucet to rinse them, the hot steaming water scalded her clinched fists.

"Ouch! Shit!" she said quickly removing her hands from the hot water.

She quickly tried to compose herself before someone else walked in. Her hands were red and the left one got the worst of it. She found herself shaking them to help relieve the pain. Parris was mad herself for being jealous and disappointed at Victor for being rude. As she reapplied her lipstick, the so-called hoochie, walked into the bathroom. She glanced at Parris' through the mirror, didn't bother to speak and went right into the first stall.

A voice told Parris to wait for her come out and ask her a few questions. But she didn't know what she would say, they were only talking and she didn't want to look foolish, so she wet a paper towel with cold water and held it on her injured hand. She hoped Victor would be waiting for her outside, but he must have finally returned to their table.

Walking quickly through the crowd, she held the damp paper towel on her stinging hand until she reached the table. When she sat down, she smiled at Victor and was thankful that the voice was silent.

"Where's the ladies room P?" Shelly asked. She noticed her friend looked a little strange.

"It's right past the entrance on your left." She replied with a blank look on her face.

"Are you okay? What happened to your hand?" Victor asked.

Parris looked down at her hand, forgetting that she was still holding the paper towel on it. "Oh, it's nothing. I turned on the hot water by accident when I was washing my hands. I'm okay."

"Are you sure, let me see." Victor said grabbing her left hand.

"I said, I'm fine." She insisted and pulled away.

There was an uncomfortable silence, so Shelly went to the bathroom and Kevin called for the waitress.

"Does anyone want anything else? Otherwise, I'm gonna get the check." Kevin said.

Victor looked at Parris who was quietly sipping the rest of her drink.

"No man, we're good. Get the check."

Chapter

17

Parris was silent the entire ride home and Victor was clueless as to what brought it on. She did not want to jump to conclusions, so thought it was best if she just kept quiet. When they pulled up to her house, Parris grabbed her purse and started to open the car door.

"Hey, hey, slow down, what's the hurry?" He said getting out of the car.

Parris reluctantly waited for him to walk around the car and open her door. He reached for her hand and helped her out of the car. He tried to give her a hug, but she coldly pulled away.

"Is something wrong? Did I do something?" he asked.

"No."

"Then what's with the cold shoulder and silent treatment? And what the hell happened back in the restaurant?"

"Nothing, I'm just tired." She said trying to avoid eye contact.

"Parris, I'm a lawyer and I can usually tell when someone is lying, especially when they're not very good at it."

"Well then figure out who's guilty, counselor." She said sarcastically and started walking towards the front door.

"Guilty? Guilty of what? What are you talking about?" he asked following her.

"If you don't know, then I'll never have you as my lawyer." She said putting the key in the door.

"Look, cut the bullshit because I don't have time. Just talk to me, please. What did I do?"

Parris ignored him as she turned on a light and kicked off her shoes. The balls of her feet were burning adding to her irritable disposition. She sat the vase on the dining room table and began arranging the roses like a professional florist.

"Are we going to talk about this or am I going to leave and be done with it?" he asked running out of patience.

Parris went and sat down on the black leather sofa and started rubbing her feet. Victor never moved from the front door, he was ready to stay or leave, depending on her answer.

"This may or may not be my place, but we can discuss that later. Who was the young girl you were talking to?" She asked wondering if he would tell the truth.

Victor started laughing and sat down next to her on the couch. Parris waited for an answer.

"You can't be serious… are you?"

"Look at my face, am I laughing?"

"Aw, come on Parris, please don't start that. Do I look like I'd be interested in a chicken head like that? Damn, give me some credit."

"Well, that chicken head kept you away from the woman you came with for almost twenty minutes."

He grabbed her feet, placed them on his lap and began to massage them.

"Her name is Tanya, she's my neighbor's, brother's daughter. She just signed with a new label and wants me to take a look at the contract. That's all. Are you satisfied?"

"Well, why didn't you introduce us, if it was so damn innocent?"

"Because I don't like folks all up in my business. It's none of her business who I'm dating."

"Oh, so are we officially dating now?"

"I certainly hope so, I spent fifty dollars on those roses!" he teased.

"Ha, ha, very funny." She said rolling her eyes at him.

He leaned over and kissed her gently on the lips.

"All you had to do was ask me and I would have told you." He said as he continued kissing her neck. "We could have avoided all the drama and your funky attitude."

"I'm sorry. You're right." She replied.

She kissed him and pulled him close, positioning his body on top of her as she lay back on the couch. She ran her nails softly down his back until she reached his tight ass. With both of her hands full, she pulled him even closer. A slow grind was set in motion, pressing firmly against her throbbing pelvis. He laced her neck with soft and wet kisses causing her heart to beat a little faster. When his tongue reached the swell of her breasts, she realized just how long it had been. He slowly moved his hand down her thigh and eased the short black dress up around her waist, exposing her sheer black thong that was hiding a secret Victoria was anxious to divulge. She assisted him in his conquest by pulling the dress off over her head and throwing it over the sofa. She was ready and every part of her body was anticipating whatever would come next. Soft kisses on her lips, then her neck, slowly made their way to her breasts. He skillfully maneuvered his tongue around each breast saving the nipples for last, teasing with every kiss. She quickly unbuttoned his shirt, baring his smooth six pack stomach. His pants soon joined his shirt on the floor. Parris admired his physique, voting him poster boy for Calvin Klein underwear. Any other time, she probably would have felt self-conscious of her own far from perfect figure, but tonight she was too horny to care. Victor's sweet kisses touched her belly button and tickled her stomach until they reached her warm chocolate center. Parris moaned in ecstasy and her body yearned to experience every inch of him. His tongue gave her pleasures never reached before and he didn't stop until she reached her peak. She silently thanked him with kisses and caressed his penis until he couldn't stand it anymore. Then he reached for his pants and removed a condom from his wallet. The anticipation of exploring each other bodies was finally over and sweet rhythm that only a man and woman can orchestrate had begun.

Chapter

18

The next morning a bright beam of sunlight was shining through the blinds, leaving streaks of gold on Victor's bare back. Parris watched him sleep peacefully and wondered if all their nights together would be so amazing. She softly kissed his shoulder before she eased out of bed trying not to wake him. She slipped on her silk robe and went out to the living room. As she picked up the clothes that were thrown all about, she couldn't help smiling at flashbacks of last night. They were soon interrupted by her stomach growling, so she went into the kitchen and took out the skillet. Eggs, bacon, French toast and orange juice were on the menu, she even sliced some fresh strawberries.

Victor was awakened by the delicious aroma coming from the kitchen. He stood in the doorway and watched her remove the coffee mugs from the cabinet. She jumped when she saw him standing behind her.

"Oh shit! You scared me."

"Sorry."

"Are you hungry?"

"Starving." He said wrapping his arms around her waist and kissing her forehead.

"Then let's eat. Do you want cream for your coffee?"

"No, I like it black like my women." He said with a smirk.

"I like mine black with a little cream, like my men."

"Oh, so you want a Latino?" he joked.

"You've got jokes. Cute."

They sat across from each other on stools at the marble island. Parris said the blessing and they both devoured the food like it was the last supper.

"How long were you married?" she asked.

"A year and a half." He answered taking a bite of bacon.

"What happened?"

"She was extremely jealous and everything I did, everywhere I went, including my clients were suspect."

"Oh." Parris replied feeling embarrassed about the interrogation last night.

"It got to a point where it wasn't worth the argument anymore. I have to defend people every day, and I don't want to come home and have to defend myself."

Parris didn't know what to say. She did know, however, that she would have to get her insecurities in check or this relationship would not last long. They continued to finish their breakfast in silence until the telephone rang.

"Hello."

"Was it good?" Shelly asked.

"Yes."

"Is he still there?"

"Yes." Parris replied looking over at him sipping his coffee.

"You go girl! Well, whatever you do, don't make him breakfast, make him take you out to eat." She advised.

"Why not?"

"Because the next thing you know, he'll be asking you to wash his drawls and pick up his clothes from the cleaners."

"You're a day late and a dollar short."

"Damn P, I knew I should have prepped you last night. I forgot you're a little out of practice."

"Well, I think it'll be alright."

"I hope so. Ken and I just came back from eating and we're getting ready for a little after-breakfast in bed. And he's a very thorough plumber I might add. My pipes are clean as a whistle." She said with a chuckle.

"You are so crazy. That is a good idea, I think I'll do the same. Talk to you later."

Parris hung up the phone and walked over to Victor and stood behind him while he read the sports section of the Sunday paper. She untied her robe and pressed her bare breast against his smooth back.

"How'd the Sixers do last night?" she asked.

"They won in overtime." He replied acting oblivious to her presence.

She reached down and put her hand in his underwear to see if he was paying attention.

"It must have been a big game. How long is overtime?" She asked placing a firm grip on his erect penis.

"Long enough to get the job done." He said turning the page.

"Oh yeah, well let's go see if you can take it to the hole!" She said running towards the bedroom.

Victor threw down the newspaper and ran after her.

Chapter

19

Monday morning was busy as usual, full of emails to return and meetings. After a wonderful weekend, Parris was finding it hard to get back in the groove. Her draught was finally over.

"Are all of the providers now available on line?" one of the older VP's asked.

Parris was back in bed exchanging kisses, with Victor's arms wrapped around her tight.

"Parris? Hello, are you with us?"

"Oh, I'm sorry. What was the question? She asked trying to regroup.

"Are employees now able to access a list of providers on line? I was told last week that the list was incomplete." he repeated with a slight attitude.

"Yes, we verified the list this morning and the link on the website is working. You can search for your provider by type, location and name." She replied.

"Good. That about sums up everything I needed to cover. Thank you all for coming. Ah, Parris, can I speak to you for a moment." Her manager asked.

The others left the large conference room, leaving Parris alone with her boss. Trying not to look nervous, she collected her papers and portfolio and held them in her arm hoping this wouldn't take long.

"Is everything alright? You seem out of sorts today and that's not like you." He asked sounding genuinely concerned.

"I'm fine Mr. Clancy. I had a busy weekend and I have a lot on my plate this morning. I apologize for what happened back there, it won't happen again."

"Alright then, good day Ms. Reed."

Parris left the conference room adjusting her suit jacket and fixing her skirt. She didn't know what had come over her; she had never drifted off in a meeting like that before. When she reached her office, she sat down in her chair and stared out the window. She knew damn well what was wrong, but was afraid to admit it.

"What is wrong with me, am I in love?" she asked herself. "No, of course not. I barely know him. Get a grip Parris. It was good, but not that good." She said checking her lipstick. "Yes it was, who are *you* kidding?" she said looking at her reflection.

By lunch time, Parris was more focused and able to concentrate. Sean emailed her for lunch and she accepted. They met at the elevator both grinning slyly at each other. There were two other people on with them, so they waited until they reached the street to start talking.

"I heard you got whip-appeal Ms. Reed."

"Is that what he told you?"

"Nah, that's word on the street."

"Stop playing Sean, what did he say? I know it wasn't much because he's not one for telling his business."

"You're right about that. I had to pry the little bit of information he was willing to give out of him."

They decided to eat at an Italian restaurant on 19th street, Sean loved their Manicotti. Parris didn't like Italian food, but didn't feel like arguing about it so she just went along with it. The waitress seated them at a small table by the window. Parris ordered a salad and Sean got his usual. Parris sipped her raspberry ice-tea, eagerly waiting for Sean to divulge what Victor had told him.

"Well, what else did he say?"

"Not much, just that you guys had a great weekend." He said looking at the menu.

"Then why were you talkin' all that whip-appeal stuff?" she asked moving the menu from in front of his face.

"Because I know Vic." He said buttering a piece of bread.

"Come on Sean, you gotta help me out here."

"He didn't say much, but from what he did say, he let me know he really digs you." He replied, chewing as he spoke. "I knew he would."

"How'd you know?"

"Because we've got history, that's all. And I know his type and you are his type." He replied.

"What's his type?"

"You!"

"Good, cause I really like him too and he's *definitely* my type."

Sean looked a little disappointed, but didn't say anything. After they finished their meal, Parris took care of the bill and asked one final question regarding Victor.

"What is his wife like?"

"What do you mean? She's okay, why?" He replied.

"Well, I asked him how long he was married and he told me a year and a half and that she was very jealous and he couldn't take it anymore so he left. That was it. He didn't say much else."

"That about sums it up, but she was more than jealous. She was off the hook and when they broke up, she took it hard. She *really* loved him."

"That's understandable, but you've gotta accept reality." Parris replied. "When it's over, it's over. Some people can't handle rejection and that's when it gets ugly."

Chapter

20

The next couple of months were the happiest Parris had ever known. She and Victor were growing closer and talking about the future, nothing specific, but very promising. Some nights he stayed at her place, others in New York. He sometimes worked lat into the night and was too tired to catch the train. Parris understood he was about to make partner and tried not to complain. The fact that he had a drawer and some closet space gave her a sense of security. Victor's house was only a few minutes away and was in desperate need of a woman's touch. His ex had obviously taken everything but the four walls when she left. It was equipped with what he called "the basics"; a 52" flat screen plasma television, DVD player, pool table, computer and a banging sound system, all worth a small fortune. Parris would bring scented candles or flowers to brighten the place whenever she came over. He told her that he kept the house because his ex-wife didn't want it. All she wanted was money in the divorce settlement. He didn't talk about his ex-wife very often and when he did, it was general and not always kind. Parris got the impression that she was very bitter. They had only been married a little over a year and had no children. From what Victor told her, she really wanted to have kids, but it just never happened and he was very thankful. She was also an attorney, earning a sizable salary, so there was no alimony, just a lump sum settlement. He didn't say how much. Victor also mentioned that he had not spoken with her since the divorce and that suited him just fine.

Even though things were going well, Parris was finding it difficult to adjust to his unpredictable work schedule. Depending how long a case lasted, he might only come home once a week and this made it difficult to make plans together. A number of his clients were new artists, who failed to read the small print of their contracts, later to find out that they haven't made a dime. Victor was very dedicated to his clients, so when he was home, he would sit for hours in his Lazy-Boy recliner with the headphones on listening to music and reading case files.

When Parris finally brought Victor to Sunday dinner at her parents, her mother immediately fell in love with him. Victor could do no wrong, even her father seemed impressed and that was no easy task. They talked for hours about golf and the stock market. Everyone was comfortable and getting along, even Kenya was already calling him 'bro'. Since his mother lived in Florida, Parris had only spoken to her twice on the phone. She was a little stuffy, but seemed nice enough. She could tell that even though she had two children, Victor was her favorite and no woman would ever be good enough. In turn, she was a saint, as far as Victor was concerned. She was very nosy and asked a lot of questions, some of them Parris thought were too personal to answer, so she did her best to avoid them. She didn't have anything to hide, but when she asked if she was using birth control, she thought that was where the line should be drawn. Victor just laughed and insisted she didn't mean any harm; she was just a little over protective and wanted to make sure she wasn't anything like his ex-wife.

Shelly and Ken were having one of those on again, off again relationships. Ken wanted to settle down and possibly get married, but Shelly still wasn't ready nor was she rushing it. Neither one of them wanted to call it quits, so they just enjoyed each other's company when they were together. Parris could not understand why Shelly didn't just take it to the next level. Ken treated her like a queen. Parris warned her that a good man like Ken is not going to wait around forever.

Victor and Ken belonged to a gym and often worked out together. Shelly and Parris decided to go along and try out a TaeBo class. The class didn't start until one o'clock, so they decided to meet the guys there.

After Parris cleaned the house, she changed into a pair of gray cut-off sweat pants and a white tank top. She tied a black and white bandana around her head, grabbed her gym bag and walked out the door.

When she got in the car, she called Shelly to let her know she was on her way. It was another picture perfect Saturday morning; warm and sunny, they were having great summer weather. She opened the sun roof to let the hot sun warm her skin. It was one of those days that made you feel guilty for riding around in a dirty car, so she made a quick detour before picking up Shelly.

A handsome Italian man was checking her out, while she waited for them to wipe down her Jaguar. He was waiting to have his Lexus detailed, he politely said hello and did not stop staring until she pulled off and was no longer in sight.

Parris honked the horn and Shelly came out with a white Nike sports bra, biker shorts with a bright yellow thong on the outside and brand new Nike sneakers. She looked like a walking Nike billboard.

"You certainly look athletic, but I know the real deal." Parris said as she approached the car. "Shelly, how can you work out with that thong all up your ass?" she asked when she got in the car.

"I'm used to it. I wear them all the time. Besides, it matches my Nikes and you know I've got to coordinate."

"Not me. I'm there to get a good workout, not look cute." She replied.

"There's no reason why you can't do both P. It's always gotta be black or white with you, you need a little gray in your life." She said while switching radio stations.

"Whatever. Just put in a CD, would you?"

The gym parking lot was packed. They spotted Victor's car right away, because it was parked all the way in the back near a bright red Corvette. Parris parked her silver Jag right next to Victor's BMW.

"What do you want to do for your birthday? It's the big 3-O, so we've gotta do it up right!" Shelly asked while walking across the parking lot adjusting her thong.

"I got another month to think about it, so I'll let you know. Maybe we can go to New York and hang out for the weekend." Parris replied holding the door open.

"That sounds like fun. Victor can let us know what spots will be jumpin'."

They scanned the first floor to see if the guys were around. Ken was working his legs, which he needed desperately and Victor was working those rock-hard abs. The first floor was mainly dedicated to free weights and most of the men were down there. There were a few masculine looking women pumping iron, along with a few would-be models profiling.

Parris waited by the stairs and waved, while Shelly went over to let the guys know they were going up to their class. Victor blew her a kiss in between crunches.

The TaeBo instructor was a young guy who was 5'3" and built like a wrestler. His arms looked like they were ready to explode. As soon as they took their places the music started. The song was Pink's "Get this Party Started". There were about thirty people, mostly women, all trying to follow the little muscle bound instructor. Parris and Shelly had no trouble getting into the groove. Shelly, however, as cute as she looked, only lasted fifteen minutes. Parris was able to go the entire thirty minutes. When she finished, Shelly was talking to a girl from her apartment complex that couldn't go the distance either.

Parris was sweating like a pig, hair was sweated out and her deodorant was on its way out to lunch, but she felt refreshed. Victor came up stairs, just as she started to get a drink from the water fountain. He playfully bumped her out of the way with his hip before she could take a sip and tried to empty the fountain himself. Parris bumped him back, but much harder and almost knocked him over.

"Ooh, baby, I'm sorry, I didn't mean to bump you that hard." She said trying not to laugh.

"Damn girl, those hips are more dangerous than I thought." He said grabbing her by the waist and pulling her close.

He kissed her on the lips and wiped the tiny beads of sweat off of her nose.

"Is Ken still working out?" she asked.

"I think he's on his last set. I told him those chicken legs aren't getting any bigger no matter how long he works them."

"Don't talk about my man's legs!" Shelly yelled overhearing their conversation.

"Oops, my bad." Victor replied heading back down stairs. "Hey P, I have to renew my membership, I'll meet you downstairs."

"Okay." Parris replied joining Shelly and her neighbor.

"Parris you remember Pam, she lives in my apartment complex."

"Yes, long time no see. How ya been?" Parris replied.

"I'm fine, girl, just trying to get this baby fat off. My son is six months old and I still look pregnant."

"I've heard it takes time, but at least you're in the right place." Parris replied.

"Not because I want to be, my husband insisted. He even bought the membership as a Mother's day gift. Ain't that something?" Pam said.

"Well, you gotta do, what you gotta do." Shelly said.

"Don't just do it for him, do you for yourself Pam. I'm sure you'll be back in shape in no time, especially if you keep taking this TaeBo class." Parris said as she stretched.

"I'm trying yall, but it's hard." Pam replied.

"It's not that bad." Shelly said.

"Shelly, you could only hang for fifteen minutes, so how can you say it's not that bad?" Parris replied with her hands on her hips.

"What I meant to say is that it's not that bad if you only do fifteen minutes."

The women laughed and said their good-byes. Parris and Shelly headed downstairs to meet the guys. There were two sets of steps and when Parris stepped down on the landing, she stopped dead in her tracks and Shelly almost bumped into her.

The girl behind the counter was no more than twenty, pretty with bleach-blonde hair and big blue eyes; she sort of looked like Heather Locklear. She was leaning on the counter, with her breasts on the verge of spilling out of her sports bra as she ran her long acrylic fingernail down his right bicep. Victor was also leaning on the counter, filling out some paper work and laughing at something she was saying and undoubtedly enjoying the view.

"Aw shit!" Shelly said.

"Aw shit is right." Parris replied continuing down the steps.

Parris immediately felt her temperature rise as she approached the desk. The girl noticed her walking towards them, but continued her conversation, laughing and flinging her over- processed hair. Ken walked over to Shelly and they both watched with anticipation waiting for the drama to unfold.

"Babe, are you almost finished?" Parris asked standing close beside him.

"Just about." He replied never looking up from the paper.

"I'll need to get a copy of your driver's license too Vic." The blond said completely ignoring Parris.

"Vic? She knows him like that?" Parris said to herself.

Parris really did not want to cause a scene, so she patiently waited another minute while Dolly Pardon's niece made a copy of his license. When he finally turned around, he either didn't notice she was annoyed or was playing it off really well.

"You want to get something to eat after we change?" he asked.

"Yeah, that sounds good." She replied never taking her eyes off the blonde.

"Oh, wow Vic! I live right around the corner from you. That's so cool! I didn't know you lived in Tavistock, I'm right on Bellevue Avenue." She said with entirely too much excitement for Parris.

"Are you ready?" Parris interjected before he could respond.

"Yes, let's go. Hey Kelly, don't forget to bring that in for me." He replied.

"I won't, see ya Victor." She replied.

Parris shot her a look and the young girl quickly turned around and went into the office. Victor put his arm around her and they walked outside. Shelly and Ken were already outside waiting, relieved that everyone was able to hold it together. Shelly decided to ride home with Ken, so Parris could go straight home. Victor followed her to her house. Parris was pretty quiet, until they got in the shower. Victor was washing her back when she decided to open up.

"What was that all about at the gym?"

"All what?" He stopped rubbing.

"Come on 'Vic', as Barbie put it, she had her fake tits all in your face and you didn't seem to mind." She said turning around to face him, giving him that "don't play stupid" look.

"Now yours are all in my face." He said touching her left breast.

"You know what I mean, but since you want to play dumb, I'll play dumb too!" she said turning back around.

"Parris you're over reacting. She was just being friendly."

"Friendly my ass! And what is she supposed to remember to bring in for you?"

"Your ass does look friendly babe." Victor joked.

"I'm trying to be serious Victor and all you can do is joke."

She quickly finished washing, barely rinsing off the soap and got out of the shower.

"Babe, she's just bringing in a new fitness magazine for me to look at." He yelled through the shower doors.

She sat on the edge of her bed and dried off with the towel. She closed her eyes tight, trying to push out the sounds. It had been five years since she last heard those voices, when they surfaced again at the restaurant, she prayed they would pass. She took several deep breaths trying to relax, but the voices just grew louder.

"Go away." she said softly. "Please, just go away."4

Chapter

21

The last time Parris heard the voices, she hoped it would be for good. She never told anyone about it, for fear they would think she was crazy. Back then, she wasn't so sure herself. It all started when she was twelve, her parents left her to baby sit Kenya while they went to the store. They were only gone an hour, but those sixty minutes were the worst Parris could ever remember. The two girls and the neighbor boy, Jimmy, from next door were playing hide-in-seek in the backyard. Jimmy was nine, and tall for his age. Kenya and Jimmy went to the same elementary school. Even though Kenya was only seven and a girl, it didn't seem to bother him because she was such a tom-boy. She played with bugs and was just as good as Jimmy when it came to sports. Everything he did, Kenya tried to copy. She was like his shadow.

When it was Parris' turn to hide, she knew just the right place and was sure they wouldn't be able to find her. The old, rusty shed. It was an old aluminum shed where her father kept the lawnmower, shovels and other garden tools. It was dirty and full of bugs, but Parris figured she could handle it for a few minutes. She knew they would never find her in there and she would win again. The shed was towards the back of the yard, on the other side of the pool, away from the house.

Kenya started counting. "1, 2, 3". Jimmy ran to his usual hiding place, behind the air conditioner and Parris headed for the shed. When she closed the door behind her, it was pitch black and smelled like moldy grass and gasoline. She could hear Kenya in the distance, "15, 16, 17". Now that she was inside, she didn't think it was such a good idea after all, but she had no time to find a new hiding spot. Her fear of the dark kicked in right away. As she tried to wipe the spider webs off her face, she noticed that Kenya stopped counting.

"Ready or not, here I come!" Kenya yelled from a distance.

"She'll never find me in here and I'll win again." She laughed to herself.

Even though only two minutes or so had passed, it felt like at least ten. It was hot in there and she was starting to sweat. There was barely enough room for her to crouch down in the corner. The snow blower was poking her in the back and she was stepping on something that felt like a hose.

"Come on Kenya, say you give up!" she whispered impatiently.

She could hear Jimmy laughing; Kenya must have found him already. Then there was silence again. The chirp of a cricket almost scared the crap out of her and she was ready to come out, but then she heard foot steps. The cricket was chirping louder now, so she couldn't tell if they were near the shed.

"I'll wait one more minute. Hurry up dummy!" she whispered.

The foul smell mixed with the heat inside the tiny space was making her nauseous. It felt like spiders were crawling all over her body. When she reached for the handle to open the door, it didn't turn. She tried it again, nothing.

"Kenya, open the door and stop playing!" she yelled.

She tried turning both handles, pulling on them frantically, but they were either stuck or the doors were locked. Her heart raced and she started to panic.

"Jimmy! Kenya! Open the door! It's not funny!" She yelled banging on the doors.

The sweat was pouring down her face and she started to cry.

"Come on you guys! Let me out! Let me out!" she begged.

She was not sure if she blacked out for a second, but when she opened her eyes, she was still in the dark, stinky shed. She had lost track of time and wasn't sure how long she had been locked in. She immediately started screaming at the top of her lungs again.

"Help! Help me! I'm locked in the shed! Please help!" she sobbed over and over again.

Parris felt like she was starting to hyperventilate. She was gasping for air and feeling very dizzy. Darkness started playing tricks and she thought she saw something move over in the corner. She waved her hands in front of her trying to push it away and cut her arm on something sharp. It felt like it was bleeding, but she was sweating so she wasn't sure. Her fear quickly turned to anger. Until now, she never thought she was claustrophobic, but she was sure she would be from now on.

Parris thought she heard someone say something, but she couldn't make out what it was. She continued shaking the handles and banging on the doors screaming for help. Still there was nothing, except a voice.

"Don't worry, we'll get them back. We'll teach them a lesson."

"I'm gonna kill you Kenya!" Parris yelled as loud as she could.

When her father finally opened the doors, the cool air hit her face and she fainted. As her father was carrying her into the house, she started coming to and could see Kenya and Jimmy watching. Jimmy was laughing. Kenya wanted to laugh, but was scared to because her father was angry.

Kenya was put on punishment for two weeks for locking her in the shed, even though she said it was Jimmy's idea. Her parents did not let him come over for about a month and Parris was thankful. Even though his parents made him apologize, to this day, she could still see him laughing.

After that day, the voices seemed to only return if she was scared or angry. Although it did not happen often, when it did, she didn't like what the voices told her to do and had no idea why they told her to do such mean and hateful things. Thoughts of hurting Kenya often ran through her mind after that incident in the back yard. At night, she would say her prayers to wish the evil voices away.

In high school, she ran track and was the fastest girl on the team. There was another incident with a girl named Tia Wilson, who was very jealous of Parris. One day during practice, she intentionally tripped her and Parris twisted her ankle. She was devastated when the doctor told her she would be out for the season. Again, she heard the voices. Two days later, Parris waited until Tia was in the locker room taking a shower. When no one was looking, she put a bunch of red ants, taken from the science lab, in her gym socks. The bites on her feet and ankles were so severe, she caught an infection and it put her out for the season as well.

That was the first time Parris had ever listened to the voices and even though she was able to get revenge on Tia, that was well deserved, her conscience soon got the best of her. She wasn't a mean and vengeful person and didn't want to become one and she feared how she would react next time, if they ever came back.

Chapter

22

When Victor got out of the shower, the argument continued when he told her she was overreacting. Parris absolutely hated to be told she was overreacting, and who was he to tell her how she should be reacting. The argument ended with him walking out and slamming the door behind him. Parris tried to call him the next day, but he did not answer his phone and his secretary said he was in court all day. Parris tried to busy herself with her own work to keep her mind off of what happened. She missed Victor and the last thing she wanted was for their relationship to end over what, in retrospect, seemed trivial. Maybe she did overreact. Sean walked into the break room while she was getting some coffee.

"Hey Parris, what's with the long face?" he asked.

"Nothing. I'm just really busy." She said making a fresh pot.

"Push the button."

"What?" she said with an attitude.

"I said, you have to push the button if you want to start another pot."

"Oh, right, the button." She said pushing the red button.

"Are you sure you're alright?"

"I will be. Did Mark Simmons retire yet?" she asked changing the subject.

"Friday is his last day. Check this out, remember my cousin Cheryl I was telling you about who was having problems with her man cheating. Well, he finally pushed her too far. She stabbed his ass and almost killed him. Ain't that some shit?"

"Oh, my God! She was serious, huh?"

"I told you, Cheryl is no joke. I talked to her last night and she was acting just like every day was Sunday. I wasn't sure before, but now I know she's got some real issues." He replied filling his mug with fresh coffee.

He continued to fill Parris' mug too. She opened the refrigerator and added creamer. Sean went over to the vending machine and bought a bag of barbeque potato chips.

"I don't understand women, you want a man so bad, and when you get one, as soon as he messes up, you want to stab him, cut off his dick or something crazy like that." He said half joking and half serious.

"Don't even try it Sean, *all* woman don't go to those extremes." She said taking one of his chips. "And don't act like he's innocent in all this. He was sleeping with the neighbor for crying out loud. I don't think anyone should tolerate that. Some of you idiots deserve exactly what you get."

Chapter

23

Victor sent a short email letting her know his case was going to keep him in New York all week. Parris decided to take a vacation day on Friday, so she could catch the train Thursday night to surprise him. They had only spoken once briefly mid-week. He still had an attitude even though she apologized several times. Guilt was getting the best of her, so she decided to pack a small suitcase with candles, strawberry massage oil, a bottle of Merlot and a new teddy she purchased from Victoria's Secret. It was a black sheer camisole with a thong that had a red cut-out heart in front. She thought for sure this peace offering would be a hit and everything would be back to normal and they would be happy again.

When she reached Penn Station, it was almost dark, but the streets were still busy like it was high noon. Hailing a cab turned out to be a project and when she finally did, they sat in traffic for fifteen minutes.

This was the first time Parris had been to the apartment. The lobby was very plush and decorated with deep maroon and gray furniture. Parris stopped at the front desk to speak with the concierge.

"Hello, is Victor Baxter in?"

"Yes, ma'am, he arrived about twenty minutes ago. Would you like me to call him for you?" The tall, thin gentlemen asked.

"No, that's okay, I want to surprise him. He's in 214 right?"

"Yes, but we're not supposed to let any guests up without notifying the tenants. It's building policy."

"I understand, but I'm his girlfriend and I really want to surprise him. Here's my ID." She said pulling out her driver's license. "I also have a credit card if you need it."

He glanced at the license, and then looked her up and down and after giving the Louis Vuitton overnight bag a nod, he gave his stamp of approval. His expression indicated that he approved of her taste in luggage, more than her credibility as his girlfriend. Parris slipped him a twenty dollar bill, to show her appreciation and just in case he tried to get amnesia in the future.

"Thank you and have a good evening Ms. Reed."

"I plan to." She replied with a smile.

When she got off the elevator, his apartment was down at the end of the hallway.

"Pizza delivery!" she said knocking on the door, trying to disguise her voice.

"I didn't order anything!" he yelled through the door.

"Well, I'm not leaving til you open the door buddy!" she yelled back. "I've gotta pepperoni pizza here with your name on it!"

He swung the door open abruptly, looking like a professor with a pencil behind his ear and glasses on his forehead.

"Look! I didn't…" he started saying until he saw her face.

"Oh, yes you did." she said with a smile.

"Aw damn, hey baby what are you doing here?" He said pulling her close and hugging her.

"I just wanted to surprise you. I felt bad about the gym episode and us arguing and I wanted to make it up to you." She said kissing his neck. "I'm sorry Victor."

"I'm sorry too. I missed you." He replied.

They closed the door behind them, kissing and hugging all the way into the living room. When they reached the couch, Victor pushed the file folders onto the floor, got on top and started unbuttoning her blouse.

"Wait just one minute." She said trying to get from under him.

"Wait for what?" he said looking at her like she was crazy.

"I told you I want to make it up to you, so just let me do my thing."

Victor reluctantly let her get up and Parris grabbed her bag and took it into the kitchen. She opened a few cabinets until she found the wine glasses.

"Do you have any matches?"

"In the top drawer near the stove." He said as he began to pick up the scattered papers and folders.

"Put those papers down Victor, I'll be ready in one minute. Go in the bedroom and get comfortable. I'll be right there."

She quickly put the scented candles on the night tables and lit them. After she poured the wine, she ran back to the kitchen got her overnight bag and went into the bathroom. Two minutes later she came out.

"Ready or not here I come!" she said walking into the empty bedroom in her new teddy.

"Oh Victor, not tonight." She said pouting like a five year old.

"I'm coming, just one more paragraph Babe. This trial is kicking my ass."

"I'm gonna kick your ass you if don't put those papers down and come over here. Do you see how hot I am right now?"

Victor quickly glanced her way and said, "The outfit looks great Babe, I'll be there in one minute."

Feeling like the air was let out of her balloon; Parris gulped down the first glass of wine and poured a second. She knew that one more paragraph meant at least ten more pages, so she got into bed and turned on the television in the meantime. After two glasses of wine and a repeat of "ER", she was asleep and Victor was still out in the living room working.

Parris woke up at 6:30am the next morning and found him in the arm chair slouched over and snoring. She took his glasses off and kissed his forehead.

"So much for making up." She whispered.

"Huh? I'm awake, come on I'm ready now." He said sounding like Froggie from the Little Rascals.

"Too late." She said as she turned to walk away.

"Girl, come here, it ain't never too late for some good lovin'." He said grabbing her from behind.

"Yes, it is. I was all ready to love you down last night. I'm ready to get something eat now. Let's go."

He pulled her down on his lap and started tickling her. She was squirming and laughing uncontrollably.

"Stop!" she begged. "It's too early for this."

"No, not until you give me some." He said continuing to tickle her all over.

"Never!" she said laughing and trying to fight him off.

Now they were on the floor and the papers were getting crushed underneath her behind. She was laughing so hard, tears were running down her face.

"Stop! Stop! Okay, I give up!"

"That's more like it." He said removing his pants.

Their loving making was full of passion, transferring heat between their bodies like an electric current. They started on the living room floor, it was fast and furious, both of them relieving their aggressions and it ended slow and tender in the bedroom. The mulberry aroma from the candles still filled the air, as they lay in each other's arms completely exhausted. Everything was back to normal.

Chapter

24

Right on schedule, the autumn breeze was getting cooler and the leaves were performing their awesome routine of changing colors. Parris snuggled under the covers and even though it was Saturday, she decided to skip cleaning the house today. It was her birthday and she wasn't doing anything that she didn't feel like doing; playing Hazel was first on the list of things *not* to do. The only thing she couldn't skip today was going to the salon and getting ready for tonight. Shelly's gift was a beauty day at a new African-American owned salon that just opened. Whenever Shelly treated or gave a gift, it was always top of the line. Manicure, pedicure, hair, facial, massage and lunch. Parris was excited about getting the royal treatment, courtesy of Ms. Shelly Jones.

Victor was in Washington D.C., but promised he would be back this afternoon. He went down to talk with a record producer to get some information on a potential client.

She lay in bed wondering what kind of gift he would give her. He had impeccable taste and she couldn't wait to see what he picked out. He was very hush-hush about the details of the evening, even Shelly was clueless. The suspense was killing her.

Around ten o'clock, Parris was just about to roll out of bed when the phone rang giving her a reason to lie back down.

"Hello."

"Happy Birthday to you, Happy Birthday to you, Happy Birthday dear Pumpkin, Happy Birthday to you!" her parents sang in unison.

"Thank you, thank you, thank you!"

"So, how old is my baby today? Twenty-two or twenty-three?" her father asked.

"Twenty-two Cole, and that makes us only forty." Her mother answered with a chuckle.

"Nice try, but the answer is thirty. I can't believe it. Good thing I don't look it, huh?" she teased.

"No you don't pumpkin. You're as beautiful as the day I had you. You know you were born at 10:15 in the evening and I was in labor for twelve long hours. Those contractions…"

"Oh boy, here we go." Her father interjected.

"Oh, hush Cole, you'd be telling that story over and over too if you had gone through that kinda pain." Helen snapped.

"Alright you guys, don't start." Parris said.

"You're right baby, what do you have planned for today, anything special?" Coleman asked.

"First, Shelly's treating me to "the works" at the salon. Then Victor has something planned for tonight, but I don't know what it is. He's not back from D.C. yet."

"He's not? Well what time do you expect him?" Helen asked.

"I'm not sure, he drove down last night, but I'm sure he'll call and let me know."

"Alright then P, we'll let you go. Have a good time tonight, love you."

She hung up the phone and went to the bathroom. She looked at her face in the mirror while brushing her teeth and decided she'd get her eyebrows waxed too. The phone started ringing again and giving her yet another excuse to get back in bed.

"Happy Birthday P, you ole' hag!" Shelly said laughing.

"Oh, you think that's funny? Your ass is right behind me, so we'll see who gets the last laugh!"

"Whatever grandma. Our appointment is at twelve. I figured we can go get something to eat afterwards." Shelly replied.

"That's cool. I'll be ready."

"So, what's up for tonight?"

"Girl, I don't know. Victor is still in D.C. and won't be back until this afternoon."

"D.C.? What the hell is he doing there?"

"He had to meet with a producer or something."

"And he had to do it today? On your birthday?" Shelly questioned.

"He left last night, either way he better have his butt back here like he said."

"I know that's right, girl. Kevin didn't mention anything to me yet, but I'll keep you posted. Be ready at quarter of."

"Okay, bye."

This time when she got up, it was for good and she made her bed to make sure. She took a quick shower and got dressed. She ironed her boot-cut faded jeans with a frayed hem and a red silk v-neck sweater. The shoes were hard because she didn't want to mess up her pedicure and it was a little too cold for sandals, so she ended up putting on a pair of clogs and hoped for the best.

Before she left, she tried to call Victor, but got his voice mail. She couldn't believe it was almost noon and he hadn't called to wish her a happy birthday. Determined not to mess up her day, she left a short message and headed for the salon.

Three hours later, she felt wonderful. Bruce was the name of the masseuse with the magical hands. In the middle of the massage, she began to laugh. He asked her what was so funny and she told him that it reminded her of a scene from the sitcom "Girlfriends", when Joan had her masseuse making house calls with happy endings. Bruce found the story humorous and let her know that he made house calls too.

After lunch, they decided to go shopping for an outfit for tonight. The King of Prussia mall was crowded as usual on Saturday. After looking in almost every store, she finally found the perfect outfit in Neiman Marcus. When she tried it on and came out of the dressing room to show Shelly, one of the sales women said she looked like a million bucks. The balance in her checking account after that purchase looked like she had spent about the same. Shelly reminded her that was her birthday and she was worth it. Parris could always count on her best friend to put things into perspective.

It was around four o'clock when they left the mall and still no word from Victor. Parris was beginning to worry.

"You don't think he's had an accident or something, do you Shell?"

"Of course not, he's probably trying to get everything ready for tonight. Don't worry, he'll call. Besides, they're never hurt when we're sitting at home worrying about them, they're just fuckin' up."

"Oh thanks, that makes me feel better."

"You know what I mean. He'll probably just show up. And if for some strange reason he doesn't, I've got your back. You've gotta wear that outfit tonight!"

"Thanks Shell." She said gazing out the window.

When she got home, there was a birthday message from Kenya and her grandmother, but nothing from Victor. She watched a little television to keep her mind off of worrying. The movie, "The Matrix" was on and Laurence Fishburne was looking good.

Around 5:30pm, the telephone rang.

"Happy Birthday Babe!" Victor said.

"Victor, where are you? Do you know what time it is?" Parris started rattling off.

"I'm sorry Parris, the guy was late and wasn't prepared and everything got all backed up."

"Where are you?"

"I'm on the road, I should be there in about an hour. I'll pick you up around nine. Okay?"

"Fine. I can't believe you're just now calling me."

"I know, I just lost track of time. I'm sorry P."

"Alright, well, drive safely and I'll see you in a bit. I love you."

"I love you too."

Chapter

25

Parris closed her eyes and sang along with Jill Scott as she soaked in the tub. She was finally able to relax now that she had spoken with Victor. It was already eight o'clock and she needed to start getting dressed. The warm pulsating jets of water felt good against her skin, but those three hundred dollar, soft leather pants were going to feel even better, she thought to herself.

She had to admit the outfit was "shitty-sharp" as Shelly put it. The camel colored pants, with a matching full-length duster, made her look like she just stepped off a New York catwalk during fashion week. The three inch heels, on her ostrich boots, where higher than what she was used to, but they completed the look and she would have to endure.

At 8:57, Victor rang the doorbell. Parris wondered why he wasn't using his key. When she opened the door, all she could see were flowers and legs. Victor's face was buried behind dozens of roses. He was holding three dozen, each one a different color, red, pink and yellow.

"Happy Birthday Baby!" he said from behind the roses.

"Oh Victor, they're beautiful!" she beamed.

She took one of the dozen and sat them on the dining room table, Victor followed her lead. They embraced and kissed like they had been apart for years.

"I'm so glad you're here." She whispered.

"Did you think I would miss your birthday?"

"Honestly? Yes. You were cutting it mighty close."

"True, but you've got to have more faith in me."

"I know." She said and kissed him gently on the lips.

"That's better. You should put these in water before we leave."

"Good idea."

He watched her walk into the kitchen, as those tight leather pants hugged her behind.

"Those pants are hot Babe. Do we have time for a quickie?" Victor asked knowing she would refuse.

"No, but wait until you see the jacket that goes with them." She yelled from the kitchen.

Victor checked his watch and helped her place the flowers a vase.

"We better get going, our reservations are for nine-thirty."

"Okay, just let me grab my coat."

When they arrived at the restaurant, the valet listened carefully as Victor tipped him twenty dollars and then gave him the do's and don'ts about the car. The hostess greeted them and they were seated immediately at a private booth. The table was beautifully set with candles and fine China. There was a bottle of champagne chilling and waiting to be popped. The waiter pulled out her chair and carefully placed the linen napkin across her lap.

"How did you manage to get reservations? This place keeps a thirty-day waiting list." She whispered.

"It was tough, but you've gotta know the right people." He replied with a wink.

"And obviously you do." She smiled back.

The waiter filled their water glasses and Victor checked his Rolex again. The wait for the appetizers was very short and the main entrée soon followed. Victor ordered prime rib and Parris got the grilled salmon and sautéed shrimp. By the time they finished, she was stuffed and the tight leather pants showed no mercy. To make matters worse, Victor requested to see the dessert tray.

"Oh honey, I can't eat dessert."

"Parris, you have to try their chocolate mousse." To the waiter he said, "Can you bring a plate of the chocolate mousse and don't forget the raspberry sauce on the side, thanks."

"Yes sir, coming right up?" The waiter smiled and when he returned with the tray two minutes later, he placed the small sterling silver tray with a lid on the table and excused himself.

"Will that be all Mr. Baxter?"

"Yes, that's fine. Thank you." He replied glancing at his watch again.

"Am I holding you up? Why do you keep looking at your watch? You've been clock watching all night, what's wrong with you?" she asked sounding a little annoyed.

"Why don't you try your dessert?" He said ignoring her.

"I told you I'm stuffed, I can't take another bite, really."

"You have to Parris, please, for me. Just one bite." He insisted handing her a folk.

"Do I have to try it now? Can't I just take it home?"

"No, it won't taste the same. Just one bite, please P." he said looking at his watch again.

"Fine."

When Parris opened the lid, there was a stunning emerald cut, platinum engagement ring surrounded by white rose pedals in the center of the silver tray. The stone was huge; her best guess was three carats.

"Oh my God!" she gasped. "Oh my God!"

"Do you like it?"

"Oh my God, Victor, you didn't." she said covering her mouth with her hand.

"Yes, I did." He cleared and throat, Parris Reed, will you marry me?"

"I'm speechless." she said still staring at the awesome piece of jewelry.

"All I want to hear is a simple, *yes*".

She looked away from the ring and directly into his eyes. Tears began to fill her own, she closed her eyes as they began to run down her cheek. She quickly took her napkin and wiped them away, when she opened them again, she gave him her answer.

"Yes."

He looked at his watch again and then removed the ring from the box and placed it on her finger. Her left hand was shaking. Now several couples, including the waiters were watching with anticipation, some even applauded and whistled.

"It's 10:15pm, the exact time you entered this world. I wanted to wait for this exact moment to ask you to enter mine."

Chapter

26

At 10:25pm, her cell phone rang. It was her parents, Kenya and Shelly all vying for a chance to talk and find out if she said yes.

"You all knew about this?"

"Of course, we did. He even asked me for permission." Coleman proudly replied.

"How do you think he knew what time you were born?" Her mother said in the background.

"You are so bad." She said shaking her finger at him.

"Are you on a speaker phone? Where are you guys at? Where's that music coming from?" Parris asked.

"They're waiting for you P." Victor answered.

"Where?" she asked with excitement.

"At the hotel, hurry up and get your ass over here so we can celebrate!" Shelly shouted.

"This is too much."

Victor reserved a penthouse suite at the Ritz-Carlton. It was decorated with dozens of balloons and streamers. When they walked in everyone sang Happy Birthday and she had to blow out all thirty candles on the cake her father was holding.

When Shelly and her mother saw the ring, they both started crying. Kenya just kept saying it was 'the bomb'. Her father, Kevin and Sean all congratulated Victor and the young men listened as Coleman gave his advice on marriage and how to make it last.

"You've got to think like they do fellas. I know it's a stretch, but if you can manage it every once in while, it works." Coleman advised.

"Think like them? Who in their right mind wants to do that? That means I'll have to multi-task and that's not my forte." Kevin said.

"Exactly, and I'll be worried about *everything*, and frankly, I don't have that kind of time." Victor replied.

"Guys, guys, it's really not as hard as you think. And I'm not talking about worrying and stuff like that, shoot, I wouldn't even try to keep up with Helen in that area. Listen, most women are naturally givers and men are takers. When they go shopping for instance, after they've gone in every store and spent up all your money, they'll usually have something in one of those bags for you. Especially, if they know you're gonna love it, they're just thoughtful like that. Men, on the other hand, can go to one store in the mall, get what we want or something close and leave. End of story."

"That's because we know what we want *before* we get there." Sean added.

"No. That's because we're generally selfish. We usually only think about ourselves, unless it's a holiday, birthday or something and even then, we have to be reminded. Meanwhile, we've passed a hundred things she'd like. It doesn't always have to be a big-ticket item either. All I'm saying is, think of her, like she thinks about you." Coleman replied. The two young men nodded their heads, pondering the thought as if it were a new found scientific breakthrough.

"You may be onto something Mr. Reed, because my closet is full of clothes Shelly got for me." Kevin said. When we first met, she bought me something new almost every week.

"That's because your wardrobe was whack!" Sean joked.

"What? Don't even try it man!" Kevin replied and then asked, "Was it really that bad?"

Meanwhile, Parris made her rounds saying hello and thanking the small group of family and friends that were invited. It didn't get any better than this, everyone she loved was there, including the man she wanted to spend the rest of her life with.

Shelly caught her having a sentimental moment and handed her another glass of champagne.

"P, that ring is gorgeous."

"I know, I can't believe it's mine. I can't believe this night, it's like a fairytale or something."

"Well Cinderella, it looks like you've got yourself a prince and you deserve it after all the frogs you've kissed."

"He is so sweet Shell. Even though it's only been six months, I feel like I've known him forever. He makes me so happy."

"I'm happy for you. He's a good guy P, so don't fuck up."

"Trust me girl, I'm not messing this one up." She said sipping her champagne. Ever since I was a little girl, I used to fantasize about my wedding. It was gonna be big, with ten bride's maids and ten grooms men. My flowers were going to be pink and white and my gown would have along train. I had it all planned out down to the invitations."

"That's funny because I never really thought about it and at this point, I would just go to the justice of peace and save the money on a ten-day honeymoon. Maybe visit Italy or Spain, nah, definitely Africa. I want to see the pyramids."

"You don't you want a wedding Shelly? You have to walk down the aisle."

"Why, P? My mom's gone and I don't know where my father is, so I really don't see the point."

"I know, but, I just think every woman deserves a special day when all the attention is focused on her and you know… I know it might sound corny, but whatever." Parris replied. She could tell the conversation was making Shelly think about her mom and she didn't want to put a damper on this happy occasion, so she quickly changed the subject.

"You know you're my Maid of Honor, right?"

"Naturally." Shelly replied with a smile.

"Ironically, now that my wedding is becoming a reality, I don't want a big wedding, just you and Kenya. I'd rather keep it simple. No kids either and I'm going to make sure I put that on the invitations."

"What if Victor wants more guys in it?" Shelly asked.

"They can ushers or something, can't they?"

"P, it's your day. They can be whatever you want. Have you talked about a date yet?"

"Not really, but I do know he doesn't want to get married in July or August because it's too hot."

"Makes sense, September is nice."

"Yeah, I was thinking the same thing."

After everyone left, Parris was worn out. All the excitement and champagne had taken its toll. Victor was asleep as soon as his head hit the pillow. She didn't bother to wake him, even though she was high and horny. Although staring at the giant rock on her finger was almost enough to make her have an orgasm all by itself.

The next morning they ordered room service. Victor had a western omelet and Parris got a Belgian waffle. They ate in bed and talked about the wedding.

"Do you want to pick a date?" she asked.

"It's up to you, but I would prefer to wait until next fall. I hate summer weddings. It's too damn hot to be in a tux."

"That sounds reasonable. The trees are so pretty at that time, they'll make a wonderful back-drop for the pictures." She replied.

Parris finished her orange juice and went into the bathroom. Victor scrambled to find his jacket because his cell phone was ringing. When she came out he was still talking. It sounded like a business call and he was ruffling though some folders in his brief case that he insisted on bringing in from the car. Parris started channel surfing while she waited for him to finish.

"When I check my schedule, I'll let you know what day is good for me." He said to the caller.

Twenty minutes later, he was still on the phone.

"You know I can't do that. Be reasonable." He said.

Parris decided to finish opening her birthday cards, since it didn't sound like he was getting off any time soon. She was trying not to get annoyed, but the longer the conversation continued, the more it started sounding like it might be personal or a little of both.

"Why don't you just do what we discussed earlier, that will work better for the both of us." He said.

She waved her hands to get his attention and he held his index finger up for her to wait one more minute. Now, she was mad, it was Sunday. What was so important that it couldn't wait until tomorrow, she wondered.

He walked into the bathroom and shut the door. Five minutes passed and then he opened the door. Parris couldn't remember if she heard the toilet flush.

"Sounds like a plan. I'll talk to you later." He said then hung up the phone.

"It's about time." Parris said.

"I'm sorry Babe. Are you ready to get outta here?"

"Well, umm, I guess, if you are. What time is check-out?"

"Probably twelve, but I've got some paperwork to finish for tomorrow."

He walked over and gave her a quick kiss, then went back into the bathroom and turned on the shower. He sat reading the newspaper while he waited for Parris to get ready. She wasn't in a rush, so she took her time. She could see that he was becoming impatient because he asked her twice, within ten minutes, if she was almost ready. The first time she said no, but the second time she didn't bother to answer. She was not going to race to get ready, just so he could go home and finish some paperwork. Parris knew she was being spiteful, but she didn't care.

The ride home was uneventful and quiet. He dropped her off, said I love you and after a quick kiss on the lips, her prince was gone.

Chapter

27

Sean almost had a coronary when she showed him the ring up close; last night he barely got a chance to see it. He got up from his desk and pulled her hand over to the window to see the brilliant stone in the natural light. Parris was still giddy. "Isn't it gorgeous?"

"He's serious." He said shaking his head.

"I certainly hope so." She replied.

"Vic always has to go all out." Sean said. "He was always good for showing the rest of us up." He walked back to his desk and sat down. "Have you guys set a date?"

"No, not yet, but it will probably be some time next fall, maybe September or October. Victor doesn't want a summer wedding."

"I guess the first wedding left a bad taste in his mouth in more ways than one."

"Why, what happened?"

"They got married in the middle of August and it was two hundred degrees outside and it was out in the park. We were sweating our balls off in those tuxes."

"Well, your balls will be nice and comfy this time. And no wonder you were sweating, they picked the hottest month of the year. What was she thinking?" she replied.

"She wasn't thinking. She was too busy trying to catch him cheating or some dumb shit like that."

Sean's last comment made her sit down, "What do you mean cheating?"

"I don't know, she was paranoid, I guess. He could barely go to work without her checking up on him. She wanted to know who he was talking to, where he was going. You know how you ladies get."

"Well, did he give her a *reason* to be paranoid Sean?"

"I don't know, but even if he did, you don't have his phone tapped and show up unexpected in court while he's working." He said as he shoved some folders into a drawer that was already too crowded. "You gotta admit that was a bit extreme."

Parris was silent for a moment, she thought about the phone call he received back in the hotel. She picked up miniature football helmet that accompanied the rest of the Philadelphia Eagles paraphernalia on his desk.

"What's wrong?" he asked.

"Nothing."

"Yes it is, because you got silent and you're still hanging around. Don't you have work to do?"

"Yes, plenty." She said looking down at the ring.

"Then what's wrong? Are you nervous or do you have doubts?" he asked.

"I little of both I guess. I don't know. Don't get me wrong, I love Victor. It's just all happening so fast and I don't know if…, never mind, I'll talk to you later." She said standing up and placing the bobbing Donovan McNabb figure back on the desk.

"Just take one day at a time and you'll be alright." He said with a smile. "There's no rush, you know?"

"I know and I will, thanks Sean." She said leaving his office.

Parris spent the rest of the day in meetings. But she could not get Sean's comment about Victor's ex-wife out of her head. Most people are paranoid for a reason, he must have done something to make her doubt him, she thought to herself, trying to rationalize the situation.

She had a lunch date with a supervisor from the claims department who was having problems with an employee. She wanted to meet so that they could go over the company policy before firing the woman.

When she returned from lunch, there was a message from Victor. He said he had to work late and might not make it back tonight. Just what she didn't want to hear after that conversation with Sean. She tried to call him back, but his secretary said she just missed him. His cell phone went right to voice mail. She left a message saying she would be home later too. Even though she was only going food shopping, she felt better letting him know.

The supermarket was fairly empty by the time she got off work and drove back to Jersey. She walked down every aisle, something she rarely did, but since she was in no hurry to get home, she took her time. By the time she finished, the shopping cart was full and it was dark outside and raining. She could see the wind blowing papers around through the window near the checkout line.

"Damn, I was hoping to beat the rain." She told the cashier.

"Yeah, it looks nasty out there. Hopefully it'll all be over by the time I get off at eleven because I've gotta walk home." She said bagging the milk. "Your total comes to seventy-seven, twenty-six."

"That's a shame, can't you take the bus or get a ride?" Parris said handing her the money.

"Not tonight, my husband's working late and he has the car and the stupid bus stops running out my way at ten." She replied looking tired and sad.

"Well, good luck." She replied not knowing what else to say.

Parris was soaked by the time she got the bags in the car and returned the cart. She was cursing the entire time because her black suede pumps were probably ruined. When she pulled out of the lot, traffic was backed up and creeping along.

"Great. I'll never get home." She said.

She could see the lights flashing from police cars up ahead, so there must have been accident. She thought about the cashier and thought about how blessed she was to have a good job and a nice car. As traffic crept along, she saw a woman up ahead trying to flag someone down. The woman was about three car-lengths away and no one ahead of her was stopping to help. Her Mercedes was on the shoulder with the flashers on. As Parris slowly passed by, she looked at the woman in her rear-view mirror and felt sorry for her. It was easy to sympathize because she was soaking wet. She appeared to be attractive and very well-dressed. For a split-second, she debated stopping to help, but then thought about all the people, women especially, who are killed helping strangers. Traffic came to a stand still and the woman tapped on the passenger side window. The tapping startled her. She looked at the woman, hesitated, and then rolled down the window.

"I'm sorry to bother you, but my car broke down and the battery on my cell is dead. Do you think I could use your phone to make a call?" She asked wiping the dripping hair from her face.

Parris was right; she was a very attractive woman. She was light-brown skinned with shoulder length brown hair and pretty hazel eyes, despite the mascara running down her cheek. Parris felt bad because she looked upset. She looked distressed, not threatening. They were about the same size, and if worse came to worse, Parris thought she could take her, so she unlocked the car door.

Chapter

28

"Oh, thank you so much. I really appreciate it." She said as she got in the car. "I'm really sorry, but I was running out of options and I'm soaked, my shoes are ruined and no one wanted to stop. You're the first person to even look my way."

Parris was glad the seats were leather because she was getting water everywhere. She took her phone out of her handbag and was ready to hand it to the woman, but it started ringing.

"Hey Babe. What's up?" (pause) "Oh Victor, do you have to? (pause) I know, I just hoped you would make it home tonight."

The woman was searching her purse for something, but stopped when she heard something familiar. Now, she was listening more intently to Parris' conversation.

"Okay." (pause) "I'm giving a woman a ride, her car broke down." (pause) "Don't worry I will." (pause) "Okay, I love you too. Bye."

"Sorry. That was my fiancé."

"Oh, really." The woman replied.

"Yes, we just got engaged over the weekend."

"Congratulations. Can I see your ring?" she asked.

Parris extended her left hand across the steering wheel, flashing the brilliant diamond.

"It's beautiful, emerald cut, that's my favorite."

"Thank you. Mine too. I don't know how he knew, it was a total surprise." Parris said adjusting the ring.

"You're a very lucky woman."

"Yes I am and he's a good hard-working man, almost too hard-working. He called to tell me he wasn't coming home tonight."

"Why's that?" She asked curiously.

"He's a lawyer and works in New York, so sometimes he works late and stays up there. It's easier."

"Oh, I guess that would be more convenient." The woman replied as she glanced at Parris' ring again. "Can I use the phone now?"

"Sure, I'm sorry, here. What did you say your name was again?" Parris asked handing her the phone.

"I didn't, but it's Leslie."

"Nice to meet you Leslie, I'm Parris."

"Likewise. I just want to call the car dealer and see if I can get it towed." She said dialing the number.

Traffic starting moving again and the rain was slowing down. After a few rings, she hung up the phone and handed it back to Parris.

"Damn it. They're not there and I can't leave a message. I'll have to call in the morning. I can't believe this. I just had it in for service two weeks ago." She said wiping her wet hair away from her face again.

"That's a shame, of all the days to leave you stranded. That car is a little too expensive to be breaking down." Parris said shaking her head. "Do you live around here? Maybe, I can drop you off somewhere."

"Oh, that's okay, I don't want to put you out." Leslie replied.

"It's no problem, let me take you home, it's the least I can do."

"Are you sure?" She replied watching Parris intently.

"I'm sure, where to?" Parris replied noticing that she was staring.

"I live in Medford, it's kind of far. I don't want to make you drive all the way out there is this weather. Just drop me off at the next gas station so I can call a cab."

"It's not that far, my parents live in that area." Parris replied. "Besides, we live in Jersey remember, catching a cab might take while. I'll just take you home."

"That would be great! I really appreciate it and I owe you. I have had the worse day, but after meeting you, it's starting to brighten up." Leslie said smiling.

"Oops, I forgot, I've got ice cream in the trunk. I live right around the corner, just let me put it in the fridge and we can be on our way."

"Sure, no problem." Leslie replied.

Parris took the bags in the house, while Leslie waited in the car. She put away the milk and ice cream and took off her soggy shoes and put on sneakers. As she walked towards the car, she noticed Leslie was smoking a cigarette and holding it out the window.

"I hope you don't mind, I had to have one. I quit last year, but, like I said, it's been a long day." Leslie said. "I keep a pack on me, just in case."

Parris did not respond, but the look on her face let her know it wasn't okay, especially in her new car.

Leslie caught the hint. "Say no more." She said as she flicked it out the window with two fingers.

"Okay, now we can go." Parris said starting the car.

"Nice townhouse, I see you have a garage, that's always nice. Is there an association fee?"

"Thanks. No, there's no fee. I've been here almost three years and I really like it."

"Where are you going to live when you get married?"

"Good question. We're not sure yet, he has a single home, but I'm not sure I want to move into another woman's house. He was married before."

"I know what you mean." Leslie replied. "That could be awkward."

"Can I take Evesham Road?" Parris asked.

"Yes, that's probably the fastest way to go."

The two women were silent for a few minutes, only the sound of the wipers moving back and forth filled the car.

"Make a left on Rt. 73 and then a right at the first light. My development is on the left."

"Oh, you live in Wiltshire Estates; I heard they were very nice."

"I'm comfortable. It's up here on the right, right here." Leslie said pointing at the large brick house.

"These are nice." Parris said pulling into the driveway. "I love the double doors."

"Thanks Parris, you're a life saver. Let me get your number and maybe I can take you to lunch or something to pay you back." She said with a smile.

"Sure, that would be nice. Here's my card. Give me a call any time. Hope everything works out okay with your car."

"Me too. Thanks again and I'll be giving you a call very soon."

Chapter

29

Victor came home the following evening, so Parris decided to give him a taste of her culinary skills. Most nights they went out to dinner or ordered take-out and she wanted him to know she was more than just a pretty face. She decided to prepare a down-home meal he could sink his teeth into, so she called her mother to get a few recipe tips.

"Hey Ma, how are you?"

"I'm fine P, how are you?"

"I'm good. I'm fixing dinner for Victor and I need to know what you put in your sweet potatoes."

"Just some butter, cinnamon, brown sugar and nutmeg, you can add some white sugar too if you want." Helen replied.

"Okay. Where's daddy?"

"He's sleeping. His arthritis has been acting up and when it starts getting cold outside, his knees get stiff."

"Give him a kiss for me. Oh yeah, have you talked to Kenya lately?"

"Not in a few days, why?"

"Neither have I. I was just thinking about her today, that's all. I'll give her a call later."

"She said she was going to stop by, but you can't count on that girl for nothin'."

"That's *your* child. Alright Ma, let me go, because I haven't even started cleaning the collar greens yet."

"Oh, I see you're going all out tonight, huh?" Helen teased.

"Yes, I gotta take care of my man."

"That's right, you know what I always say, if you don't, some other woman will."

"I'll talk to you later Ma, love you." She said and hung up.

Parris got started preparing the meal. It took her while to clean the greens, but once she got them in the pot, she was able to concentrate on the rest of the food. It was only six o'clock and Victor's train didn't arrive until six forty-five, so she had a little bit of time. The phone rang just as she was putting the chicken in the oven. She checked the oven temperature and wiped her hands on her apron before she picked up.

"What took you so long to answer?" Shelly asked.

"Jeez, I was wiping my hands off. You are so impatient. What's up girl?"

"Not much, I was just calling to see how the newly engaged couple is doing."

"We're fine. I'm fixing a home cooked meal for my baby tonight." Parris said with a smile.

"Since when do you cook?"

"Don't even try it Shell, you know I can cook." She said stirring the cheese into the macaroni.

"I know you can, I said, since when *do you* cook P, don't front."

"Shut up Shelly. How's Kevin?"

"On my last nerve. I don't want to talk about him right now. What are you doing on Saturday morning?"

"Nothing that I know of, why?"

"I need you to help me redo my resume. They are starting to trip on my job and I've gotta start looking." Shelly replied.

"Sure no problem, what time?"

"Around ten, I guess?"

"That's good. Hey, guess what?"

"What?" Shelly replied.

"I met a nice sistah the other night. Her car broke down and I gave her a ride home."

"You did what? What the hell made you pick up a perfect stranger?" Shelly asked is disbelief.

"It was pouring outside Shelly!" Parris said taking the Pillsbury dinner rolls out of the refrigerator.

"So! Damn that. People are too crazy out here to be giving strangers a ride, woman or not. What's wrong with you P?"

"Shelly listen, she was driving a Benz, well dressed and harmless. She lives in Medford."

"So."

"Stop being so paranoid. The woman needed help and I helped her out. Besides, I would have wanted someone to do the same for me."

"Alright, Miss Good Samaritan."

"Whatever. She was nice and she offered to take me to lunch to thank me."

"Okay P, you're better than me, because I would have left her ass right there. Anyway, I've gotta go, tell Vic I said hello."

When Victor came through the door, Parris had the table set, candles and all. He threw his briefcase on the sofa and plopped down in the chair looking exhausted.

"Hi Babe." Parris said greeting him with a kiss.

"Hey. I have had the worse day." He said rubbing his temples.

"Well, I cooked you a nice dinner, so go get washed up."

"You cooked?" he asked sounding surprised.

"Yes! Why is everyone acting so surprised?"

"Because in the time I've known you, you have never cooked me dinner, only breakfast. I thought I was going to have to eat eggs and bacon for the rest of my life." He said laughing.

"Very funny." She said rolling her eyes at him.

Dinner turned out perfect and Victor cleaned his plate. Their conversation was all about Victor's cases. After thirty minutes, she wasn't even listening anymore. She was tired of hearing about his clients and she tried changing the subject several times, but it kept going back to his job. He didn't once ask her about her day.

After having more than an ear full, Parris started clearing the table and washing the dishes. Victor went into the living room and started working.

"Dinner was delicious, Babe." He yelled from the living room.

"Thanks." She said with no enthusiasm.

Parris put away the last dish and was about to go take a bath, when the telephone rang.

"Hi, can I speak to Parris?"

"Speaking."

"This is Leslie, from the other night. How are you?"

"Oh hi, I'm fine. How did you make out with your car?"

"They forgot to reconnect a cable or something. I'm back on the road now, thank goodness."

"That's good." Parris replied.

"Did I catch you at a bad time?" Leslie asked.

"No, not at all, I just finished washing dishes."

"I wanted to know if you would like to go to brunch on Saturday?"

"Sure, that sounds nice. What time?"

"How about ten?"

"That's fine." Parris replied forgetting about the plans she had already made with Shelly.

"I'll pick *you* up this time, if that's okay?"

"That'll work. I'll see you then."

When Parris finished her bath, Victor was still reading.

"Why don't you come to bed, honey?" Parris said.

"In a minute." He replied.

"I've got dessert waiting for you."

"What kind?"

"It's hot, chocolate and starts with a P."

Victor jumped up, walked to the bedroom and stood in the doorway. Parris was lying in the bed under the covers.

"Is it chocolate pudding?" he asked with a smile.

"You're getting warmer, maybe this will help." She said removing the sheet and revealing her naked body.

"Oh yeah, Ummm, that's my favorite." He said jumping on top of her.

Chapter

30

When Leslie rang the doorbell fifteen minutes earlier than expected, Parris was in her bra and panties, brushing her teeth thinking about Victor. Their a.m. love-making session lasted over an hour. Surprisingly, he still had enough energy to go to the gym, while Parris laid in bed feeling spent. She rinsed her mouth and quickly grabbed her silk robe to answer the door.

"I know I'm early." Leslie said. "I'm sorry. I've got a thing about being on time."

"I'll be ready in a minute. Come on in and have a seat." Parris replied. "I have the same "hate to be late" disease."

"Please, take your time." Leslie said looking around the living room. "Nice place you have here. You have exquisite taste, I see you like African art, me too. If you ever get a chance to visit, you should, you'll love it."

"You've been to Africa? That's on my list of things to do, I'm jealous."

"It's an experience you'll never forget. The people, the culture, its unbelievable, Oh my God and the pyramids, they're breath-taking!"

"You'll have to tell me all about it over lunch. Let me go finish getting ready, make yourself at home, I'll be right back." She said disappearing into the bedroom.

Leslie slowly walked around the room admiring the black art work and unique sculptures.

"You really have some great pieces here." She said.

"Thanks, I enjoy collecting them from all of the different places I've visited." Parris yelled back from the bedroom.

A photograph on the mantle above the fireplace, made Leslie freeze dead in her tracks. It was a picture of Parris and Victor that was taken on her birthday. Leslie picked up the frame and stared at the photo trying desperately to suppress the thoughts that were swirling around in her head. The picture reminded her of how happy they once were. They were in love and planning to live a long, happy life together. They had it all, money, successful careers and each other. She once thought that was all she would ever need, and then in an flash, it was gone. She hated him for what he had done and seeing him look so happy made her furious.

"Okay, I'm ready." Parris said walking into the living room.

Looking startled, "Oh, great. Is this your fiancé?" she asked still holding the picture.

"Yes, that's my baby Victor." She beamed.

"You guys make a nice couple." She replied placing the picture back on the mantle. "Shall we go?"

"I'm ready when you are."

Leslie decided to take Parris to an expensive and well-known restaurant located on the roof top of Rittenhouse Square. They served a variety of health-conscience meals ranging from salads to pasta dishes. Fresh flowers and exotic greenery adorned the off-white room. Today, the brunch clientele was full of distinguished women, many of which appeared to be associated with sororities or private clubs of some sort. Leslie was obviously a regular there because the hostess greeted her with a kiss and seated them at a wonderful table overlooking the city.

"This is a beautiful place and the view is great." Parris said.

"It's my favorite. I try to come at least once a week." Leslie replied as she scanned the menu. "Do you like salmon?" she asked.

"I love it." Parris said looking at her own menu.

"They have a grilled salmon and pasta dish that's fabulous, you should try it."

"Sounds good, maybe I will."

The waiter took their orders and returned a few minutes later with a small bouquet of miniature pink roses. He placed them in the center of the table.

"Thank you Pierre. They're beautiful." Leslie replied.

"And pink, your favorite." He said with a smile. "Your food will be out momentarily."

"Thanks. I love pink roses, my 'ex' used to buy them for me all the time and it's been a habit I can't seem to break." Leslie said as closed her eyes and smelled the roses.

"How long were you married?" Parris asked.

"Not long, he wasn't the man I thought he was." She said as she nibbled on some fresh fruit. "He had an insatiable desire for beautiful women."

"I'm sorry to hear that. I don't understand, you're a beautiful woman, why wasn't that enough." Parris replied.

"If I knew the answer to that question honey, I'd still be married, now wouldn't I?" she said with a tinge of sarcasm. "Hell, I never expected him to have an affair." her voice began to rise. "He claimed to be so fuckin' busy working, I don't even know when he had the time!" she said even louder and drawing attention.

Two older women at the table next to them looked over at Leslie and one of them whispered something to the other.

"What the fuck are you looking at?" Leslie snapped at them.

Shocked, they both turned their noses up and quickly looked away. Leslie rolled her eyes, took a sip of water and adjusted her linen napkin on her lap. Parris was stunned. Leslie's rude reaction was totally out of character, but she regained her composure immediately. Parris saw that it was very apparent she was still hurt and could not image who wouldn't be, given the same situation. The waiter returned with their food and Parris was grateful for the interruption. Leslie smile and thanked the waiter and then began eating her salad.

"Are you ladies okay, do you need anything else?" the waiter asked.

"No, everything's fine, thanks." Leslie replied with the same pleasant smile and demeanor as before.

"I'm fine too. So, Leslie, what do you do for a living?"

"Oh, uh, I'm an advisor." She answered quickly. "How's the pasta? Isn't it delicious?" she replied.

"It's great, thanks for the recommendation."

"How about you? What do you do?"

"I'm the Human Resource director at an insurance company downtown."

"That sounds interesting." Leslie said.

A cell phone began to ring, several women stopped to check their phones. Parris pulled out her phone and answered it.

"Where are you at?" Shelly asked sounding very annoyed.

"I'm in Philly having brunch with Leslie."

"Who?"

"Leslie, the woman I met the other day. I told you about her." Parris replied and smiled at Leslie.

"I thought you were going to help me work on my resume?"

"Oh my God Shell, I completely forgot. I'm sorry. Maybe we can hook up later."

"I can't, that's why I wanted to do it early. Never mind P, I'll talk to you later." Shelly replied and hung up.

"Damn, I can't believe I forgot." Parris said putting the phone back in her handbag.

"Is everything okay?" Leslie asked.

"Yes, I forgot about plans I made with my best friend."

"If she's your best friend, I'm sure she'll forgive you." Leslie said with a smile.

"Oh yeah, I'm not worried about that, I just can't believe I completely forgot. I don't usually forget appointments like that."

"Well, there's a first time for everything." Leslie replied.

After lunch, Leslie wanted to go window shopping on Walnut Street. They ended up doing more than looking and after a few purchases, they discovered they had the same taste in shoes and clothes. Leslie had very expensive taste and she did not seem to be concerned about the price. She dropped Parris off back at home around one o'clock. Parris didn't see Victor's car and wondered if he was coming back over after he finished working out.

"Thanks for a great afternoon Parris. I really enjoyed your company."

"Me too. We'll have to do it again soon." Parris replied as she got out of the car.

"Sounds good. I'll talk to you later."

Parris watched her pull off in the champagne colored Benz and wondered what kind of advisor could afford to shop til she dropped, live in the Wiltshire Estates and drive a car like that.

Chapter

31

Parris spent the next couple of months planning her dream wedding. She and Victor decided on the month of September to commit their lives to one another. It was already December, which left only nine months to plan. With Shelly's help, Parris was able to reserve a beautiful ballroom at BlackTie Catering in Cherry Hill. They also decided on a soft copper color for the girls dresses. Her mother tried to convince her to ask her two cousins, April and Dana, to be in the wedding, but Parris wasn't having it. April was extremely overweight and loved to complain about everything and Dana was only thirteen, neither of them were part of the vision she had for her big day. She told her mother that dealing with Kenya was all the drama she needed.

Right after Thanksgiving dinner, her parents made an announcement and surprised them with a gift, a check for ten thousand dollars that they had been saving for this special occasion. Fortunately, with her and Victor's salaries, they really didn't need the money to have their dream wedding, but her parents insisted they use it towards a new house. Victor was busy working and in court almost everyday, so he did not have much time to help with the arrangements. He said he trusted her judgment and that was just fine with Parris, as long as he signed the checks when she needed him to.

Christmas was only two days away and as usual, Shelly and Parris were just starting their shopping. They both took the day off from work and were at the doors of the mall at 9am when they opened. It was cold and snowing just enough to put a light coating on the grass.

"So, who do you have on your shopping list Shell?"

"It seems like everybody. I said I wasn't going to spend a lot of money this year, but I can never stick to it." Shelly replied.

"I know, but its Christmas and it only comes once a year. Remind me to get the gift certificates for my staff. I want to get something special for Maria's son." Parris said as she stopped to look at some tree ornaments.

"That's easy for you to say money bags. With the kind of money you and Vic make, you two should be Mr. and Mrs. Claus this year." She teased.

"Well, my dearest friend, if you need some extra cash, I've got your back!" Parris said giving her a kiss on the cheek.

"Thank you Mrs. Claus, but I don't really have a lot to get, just Kevin, Granny, you, Kenya, your parents, my boss and my neighbor, Mr. Jackson, I don't think he has any family and he's always so nice to me."

"Yeah, he is sweet. Let's go in Bloomingdale's first, I'm sure we can both find something for Kenya in there. You know how she is, it's gotta be designer." Parris replied.

Two hours later, each with several bags in hand, they made their way through the other last minute shoppers to the free gift wrapping station. Amazingly, there were only two people in line and they only had a few gifts to wrap.

"Mommy's gonna love this dress." Parris said as they waited in line. "And the hat matches perfect!"

"It's pretty and the color will look good on her." Shelly added.

The man in front of them had two small kids with him and they were restless and one was crying.

Whispering, Shelly said, "Why did he bring the kids with him? Now they already know what they're getting."

"It doesn't make sense, but I see a lot of parents do it." Reaching in her handbag, Shelly asked, "Do you want some gum."

"Yes, please." Parris replied.

"They take all the fun out of waking up Christmas morning." Shelly said.

A woman at the register finished paying and was having trouble putting the large gifts in her shopping bag. When she turned around, Parris recognized her.

"Leslie? Hey, how are you?"

"Oh, Hi Parris how's it going?" Leslie replied.

"Good. I'm trying to finish up my shopping. Leslie, this is my best friend Shelly."

"Nice to meet you. I just finished and I'm getting out of this crazy mall!"

"We're right behind you." Shelly added.

"Have you guys set a date yet?" Leslie asked Parris.

"Yes, September 20th."

"Congratulations, the weather should still be warm." Leslie replied.

"Not too warm I hope, my fiancé got married in August the first time and he hated it. And he said it was the first sign that the marriage wasn't going to work. So, I'm praying for comfortable weather."

"Oh, really, a sign, huh?" Leslie replied. "Well, let me tell you, the weather will be the least of your worries."

Shelly looked at Leslie strangely when she said that and moved their bags up in line hoping she would hurry up and leave.

"You're right. Look, have a nice holiday, if I don't talk to you before then." Parris said.

"You too, but I'll be in touch. Nice to meet you Shelly." Leslie said as she turned and walked away.

"Yeah, you too." Shelly replied shrugging her shoulders. "What's her deal? She's a little strange, don't you think P?"

"I guess. I feel sorry for her, her ex-husband had and affair and she hasn't gotten over it."

"She's very pretty. She shouldn't have a hard time finding someone else, even though she seems like she might have some issues."

"Who doesn't have issues Shell?" Parris said placing the gifts on the counter.

"Me." Shelly said without cracking a smile.

Chapter

32

On Christmas Eve, Parris decided at the last minute to invite a few friends over for some holiday cheer. There was three inches of snow on the ground and Parris was really starting to get into the spirit. Victor got off work around noon and called to say he needed to finish some last minute shopping, but would be there as soon as he was done. In the meantime, Parris prepared some finger foods for their guests. She even baked some chocolate chip cookies from scratch; the delicious chocolate scent filled the entire house.

As Donny Hathaway's, *This Christmas*, played in the background, Parris danced around the room singing and trimming her five foot artificial tree. Victor wanted to get a real tree, but Parris was happy with her fake one. She pulled out ornaments that her mother had saved since she was a little girl. She even had a picture with Santa that was taken when she was two years old. She placed it on the mantle next to the picture of her and Victor. She loved this time of year and was glad she had friends and family to share it with.

While hanging some of the garland, the doorbell rang. It was a Federal Express deliveryman with a package addressed to Victor. Parris signed for it and admired the pretty wrapping paper. It was a small gift box about the size of a cigar box, with a large red and silver bow. When she placed it under the tree with the rest of the gifts, she noticed there was no card or return address. She figured it was probably from his mother and she forgot, although she wondered why it was sent to her house instead of his. She didn't think his mother even had her address.

She finished decorating around six-thirty and was admiring her work, when the telephone rang. She thought it might be Shelly asking what she should bring tonight, but to her surprise, it was an unfamiliar voice.

"Hello?"

"Hello, may I speak to Victor?" the woman said.

"He's not here right now, may I ask who's calling?" Parris replied.

"No that's okay, I'll call back."

"Well, can I take…" (click) Parris stood in the middle of the living room, staring at the phone and wondering who just hung up on her. As soon as she put down the phone, it rang again.

"Hello?" she said abruptly.

"What's wrong with you?" Shelly asked.

"Oh, nothing. Some woman just called here asking for Victor. She didn't leave a name, said she would call back and then hung up on me before I could ask to take a message." Parris said with an attitude.

"Why is she calling *your* house?"

"Exactly! More importantly, how did she get my number? She better not call back!" Parris replied.

"Did her number show up on caller ID?" Shelly asked sounding like a detective.

Parris looked at the box and it read 'private'.

"No, it's a private number." Parris replied.

"It figures. Well, look P, don't let it get to you, just ask Victor who he gave your number to. It's probably a client or something. You know what a workaholic he is."

"Yeah, don't remind me." She said still sounding disturbed.

"What time?"

"What time what?" Parris asked.

"What time do you want us to come over?"

"Anytime, after eight is fine Shell."

Parris ran a bath so she could relax. The mysterious phone call made her uptight and she didn't want it to spoil her evening. She tried to call Victor to see what time he was coming home and got his voice mail instead. She didn't bother to leave a message, but brought the phone into the bathroom just in case he called her back.

She turned on the whirlpool jets and leaned back on the bath pillow. The bubbles multiplied over and over again as the water jets bounced off of her skin. *Let It Snow,* by Boys II Men, was playing now and their smooth, mellow voices along with the warm water almost lulled her to sleep. Just when she was about to drift, the telephone rang. She hoped it was Victor, but when she leaned over to answer it, they hung up.

"He'll call back." She said to herself, feeling sure it was Victor who accidentally got disconnected. She leaned back again on the pillow and closed her eyes.

"That bitch is trying to take your man!"

The voice made Parris jump into an upright position. Water and suds went splashing everywhere. She looked around the room, quickly stepped out of the tub and stood naked next to the sink dripping water all over the floor. She stared at the large tub full of bubbles, like she was waiting for it to say something else, but all she could hear was the motor from the bubble jets.

Chapter

33

Shelly and Kevin were the first to arrive. They brought with them all the fixins', including martini glasses, for Shelly's famous Cosmopolitans. Sean and his date, Brenda, arrived a few minutes later carrying bottles of Kaluha, Bailey's and a peach cobbler that Sean's mother had made. Unpredictable Kenya called and promised to stop by if she got a chance.

"Where's Vic?" Kevin asked.

"Can you believe he's at the mall? He said he had a few more gifts to get. Let me try to get him again on his cell." Parris said picking up the phone.

"He's crazy, out there shopping with all those people. You wouldn't catch me out there!" Kevin said shaking his head.

"Nah, Kev man, that's what makes it fun. Traffic jams, long lines and fighting over the last toy in the store." Sean said.

"Then why aren't you out there, Kris Kringle?" Shelly asked Sean.

"Because I started my shopping right after Thanksgiving and I know Brenda would be cussing me out right now if I wasn't home. That's why, Grinch."

"That's right honey." Brenda said, giving him a kiss on the lips.

"He must have the damn thing turned off." Parris said tossing the phone on the counter.

She busied herself warming up the Buffalo wings and setting the table. The voice earlier made her uneasy and she was trying to keep it together. Shelly starting making everyone drinks. Parris gulped hers down and asked for another one.

"Slow down P, it's still early." Shelly told her.

"Just make me another one." Parris snapped.

"Don't get all funky with me."

"Sorry, I just don't understand why he's not answering the damn phone."

"I don't know, but, here, you're right, you do need another one." Shelly said refilling her martini glass.

Sean was in the middle of telling a dirty joke when Victor walked through the front door. Parris immediately noticed he was empty handed.

"Hey everybody!" he said rubbing his hands together in an attempt to warm them.

"Hi, Babe. What took you so long? I tried to call you two or three times. Is your phone on?" Parris said giving him a kiss.

"No, I turned it off." He replied shaking Kevin's hand. "What's up man?"

"Why did you do that?" Parris asked.

"I wasn't getting a signal P, okay. But I'm here now, right?"

Victor took off his coat and walked away to greet the rest of their friends. "Yo, man, the malls are packed! Traffic is all fucked up and I could kick myself for waiting to the last damn minute to go shopping!" he replied.

"Especially, since you didn't buy anything. Where are all your bags?" Kevin asked.

"Mind ya business Kev." Victor replied smiling.

It took all the strength she could muster, to let the subject drop, so Parris took another sip of her Cosmo.

"Yo man, Merry Christmas. Long time, no see." Sean said greeting him with a handshake and a hug.

"Man, I've been busy as hell." He replied sitting down and taking off his boots. "Every brother who raps thinks he's Jay-Z and all the chicks think they're Mary J. The record companies are making out like fat rats off of these kids, who won't be around next year because they're too eager to sign on the dotted line without reading the small print."

"That's messed up." Kevin replied.

"Tell me about it, I'm representing this heavy metal dude who won't make a dime for five years, meanwhile he's number one on the charts. It's crazy."

"Aren't you representing that fine sistah named Cleo?" Kevin asked. "Is she as fine as she looks in the video?"

"Yeah man, she looks good and she's one of the few, who can really sing, but all her people want her to do the T&A thing and she's not about that." Victor replied.

"What's T&A?" Brenda asked.

"Tits and ass." Shelly replied.

"Oh, I should have known." Brenda replied.

"You know Bren, shake whatcha momma gave ya!" Sean said smacking her on the butt.

Parris shook her head laughing as she picked up his wet jacket and boots and put them in the closet. Shelly handed Victor a drink, while Sean formally introduced him to Brenda.

"Is everyone ready to eat?" Parris asked after she finished her second drink.

After everyone ate, Victor started a fire; the heat from the fireplace warmed the entire room. Tim and Stephanie arrived; they were a married couple who lived a few doors down. Tim was a high school principal and Stephanie was a stay at home mom. They've been married for six years and have two kids. Stephanie was twenty-seven, ten years younger than her husband. As they joined the conversation, Shelly and Parris noticed that Tim treated her more like a child than his spouse and he kept correcting her. Shelly couldn't take it any more and at one point told Tim to let her finish the story and after that he seemed to relax. The eight of them sat around for the next couple of hours drinking, laughing and reminiscing about the good old days. The guys decided to entertain themselves with a game of spades. Sean kept winning and Kevin was accusing him of cheating. Parris showed the women a picture of the gowns she had chosen for the girls.

"They're very pretty and I love the color. It's like coral, right? This one reminds me of the gowns I picked out for my wedding." Brenda said pointing at the magazine.

"I think it's more copper, than coral?"

"You're married?" Shelly asked.

"I was. I'm divorced." Brenda replied.

"I'm sorry to hear that." Parris said.

"Would you do it again?" Shelly asked.

"Only if he comes with a money-back guarantee in case it doesn't work out." Brenda replied with a chuckle. "I refuse to be left broke and disgusted a second time."

"I know what you mean." Shelly said. "I guess you're an old pro at marriage, aren't you Stephanie?"

"Oh yeah, an old pro, yippee." Stephanie replied.

Parris already had one drink too many and was starting to get a headache. She definitely wasn't in the mood for a negative conversation about marriage, so she went into the kitchen and started cleaning up. Victor came in to get another beer out of the refrigerator. He walked up behind her, as she washed the dishes and started kissing the back of her neck.

"Ummm, you smell good." He said.

"Ummm, you *feel* good." She said when she felt his erection.

"Did you give one of your clients my number?"

"No, why?" he said feeling on her breasts.

"Well, some woman called here this afternoon. She asked for you and when I tried to ask for a name and number, she hung up." She said turning around to look at him.

"That's strange and I wouldn't give anyone your number. My clients call me enough at work; I don't need them calling me at home too." He replied as he took three Heinekens from the refrigerator.

"Then who else would be calling *my* house asking for you?" she asked with her hand on her hip.

"I don't know P, but if she calls back, you can ask her. Now leave those dishes alone and come join our guests." He said as he kissed her on the forehead and walked back into the living room.

Chapter

34

Parris and Victor stayed in bed until noon Christmas day. Another inch of snow had fallen overnight and icicles had formed over the top of the bedroom window. Looking out across the yard, the wintry scene was like a Christmas card. Parris was anxious to exchange gifts, so she went out into the living room to get one of the many gifts she had purchased. Victor was pretending to be asleep when she returned and was hiding his head under the covers. Parris started jumping up and down on the bed like a child trying to force him to get up.

"Come on Babe, let's open our gifts! Here's one for you!" she said still jumping up and down.

"I'm still asleep." His voice was muffled under the covers.

"You are not, stop playin'! She said out of breath. "Okay then, I'll open it for you!"

"Oh, no you won't!" he said throwing the covers off and grabbing the box out of her hand.

Parris sat down on the bed with her legs crossed Indian style. Victor laughed when he saw her get into position.

"How the hell do you do that?" he asked.

"Do what?" She said happily.

"Sit with your legs like that? It looks like it hurts." He said examining the present. Then he got up and walked out of the room.

"Where are you going?" she asked looking confused.

"Out into the living room. We're supposed to open the gifts in front of the tree, even if it's fake. But first, I gotta take a piss." He replied.

Following him, "So what it's fake, leave my tree alone. You know, you can be so difficult some times." She said.

"What's so difficult about a man taking a piss?"

"Whatever Babe, you know what I mean." She said as she passed the bathroom.

Parris turned on the Christmas tree lights and the television hoping to catch some of the Macy's Day parade.

"We should have gone to the parade this year. Do you want some coffee?" he asked walking into the kitchen.

"Yes please, and no we shouldn't have, there's at least five inches of snow out there. We should be watching it right here in the comfort of our home." She said counting and sorting the gifts that had a tag with her name on it.

"A little bit of snow isn't gonna kill you P. The cold air is good for you."

"Whatever. Which one can I open first?" she replied shaking a smaller box.

"That one." He said pointing to the big box.

"Oh goodie!" she said with a big smile. "When did you bring this stuff in?"

"I didn't, Santa did." He said handing her a cup of coffee.

"Well, I hope Santa got me everything I wanted."

When she opened the big box, it was a pair of black suede boots. She tried them on and walked around the room like model.

"Oh Santa, thank you." She said striking a pose.

Now, it was Victor's turn and Santa brought him a portable DVD player.

"Thanks. I was going to get one of these." He replied. "Now I can watch movies on the train."

Santa had checked his list twice and Parris must have been a good girl because by the time she was finished opening all her gifts there was Victoria's Secret lingerie, a Movado watch, a black leather jacket, and a bottle Chanel perfume were all piled up on her side of the tree. Victor didn't make out too bad himself, he received, a briefcase, a box of his favorite cigars, a Nike sweat suit, a pair of Jordans and cologne.

"Thank you sweetheart, I love everything and I love you too." She said sitting on his lap.

"Me too." He said kissing her on the lips.

"Oh yeah, I almost forgot. Something came FedEx for you yesterday. She said getting up to look for the box.

"From who?" he asked lighting a cigar.

"I don't know, there wasn't any information on the box." She replied handing it to him. "Pretty wrapping though."

Victor was taking his time unwrapping the box. He switched the channel to ESPN and leaned back on the sofa enjoying one of his cigars.

Parris decided to start making her holiday phone calls, starting with her parents.

"Merry Christmas!"

"Merry Christmas to you too, Pumpkin. Did Santa bring you what you wanted?" Helen asked.

"And then some. How 'bout you?"

"It's wonderful! This year, your father has really out done himself. He got us tickets to cruise the Virgin Islands! And I can't wait, we leave in two days."

"Oh Ma, that sounds nice." Parris said sitting down at the kitchen table. "Did you like my gift?"

"Oh, yes, Parris, the dress fits perfect and the hat! Girl, where did you find that hat?" Helen replied.

Victor yelled from the other room, "Hey, Babe is this some kind of joke? If it is, I like it, I like it a lot!"

"Hold on Mom. What are you talking about Victor?" she replied sounding distracted.

"It's very cute P, I can't wait to get my kiss." He said.

"Tell Victor I said Merry Christmas." Helen interjected.

"I will. What kiss?" she yelled back.

When Parris walked into the living room, she didn't know what to make of the gift he was holding in his hand. She knew she didn't buy it for him and she wasn't going to be satisfied until she found out who did.

"Mom, I'll call you back."

Chapter

35

"What the hell is that in your hand?" she asked walking over to the sofa.

"Oh, like you don't know." He said grinning. "Here try it on."

"No, I don't. I didn't buy that!" she said getting angrier by the second.

"Stop playin' P."

"I'm serious Victor, I did not buy that. You know I don't even play like that."

"Then who did?" he said putting it back in the box.

"I think that's what you need to be telling me?" Parris said snatching it up out of the box.

"How the hell should I know! I thought it was from you."

"Well, it's not Victor. Who the fuck is sending you their panties for Christmas?"

"Babe, I honestly don't know." He said shaking his head.

"Yeah, well you better fucking find out!"

Parris stormed into the bedroom and slammed the door. She threw the red, crotch-less panties on the dresser and stood staring at them. Tears began to roll down her face. She looked at herself in the mirror on the wall and could not believe how quickly their wonderful morning had turned to shit. Not only were the panties crotch-less, they had a picture of mistletoe on the front, with the words, "*Kiss me it's Xmas*" on them.

Victor knocked on the bedroom door.

"Parris, are you okay? Can we talk about this please?" he asked.

Parris was silent.

"Babe, come on, you gotta believe me. Open the door. I have no idea who sent that shit. Maybe it was Sean or Kevin playing a joke. You know how they are."

"*He's lying.*" The voice said.

"Parris please, open the door." He begged.

"It's not locked Victor." She replied.

When he opened the door, Parris was sitting on the floor in front of the dresser holding the panties. He sat down beside her and handed her a tissue.

"Don't cry P, you know I hate to see you cry. I will call Sean and Kevin right now and find out who did this. I'm sure there's a logical explanation. Please don't cry." He tried to touch her, but she pulled away.

"Victor, I don't think either one of them is that clever. Besides, it's not funny and why would they play a joke on Christmas? It was a woman and you know it. I would appreciate it, if you would just tell me the truth."

"I am telling the truth!" he yelled.

"Then why are you getting so upset?"

"Because you don't believe me." He said trying to calm down.

"Okay, Victor, let's flip the script for a second. Would you believe me, if I received a box with a pair of red, boxer shorts that had, *"Suck me it's xmas"* on them?" she said as she stood up and threw the panties at him.

Victor stood in the middle of the bedroom speechless. She had a point and he knew it. He also knew there was no way he was going to get out of this until he found out who sent them.

"No! I didn't think so." She said and then got back in bed and curled up under the covers.

Victor started putting on his jeans and grabbed his sweater from the chair.

"Well, it's clear you've made up your mind and there's nothing I can say right now to change it, so I'm going to my place. I've got some work to do anyway. I'll talk to you later." He turned to walk out of the room and then stopped at the door. "I love you P and I would never do anything to hurt you. You should know that by now."

Parris was quietly crying and did not bother to respond.

Chapter

36

The next few days went by with little conversation, no affection and no sex. Neither of them brought up the panty incident again, especially since both Kevin and Sean denied sending the gift. Victor apologized again and even gave her an after-Christmas gift to make up. The platinum diamond tennis bracelet amazingly enough, in all of its brilliance, had a way of shedding new light on things. Parris figured it was better to let the subject drop for now and if he really was cheating, the truth would come out eventually.

They spent New Year's Eve at home watching Dick Clark's count down and drinking champagne.

"Happy New Year P." he said giving her a kiss at twelve o'clock.

"Happy New Year to you too. I can't believe how fast the year went by. The wedding will be here before we know it."

"Yeah, it's only nine months away. Have you decided where you want to go on our honeymoon? I was thinking Hawaii."

"That sounds nice. I'll start looking at some brochures next week." She said. "Five or seven days?"

"Five. I heard Waikiki was nicer than Honolulu, so check that out first. Oh, yeah and I almost forgot. I've got to fly out to L.A. next week to meet with Cleo." Victor said.

"Why can't she come to New York? Doesn't she live there?"

"Because she's in the studio recording her new album and it's more convenient." He replied.

"How long will you be gone?"

"I'm not sure, but probably a few days. I'm going to have to meet with her in between sessions."

"I hope you'll be back by Thursday because that's the night of the annual awards dinner at work, remember?"

"That's coming up already? I'm glad you reminded me because I almost forgot. Well, I'll do my best to be back." He replied changing the channel.

"This is really important to me Victor and I told you I'm supposed to be getting an award." She said.

"I know P. I said I'll do my best."

Parris looked at the clock and it was only 12:15. She didn't want to start the New Year off with an argument, so she decided to go to bed instead.

Her work week was not starting off much better. A manager that has been with the company for twenty years was being accused of sexual harassment and his job and pension were in jeopardy. Three women had come forward with accusations of him touching them inappropriately and telling distasteful and offensive jokes, he even sent one of them a naked picture of himself. Parris had to meet with each of the women and the manager in question. She didn't finish the interviews until after six and was completely exhausted. When she finally got back to her office, Victor called from L.A. to let her know he had arrived safely. He said he was planning to meet with Cleo tonight for dinner to discuss her case. Parris felt a tinge of jealousy when he said it, but at the same time, appreciated the fact that he told her. He also asked her to pick up his mail because he was waiting for a check to come.

On her way home, she stopped and got some Chinese food. She sat at the kitchen table and quickly ate the chicken and broccoli that tasted really good tonight. She wasn't sure if it was because she was hungry or just dog tired. There were three messages on her machine, one from Kenya, Shelly and Leslie.

Kenya was checking in and Shelly wanted her to see something on the television. Leslie was calling to see if they could get together this week for lunch or dinner. She also mentioned a friend of hers that does beautiful wedding invitations. Parris was too tired to call her back, everyone could wait until tomorrow, so she took a shower and got in the bed.

At 11:35pm, the telephone rang and woke her out of a deep sleep. She figured it was Victor calling to say good-night. When she picked up, the other end was silent and then they hung up. Parris looked at the caller id, but it read 'private' again. She got up to get a drink of water and she tossed and turned for an hour, before falling back asleep, wondering who kept calling and hanging up and if it was the same person who sent the mysterious Christmas panties.

Chapter

37

By Wednesday evening, Victor still wasn't sure if he was going to make it back in time for the banquet. Cleo's schedule was more hectic than he expected and he said the only time he could catch her was at her hotel.

"Her hotel? I think that's a little more than accommodating, don't you?" Parris asked.

"Babe, she has a zillion people around her all the time." He claimed.

"I'm not concerned about a zillion people, I'm concerned about you!"

"Look Parris, I've got to do my job the best way I can and sometimes it requires me to be available to my clients at *their* convenience, not mine. Some of my clients expect and demand special attention and again it's my job to see that they're represented properly and if that means I have to meet with them at their hotels, then so be it. That's how I get paid, remember?"

"Just call me as soon as you finish up. You can probably catch a red-eye back and still make the dinner."

"Okay, I'll call you. You still love me?" he asked.

"I guess so." She replied trying to get a rise out of him.

"You guess so? Oh, it's like that?"

"No, it's like, I don't appreciate you meeting a pretty, young woman with big breasts and a big behind in her hotel room?"

"P, you are trippin'. I'm not thinking about that fine-ass girl with the big boobs and juicy butt." He replied laughing.

"See, you think it's funny Victor and I'm not laughing. I'm serious."

"I know baby, I'm sorry, but I couldn't resist. You know you're the only woman for me, don't you?"

"I hope so." She replied.

"I know so. I love you Parris."

"I love you too."

"I'm gonna go work out, they have a small gym in my hotel. I'll call you later. Oh yeah, did the check come yet?"

"I don't know; I haven't checked yet. Sorry, I forgot. I'll go by there on my way out."

"Where are you off to?" he asked.

"I'm just gonna grab some dinner, no biggie." She replied.

They said their good-byes and Parris changed out of her suit and into a pair of jeans. She called Leslie to tell her she was on her way to pick her up. On the way to the restaurant, Parris decided to swing by and pick up Victor's mail.

"Leslie, do you mind if I make a quick pit stop? I was supposed to do this yesterday, but I forgot." Parris said.

"I don't mind." Leslie replied.

Parris pulled into the driveway and turned off the ignition.

"I just have to pick up his mail, I'll be right back."

"Victor lives here? I didn't realize you guys lived so close to each other. That's sweet. When will he be back?" Leslie asked looking around the yard.

"I'm hoping tomorrow, but unfortunately, work may keep him there a little longer."

Leslie could not believe she was sitting in front of the home she once occupied. Everything looked exactly the same. Even the big ceramic flower pot on the porch was still there, she had planted the flowers herself and would have taken that too, but it was too heavy. She hired a home decorator to help her furnish the place as well as a professional landscaper. Looking at the house again, brought back memories of what could have been.

When Parris returned to the car, she put the mail up in the sun visor, there were only a few letters, including the check. During the ride to the restaurant, Leslie asked a few questions about the wedding and Parris was more than happy to discuss the details. Dinner was uneventful, but the bottle of Chardonnay Leslie ordered, made up for the lack-luster meal. Leslie gave her the business card of her friend who owned a custom stationary store and they discussed different decorating ideas for the reception. She was very helpful and came up with several good suggestions. She actually sounded more enthusiastic about the wedding than Shelly; she even suggested that Parris take notes so she wouldn't forget anything. Parris was almost tempted to ask her to be in the wedding.

"I think you're right about the long-stem candles on each table, they'll add a nice touch." Parris said sipping her wine. "I'm really glad we had dinner tonight. The food was so-so, but the wine is very good, good choice. I've made more progress tonight, than I've made in months."

Parris let out a sigh and continued to review her notes. "Leslie, you should be a wedding coordinator. You have given me so many great ideas. Some of this stuff, I would have never thought of. I mean, don't get me wrong, Shelly's my girl and I love her, but she's not one for details."

"Well, I'm glad I could help. I'm also glad that we have become friends. Who would have ever thought picking up a total stranger would turn into this?"

"I know what you mean." Parris laughed. "Shelly cussed me out for picking you up that night. But I told her how pitiful you looked out there soaking wet and I told her she would have done the same thing."

"Did I look that bad?"

Parris laughed, "Yes, you really did."

"That just goes to show that you can't judge a book by its cover." Leslie said finishing the last of her wine.

"Exactly."

Parris dropped Leslie off and headed home. She called Shelly on her cell phone while she was driving.

"Hey girl, what's up?"

"Nothing, I'm just sitting here trying to figure out how to tell Kevin I don't want to see him anymore." Shelly replied.

"What? What happened, Shell?" Parris said.

"Nothing happened, I'm just not feeling him anymore P. He's very nice, but he's boring as hell. We don't do anything and we barely go out anymore. In the beginning, we were out every other night, now, all he wants to do is snuggle in front of the T.V. and watch videos or play that stupid Game Cube. I think I've seen every damn movie there is out on DVD."

"Well, have you told him that?"

"Several times, but he's not hearing me and I'm tired of talking. I need a little more than him constantly breathing down my neck all the time. All that cuddle shit gets old P."

"I'm sorry it's not working out, Shell. I like Kevin and I hope you guys can find a way to make it work. Look at it this way, at least you know where your man is and what he's doing, unlike myself." Parris replied.

"What do you mean?"

"Victor's all the way out in L.A. meeting with that Cleo chick in her hotel room, so consider yourself lucky."

"That is kinda messed up P, but you know he's working and besides, he didn't give you that big-ass rock on your finger and a tennis bracelet, just so he could screw around with some video chick."

"They're just material things. Men, do it all the time. Look at Kobe Bryant, after that affair with the white chick; he bought her a huge rock to shut her up. But, I guess you're right. I really have to trust in him more. By the way, are you free tomorrow night?"

"I think so, why?"

"Because I have a feeling he's not going to make it back in time for my company dinner, so I may need you as a stand-by."

"No problem, just give me a call." Shelly replied.

"Thanks Shell."

"Where are you? You're usually home by this time."

"Oh, I had dinner with Leslie. She gave me so many great ideas for the reception. She knows a lot of people as well. I told her she should be a wedding coordinator. She is really nice Shell, you should come next time we go out, you'll like her." Parris said getting all excited again just thinking about it.

"No thanks, I'll pass. There's something about her that doesn't sit right with me, but I can't put my finger on it." Shelly said.

"That's because you're just looking for something not to like." Parris insisted.

"I'm not looking; it's just a feeling, that's all."

Chapter

38

When Victor arrived at the Hyatt Hotel, he called up to Cleo's room to ask if she preferred to meet in the hotel lounge. The conversation with Parris was on his mind and he thought it would be just as easy to meet downstairs. Cleo, however felt otherwise.

"I don't think that's a good idea. I'm tired and there are too many people down there, besides I don't want us to be interrupted by the fans and stuff." She claimed. "Just come up, room 345."

When Victor got to her door, the latch was turned out keeping it from closing completely. For some reason that made Victor's muscles tense up.

"Cleo? It's Victor." He said before going in.

"I'm in the bathroom, come on in Vic. I'll be out in a minute."

"Okay." He replied as he walked into the room.

There were fresh flowers, a bottle Grey Goose, a carafe of cranberry juice and a bucket of ice sitting on the small table. The television was on BET and a Ludacris video was playing.

"Help yourself to something to drink and pour me a glass too!" she said before flushing the toilet.

"I think we should take care of business first." He said sitting down at the table.

"Oh, Victor, relax. Business between us will get taken care of, believe me." She assured him as she opened the bathroom door wearing a pair of tight cut-off denim shorts and a white tank top. Cleo might not have been willing to show a little T&A in her music videos, but she was more than happy to show them in private.

When Victor looked up and saw her standing in front of him, he couldn't help but stair at her large, bra-less breasts that were pointing in his direction. Cleo only stood 5'4" and weighed about 115 pounds. She was young, fine and built like a brick house. Victor quickly regained his composure and stood to greet her. She stood on her tippy-toes and wrapped her arms around his neck, intentionally making sure her D-cups pressed against his chest. He could see her dark areolas threw the thin tee shirt and was instantly aroused, but dared not let her know it.

"I'm sorry we couldn't meet earlier. I've been mad busy and you know how Flex is once we get in the studio." She said as they parted.

As she walked over to the night stand to get the remote, Victor noticed that she was barefoot and that her smooth, brown legs were just as shapely as the rest of her body. She was definitely a tenderoni he thought to himself. The sweet smell of her perfume lingered as she walked away.

"I think we should get started. I've got a plane to catch."

"Oooh, this is my song! I really like this jam. Kanye West can't rap, but his tracks are hot!" she said swaying her hips to the beat. "Do you know him? I wouldn't mind working him on a track or two!"

"I met him once at a party, but that was before his album was released." He replied as he watched her dance. "Uh, look Cleo, I want to talk to you about your contract and go over some of these papers in more detail."

Cleo was acting like she was oblivious to what Victor was saying, all she was hearing right now was the music.

"Cleo." He paused. "Cleo, did you hear me?"

He didn't want to get angry or cuss her out because she was a new client with a huge contract from Def Jam and it was in his best interest to patient and handle her carefully, so he decided to sit back down and wait. Maybe a drink wasn't such a bad idea after all, so he opened the bottle of Goose.

"Pour me one too." She said snapping her fingers and dancing her way over to the where he was sitting. "Easy on the cranberry."

Victor handed her the glass and took a drink of his own practically finishing it. As he refilled his glass, he thought about Parris and how she had every right to be concerned about a young, beautiful girl like Cleo. She could be dangerous for any man or woman for that matter. He took another sip and opened his portfolio hoping she would follow his lead, unfortunately it didn't work.

"I was thinking we could shoot the second video in the Bahamas, right on the beach. Whatcha think Vic?" she asked as she maneuvered her body directly in front of his chair and stood in between his legs. Her breasts playfully bounced, inviting him to touch them and the look on her face let him know she wanted him to.

"I could wear a bikini or maybe a thong. How do you think I'd look in a thong Victor?" she asked as she turned her back to him so he could get a better view.

Victor had to laugh to himself because she was so young and trying so hard to seduce him. Little did she know that with a body and face like hers, she seriously didn't need to try very hard.

"I think you'd look just fine." He replied.

"You don't think my ass is too big do you?" she said poking it out some more.

"No Cleo, I think it's just fine. Now, are you finished? Because I really need to catch that flight and get home."

Without answering, she quickly turned around and pulled the skimpy tank top off over her head. Before he could respond, she was strattling his lap and allowing her nipples to brush up against him.

"I'm not finished, I'm just getting started." She replied licking her lips and slowly grinding her hips against the bulge in his pants. Victor knew he let this go much farther than it should have and even though he was enjoying her little show, he was going to have to stop it before something happened that he would regret.

"Stop!" he said grabbing her by the waist and lifting her off of him. "Put your top back on Cleo. Please." He said calmly.

She looked stunned that he said no and he was sure rejection was something she wasn't used to.

"Oh, you want to take them off yourself, huh?" she said smiling. "I get it. Whatever you're into baby, I'm down." She replied taking a sip of her drink.

Victor stood there for a minute looking at her and he was very tempted. This fine black woman was ready to hand it over on a silver platter and he could not believe he was actually going to turn her down. There was a time in his life when there wouldn't have been a question, no hesitation, no regrets. But now, things were different and the difference was Parris. He loved and respected her and didn't want to risk loosing her. He had seen a lot of guys loose good women for some quick pussy and he didn't want to join the club.

"Cleo, you are a beautiful, young woman and there was as time in my life when I would have gladly taken advantage of this situation, but tonight, I just can't. So please get dressed."

"You're kidding right?" she said putting her hand on her hip.

"No, I'm serious."

"What are you gay or something?"

"No."

"Then what's the problem? I mean, I'm really feeling you and I know you like what you see."

"It's not that."

"Then what is it? You got a problem getting' it up?" she said rubbing his groin. "I can help you wit that."

"No, as you can see, I'm good in that department." He replied moving her hand away. "We have a professional relationship and I would just like to keep it that way, okay?"

Cleo took a sip of her drink and looked him up and down for a second.

"I realize we have a *professional relationship*, I'm not stupid. But damn! What's wrong with adding a little pleasure into the mix? It's just sex!"

Victor laughed. "Are you serious?"

"As cancer." She said sarcastically. "And I hope you don't think I do this shit for every good-lookin' brother that comes my way, cause I don't! I ain't no ho!"

Victor walked over to the bed, picked up her tee shirt and handed it to her. Her attitude immediately turned funky and she was pissed now.

"Fuck you too! You need to leave." She shouted.

"We really need to go over these contracts."

"Fuck the contracts and fuck you! I'm not in the fucking mood to go over shit! Now get out!"

Victor picked up his portfolio, took one last sip of his drink and headed for the door. Before he opened it, he stopped and turned to look at her. She was standing there, topless, with her arms folded.

"What?"

"Cleo, I'm engaged. I'll call next week." He said and walked out the door.

"Fuck you and your fiancé!" she yelled as the door shut.

Twenty minutes later, Cleo called Victor's cell apologizing and asked him to come back to the hotel, so they could go over the contracts. This time they would meet in the lounge located in the lobby. Victor knew he was running short on time and might not be finished in time to catch his flight, but she was an important client and right now, business was more important.

Chapter

39

Just as she suspected, Victor wasn't going to make it home in time for the awards dinner. He left a message apologizing. Parris called Shelly and told her to be ready by seven-thirty because the dinner started at eight. After scanning the closet for fifteen minutes, she was totally frustrated because this would have been a perfect opportunity to introduce Victor to her colleagues. She finally decided to wear her black Donna Karan dress she purchased six months ago, but never wore, it still had the tags on it. As she was putting on her sheer stockings, her engagement ring got caught and put a big hole in the right leg. She desperately searched for another pair in the bottom of the sock drawer, but wasn't having any luck. Now, she was beginning to get angry and tiny beads of sweat were forming on her nose and forehead. She haphazardly threw old stockings, leotards and socks all over the room hoping a new pair would eventually turn up. First Victor, now this, she thought.

"Damn it! I don't believe this shit!" she yelled. "I don't have time for this!"

She reached across the bed to pick up the phone to call Shelly to ask her to pick up a pair, but it rang before she had the chance.

"Hello."

"Hi Parris, it's Leslie. I just wanted to wish you good luck tonight."

"Thanks. I need some luck right now." She said sounding totally defeated. "Wow, your phone has a lot of static, are you in the car?" she said holding the phone away from her ear.

"Yes, sorry about that. What's wrong?" Leslie said concerned.

"For starters, Victor's not going to make it back in time and to make matters worse, I just put a huge hole in my last pair of stockings. Needless to say, I'm pissed and ready to just forget the whole thing and stay home."

"Oh Parris, don't do that. You've gotta go, didn't you tell me you were getting an award?"

"Yes, but…."

"Well then, you have to be there to receive it. You don't want them to think you don't appreciate the recognition." Leslie said.

"You're right, I don't want that to happen. I'm gonna call Shelly and have her pick me up a new pair." Parris said sounding more hopeful.

"That's it girl! Don't let a man or some nylons stop you from doing your thing."

"Thanks Leslie, I needed that. I'll call you tomorrow and let you know how everything went."

"Okay, have a good time."

Parris pressed the speed-dial for Shelly and asked her to pick up a pair at the WaWa convenience store, since it was too late to catch the mall before it closed.

"WaWa? I'm sure they only have the cheap ones P, if they have any at all. You don't have a pair that you can put on where the hole won't show?" Shelly asked.

"No Shelly. Just get them, size B, black and sheer if they have them."

"Be for real Parris, we're talking Wa-Wa, where you get milk, not black, sheer, nylon pantyhose." Shelly said sarcastically.

"Whatever, just get them okay. Bye!" she said throwing the phone on the bed.

In the meantime, she finished doing her makeup. She really needed to get her hair done, but her appointment wasn't until Saturday and it would have to do. She slipped on the silk dress that was clinging in all the right places and then transferred all the necessities into her black beaded purse. The telephone rang, just as Shelly's car was pulling up in the drive. She checked the caller id and saw Victor's cell phone number. She was still mad and didn't feel like talking, so she let it go to voicemail.

(beep)

Hey Babe, I'm really sorry I couldn't make it. The next flight doesn't leave for another hour. I'll make it up to you, I promise. Good luck tonight. I love you P and I can't wait to taste your sweet lips. Keep it warm for me baby, I'll be there as soon as I land.

"Whatever." She said as she opened the front door.

"Whatever what?" Shelly asked handing her the generic pantyhose.

"Nothing. Victor just left me a message." She frowned when she removed the pantyhose from the package.

"I told you." Shelly replied rolling her eyes.

Parris quickly put on the thick, black stockings, frowning her face the entire time.

"How do they look?" she asked.

"Like scuba pants." Shelly said laughing.

"You get on my nerves sometimes Shell, you really do." Parris said grabbing her purse. "Come on let's go."

The phone rang again when Shelly opened the front door.

"Let the machine get it." Parris said.

When the door closed, the answering machine clicked on, but they were already out the door.

(beep)

Ms. Reed, this is the First Alert alarm company, if you're there, please pick up. Hello?

Chapter

40

Parris gracefully walked up to the podium and gave thanks to her supportive staff and upper management for their continued support. Her speech was great and you would have never known how disappointed she was that Victor wasn't there to see her receive it. The audience gave her a warm applause when she finished. She returned to her table holding a gold trimmed crystal plaque thanking her for all her hard work. She had no idea she would be first on the list to be honored and was thankful they didn't arrive too late.

"Good job P." Shelly said giving her a kiss on the cheek.

"Thanks."

"Your phone keeps vibrating." Shelly said sipping her water. "When do we eat? I'm starving."

"Me too, soon I hope." She said looking at the phone. "There are three urgent messages, I'll be right back."

When she returned to the table, she whispered something to her boss and grabbed her purse.

"Come on Shell, We've gotta go?" she whispered.

"What's wrong? Is everything okay?"

"No. Someone broke into Victor's house and the police called me."

When they reached the house, there were two police cars out front with their lights flashing. An older, gray-haired officer made his way over when Parris stepped out of the car.

"Good evening, I'm Officer John Stone. Are you Parris Reed?"

"Yes I am. What happened officer?"

"Well, it appears that someone broke in around 7:45pm, but they were gone by the time the alarm company dispatched the department. We tried to contact the owner, but the cell number he gave us is no longer in service. Mr. Baxter had your name down as an emergency contact. Do you know where he is or how to get in touch with him?"

"Yes, he's my fiancé and he's out of town right now. He should be returning sometime this evening. He must have forgotten to give the security company his new cell phone number." Parris replied.

"Well, Ms. Reed, we need you to take a look around and see if there's anything missing. We'll obviously have Mr. Baxter do the same when he gets back, but for right now, we need to have someone check it out." He said.

"Sure officer, no problem. How did they get inside?"

"We're not exactly sure, but it looks like they may have come in through the basement window because it was open and a few things were knocked over.

Officer Stone followed Parris and Shelly into the house, while the other officer questioned one of the neighbors to see if there were any witnesses.

"That's strange; I guess they didn't have time to take the most expensive thing in here." She said pointing at the sound system still in tact.

Parris started in the kitchen and then made her way into the living room. The VCR and camcorder were still in the entertainment center, but the DVD player was missing.

"It looks like the only thing they took was the DVD player out of this room. I'll check the bedroom next, he has several expensive watches and maybe some cash in there."

"Why the hell didn't they take the camcorder too? That was stupid. They need to go back and take a Stealing for Dummies class." Shelly said.

The officer took notes as they walked up the stairs. When they entered the bedroom, Parris immediately checked his top dresser drawer, where he keeps his watch case. Victor collected watches and some of them were worth thousands of dollars. Surprisingly, the case was still in there locked and appeared untouched.

"It doesn't look like they took anything out of here." Parris said looking around the bedroom.

The waterbed was unmade and a couple of his dress shirts were on the bed. Shelly was checking out the variety of cologne bottles on the dresser, when the officer asked her not to touch anything.

"Sorry." She said embarrassed.

Parris checked the night table drawers next. He sometimes left money in there. When she opened the drawer there was no money, so they might have taken that, but there was an open 3-pack box of Trojan, glow-in-the-dark condoms, that she had never seen or used before. She peeked in the box and found only one remaining. Victor was a Magnum man and has never used any other kind when they made love and now that they were engaged they hadn't used a condom in a while. She also noticed a piece of pink stationary that was folded half way. From what she could see, it looked like a personal letter, with a woman's handwriting, so she thought twice about it, but then inconspicuously slipped the piece of paper into her purse and closed the drawer.

"Well, Officer Stone, they might have taken some money out of this drawer, but I can't tell. You'll have to wait for Victor."

"That's fine Ms. Reed, we appreciate your time." The officer said as they left the room.

Parris was cussing under her breath when she got back in the car. She was also driving too fast.

"Parris what is wrong with you? Slow down!" Shelly demanded.

"I'm gonna kill him Shell, if he's cheating on me." She said with enough venom to almost make Shelly believe her.

"What are you talking about?"

"I found an opened box of condoms and a letter in his night table drawer." She said gripping the wheel.

"A letter, what letter? What did it say?"

"I'll let you know as soon as I read it, it's in my purse."

"You took it?" Shelly asked in disbelief.

"Yes!"

"My girl!" Shelly said snapping her fingers. "Hey, are you sure you guys didn't use the condoms?"

"Positive. I don't do glow-in-the-dark and neither does Victor, and if he does, its news to me."

The women were silent the rest of the way home. Parris told Shelly she would call her as soon as she read the letter and got her thoughts together. Shelly didn't want to leave her friend, but Parris insisted she would be alright and wanted to confront this alone.

Parris kicked off her shoes and sat down on the sofa.

Her stomach was turning and her head was starting to ache. She rubbed her temples trying to relieve the tension. She stared at the black beaded purse beside her. She silently prayed that the words on that letter were not those of another woman.

Chapter

41

At least ten minutes had passed before Parris got the nerve to open the letter. The last two hours had distracted her so much that she failed to turn on any lights. The living room was completely dark, except for the full moon outside, whose light was casting a spotlight directly on the folded piece of paper. She reached over and turned on the light as her stomach ached with anticipation. When she unfolded the letter, she noticed it was dated two weeks ago and had a faint scent of potpourri.

The perfectly hand-written, *"Hello Sweetie"* salutation made her bite her lip, but her anxiety quickly subsided when she glanced at the signature and read the first sentence asking when he was coming to Florida to visit. The letter was from his mother. Lillian Baxter was a retired English teacher who preferred communicating in writing rather than by telephone for some reason. After the engagement, she even wrote her a congratulatory note, but it wasn't on this fancy stationery. Victor would even write her back sometimes, it was some mother-son thing they had going on.

"Thank you God." Parris whispered.

She folded the letter back up and put it in her handbag. She knew it would have to be returned before he noticed it was missing. Even though she was glad that the letter was not from another woman, that still didn't explain the box of condoms, two of which were missing.

Shelly called a few minutes later to get the scoop, she couldn't wait any longer. Parris was in the kitchen fixing a baked potato in the microwave, since they never got a chance to eat at the banquet.

"Well?" she asked.

"False alarm, it was from his mother." Parris replied adding a spoonful of butter.

"Thank goodness. 'Cause home-boy was going to have some serious explaining to do."

"He still does. Don't forget the condoms." She replied adding sour cream.

"Aw damn, that's right! Forget the letter, who were the condoms for?" Shelly said agreeing. "I don't know P, what reasonable explanation could he possibly have?"

"I don't know either, but I just want the truth."

"You don't *really* think he's going to tell you, do you?"

"I don't know."

"Well, take it from me, chances are he's going to lie. They always do. So, why don't you wait until you're at his place and the next time you get ready to have sex, reach into the drawer for one of the condoms? His facial expression alone, will tell you what you need to know." Shelly said.

"Good idea, but what if he gets rid of them before I get a chance?" Parris said with her mouth full of potato.

"He won't. Most men aren't that thorough and if he was, he never would have left them in the drawer in the first place. Just do it soon, like tomorrow night or something. He's going to be distracted by the break in, so I wouldn't sweat it." Shelly said confidently.

"Okay, sounds like a plan. When did you become so clever?"

"Sometimes you've gotta beat them at their own game and I've had lots of practice."

"I guess you're right. Did you eat anything?"

"No, and I'm starving. There ain't shit in here to eat, but cereal, I need to go food shopping."

"That's a shame, because this baked potato with butter and sour cream is delicious!" Parris teased.

"Thanks Parris, just rub it in."

"Go ahead and enjoy your Captain Crunch. I'm going to get off the phone now, so you don't have to hear me smacking my lips."

Chapter

42

Around 11:30pm, Victor was leaving the airport on his way to the house when he called Parris on his cell phone. She told him about the break-in and she could tell he was tired and upset about something, but wouldn't say, so she agreed to meet him at his place. All of his electronic equipment was insured, so he wasn't concerned about that, it was the thought of a stranger violating his privacy that really ticked him off.

"People are really fucked up! I can't believe the audacity of these assholes that think they can just take your shit! They have no regard for how hard you work and the sacrifices you've made to acquire nice things!" He yelled into the cell phone.

"I know honey. If it makes you feel any better, it looks like they only took the DVD player. I didn't notice anything else missing." Parris said trying to console him. "Oh yeah, you need to get a lock on the basement window. The officer said he thinks that's how they got in."

"They probably grabbed some of my movies too. I have some real classics, you know." He said with a sigh. "If those mother-fuckers took my Bruce Lee and Richard Pryor DVDs, I'ma hurt somebody!"

"Well, just wait until you get there and check it out before you get yourself all worked up." She replied.

"You're right. I'm just pulling up. I'll see you in a few."

Parris arrived a few minutes later and found Victor sitting on the floor surrounded by every DVD and CD he owned.

"It looks like they're all here." He said amazed.

"That's good." She said taking off her coat and walking over to where he was sitting.

She bent over and gave him a kiss. As soon as their lips touched, that fuzzy feeling in her stomach reminded her how much she loved and missed him.

"I missed you Babe." She said gently touching his brow.

"I missed you too." He said squeezing her butt as she strattled his lap. "Did you check the bedroom? Is my watch case still there?"

"Yes." She said pulling off his sweater.

He kissed her on the lips allowing his tongue to explore her mouth. She eagerly accepted and started to remove his shirt, but he stopped her.

"Wait P. I want to check out the rest of the place before I relax." He said moving her off of his lap so he could stand up.

Parris was a little disappointed because she was horny, but figured this would be a good time to put the letter back before he noticed. He went into the kitchen to grab a beer and she headed upstairs. When she reached the night table and opened the drawer, he was entering the bedroom, but not paying attention. She dropped the letter in and closed it with her knee as he walked over to the dresser, where he kept his watches. She took off her jeans exposing a pretty lace thong and laid across the bed hoping to entice him. He seemed unaware as she watched him carefully examined each drawer and then the shelves in the closet.

"I wonder why they didn't take the gold cuff-links. They're sitting right on top of the dresser." He said walking into the master bathroom.

Parris decided to get completely undressed knowing that he'd have a harder time resisting. She quickly checked the drawer again to make sure the condoms were still there and then got under the comforter.

"Come on Victor, you can check the rest later. I want to show you how much I missed you."

When he came out of the bathroom, he was already butt naked and standing at attention.

"Oh yeah, that's what I'm talkin' about. Come to momma Big Daddy!" She said with a smile.

Victor joined her under the covers and began kissing her neck and shoulders, slowly moving his way down to her breasts. His tongue circled each nipple leaving them wet and erect. Parris ran her finger nails gently up his back as his tongue found her belly-button. The sweet sensation made her giggle. He let his fingers do the walking into the wet and warm gap between her legs. She let out a moan to let him know that was her spot. He took his time and pleasured her with the magic of his tongue and when she climaxed, they flipped the script so that she could please him too. Parris worked a little magic of her own and just when he was on the verge of letting loose, she stopped and asked if he had any condoms.

"Yeah, in the drawer. Why'd you stop?" He said with his eyes closed trying to savor the moment. "What you forgot to take your pill or something?"

Parris watched his face carefully waiting for his expression to change. Then she reached into the drawer and pulled out the box in question.

"Where did these come from?" she asked never taking her eyes off of his.

"What?" he said opening his eyes and lifting his head. "What are they, glow-in-the-dark?" he said grabbing the box and pulling the single condom out.

"Since when do you buy glow-in-dark condoms?"

"I didn't, but I'll use it." He said ripping it open and putting in on. "Come on before I go down."

"What do you mean you didn't? You obviously did because the other two are missing." She said shaking the empty box in his face.

"No I didn't, now, are we going to do this or argue?" He said holding his penis.

Parris was stunned. His expression never changed and she couldn't believe he was acting like condoms just magically appear in his drawer. She wasn't sure what to do next, have sex anyway or argue until he confessed. What she did know was that they couldn't do both. While she sat there staring at him trying to decide, he pulled her to him and kissed her. He rolled her over and entered her before she could say another word. Her weak flesh gladly gave into him, slowly pushing thoughts of the controversial condom deeper and deeper into her subconscious with each thrust.

Chapter

43

Parris woke the next morning feeling rested and refreshed, but she didn't forget about the condoms. She tip-toed around the bed, gathering her clothes, she didn't want to wake him. He had definitely put his thing down last night, so she couldn't blame him for sleeping in. Before leaving the bedroom, she glanced back and saw him lying on his stomach snoring lightly. Parris stood at the door for a minute admiring his handsome face and realized how fortunate she was to have him in her life.

It was after nine by the time she got home and changed for work. Grateful it was Friday and dress-down day, she threw on a pair of jeans and a gray turtleneck. Once she got over the bridge, she called Maria to let her know she was on her way.

The air was cold and whipping through the parking garage, as she headed towards the elevator. She wished she had put on her heavier coat instead of the leather jacket, trying to be cute. Her cell phone started ringing and she had to take her glove off to answer it.

"How did it go?" Shelly asked, getting right to the point.

"Let's just say the glow-in-the-darks, have me glowing this morning." She replied gripping the collar of her coat. "It's cold as shit out here!"

"Parris, I can't believe you tampered with the evidence." Shelly said.

"Girl, I did more than tamper, I destroyed it!" she laughed.

"So, I guess you're going to just let this one slide?"

"No. I'm going to talk to him about tonight."

"No you're not, stop lying."

"Yes I am Shelly, oh wait, hold on, that's my other line." She said clicking over.

"Hello."

"Hi Parris, it's Leslie."

"Oh, hey girl, hold on. (click) Shell, let me call you back." (click) "Leslie, what's up?"

"I was just calling to see how the award dinner went."

"Oh, it was very nice. I got my award, but I had to leave early. Victor's house was broken into and I had to go talk to the police." She said getting on the elevator.

Sean was also getting on and he pointed to his watch to remind her that she was late.

"I know, mind your business." She whispered to him while covering the phone.

"That's a shame, did they take anything?" she asked.

"Well, the only thing we noticed so far was the DVD player." Parris replied.

"That's good, but sometimes you don't notice other things for weeks. So you should keep an eye out." Leslie advised. "And I guess things are okay now that Victor's back, huh?"

"Yeah, we're good. Look, I'm already late, so let me go. We should try to get together soon, okay?" Parris said waving at Maria and walking into her office.

"Sure, I'll talk to you later."

She scanned her daily planner and found that her schedule was free all day. She pulled her award from the tote bag and sent a short email requesting facilities to come hang it. After reading and replying to the twenty messages in her inbox, Parris took a coffee break and called her mother. No one was home, so she left a message. Sean stuck his head in her office to see if she was busy.

"Hey Parris, what's happening?" he asked as he sat down.

"Not much Sean, how are you? Wanna see my award? She said handing it to him.

"That's nice. Who'd you have to sleep with to get this?"

"Your daddy Mr. Funny Man." She said snatching it back. "How's Brenda? Are you still seeing her?"

"Yeah, we're still kickin' it. It's been two months and things are going well, thanks for asking." He said proudly. How 'bout you and Vic? Did he get back from L.A. yet?"

"He got back last night and you know he got robbed." She said taking a sip of coffee.

"Get out! Was it bad?" he asked. "They didn't take the Richard Pryor collection did they?"

Parris laughed. "No, Richard's safe. Just the DVD player."

"Damn, that's fucked up! What about Bruce Lee, is he straight?"

"Yes Sean, Bruce is cool too. You guys are unbelievable."

Parris stared out the window for minute, wondering if and how she should ask her next question. She knew that Sean probably knew Victor better than anyone, but because they've been friends for so long, he probably wouldn't say anything against him. But she figured she had nothing to lose, so she went for it.

"Parris, earth to Parris." He said.

"No, I said, they didn't take any movies." She said turning back around to him. "Let me ask you a question and please be honest, okay?"

Sean looked at her with apprehension, "Yeah, okay."

"Did Victor ever cheat or talk about cheating on his ex?"

Sean scratched his head and Parris swore she could see the wheels turning, as he carefully thought about his answer.

"Parris, you know Vic is my boy and I learned a long time ago, not to get in the middle of other people's relationships. Besides, if he did, and I said "if", that doesn't mean he'd do the same thing to you." he said, sounding unsure if that was the right answer.

"If? If, means there's a possibility." She said trying not to raise her voice. "Look Sean, I realize you two have been friends for a long time and I respect that. But, you and I are also friends, right?"

Sean nodded. "Sure."

"Okay then, I'm simply asking you a question, about a mutual friend, that requires a yes or no answer."

Sean started laughing and shaking his head. "You are not going to trick me into this Parris."

"Trick you into what Sean? Just answer the question, yes or no."

"No. Are you satisfied? Why? Do you think he's cheating? What? Did he do something stupid?"

"Cheating, I'm not sure, something stupid, possibly. Do you think I would be asking you this, if I didn't think there may be a problem?"

"I guess old Vic's not perfect after all."

"Far from it." Parris replied.

Sean stood up and walked over to the window. Parris could tell he wanted to say something, but was afraid to.

"Never mind Sean. I don't want to put you in the middle of this. I'll work it out by myself." She said trying to look busy. This is something I'm going to have to deal with on my own. Thanks anyway."

Walking over to the door, Sean paused and said, "Parris you're a smart and beautiful woman and if I had someone like you, they couldn't pay me to mess up. Just know that if it walks like a duck and talks like a duck, it's a duck. Does that help?"

Parris looked up from the file.

"Quack, quack." She replied with a fake smile.

The ride home was long and traffic was terrible. Even though Sean did not directly answer the question, he definitely gave her plenty to think about and she couldn't deny that Victor was beginning to grow some feathers. She called her mother to try to take her mind off of the traffic.

"Hey Mom."

"Hello P, how are you?"

"I'm fine."

"You don't sound fine, what's wrong?" Helen asked.

"I don't really want to go into it, but, did Daddy ever get out of line?"

"What do you mean out of line?"

"You know, stay out too late, or maybe give you a reason to think he may be cheating?"

"Where's all this coming from? You and Victor okay?"

Parris was silent.

"Well, now Parris you know men are going to be men, don't make it right, but it's true. Lord, have mercy girl, is Victor showing off already?"

"I'm not sure, but his behavior is a little suspect."

"Well, whatever you do, don't say anything until you're sure. If he's screwin' around you'll find out soon enough. Time tells every story. He's bound to mess up and forget to cover his tracks, they always do. Then, once you have enough evidence and he can't deny it, Wham! Sock it to him!" Helen said getting excited. "That's if he's guilty, of course."

"I don't understand why it even has to get to that. A good woman tries to do the right things by feeding, sexing and supporting her man and they still aren't satisfied. And on top of that, you've gotta worry about some tramp trying to steal him."

"What tramp?" Helen asked.

"I don't know? All of them. Don't forget he works with these artists who are young and beautiful. He just came back from a trip with a new client who is gorgeous Mom."

"So are you Parris. I think Victor's a smart and mature man and isn't easily swayed by a pretty face."

"I hope your right." she replied.

"I know it's hard, but you've gotta be smart and strong in how you handle your relationship and more importantly, you've got to trust him baby? Do you trust him?"

"I want to Ma, I really want to but...with all that temptation out there, I'm not sure."

"I know P, but you have to remember, the serpent tempted Eve and Eve turned around and tempted Adam. Adam had a choice and so does Victor. I pray that he makes the right choice. It's a vicious cycle and only a strong, God-fearing person can resist the temptations of this world and even *they* fail sometimes, but that doesn't always have to be the end all. There is a such thing as forgiveness, remember?"

"Thanks, Reverend Reed. Now, will you answer my question?" Parris insisted.

"What question?" Helen asked innocently.

"About Daddy."

"Let's just say I shot that shiny red apple out of his mouth before he could take a bite."

Chapter

44

Parris decided to take her mother's advice to watch and wait. For the next few months, she put all her energy into planning the wedding. Valentine's Day came and went quietly with candlelight dinner and flowers. Victor refused to give into all the commercialism that came with the holiday and Parris didn't blame him, it was very overrated. On Easter, they went to church and had dinner at her parents; everyone was shocked when her father let Victor carve the ham.

All and all things were going well. Plans were falling into place and most of the arrangements were completed. The only thing remaining was the bridesmaid's gowns. Victor's client, who was a designer to stars like Jennifer Lopez and Queen Latifah, offered to make the girls' gowns. Parris didn't know if she wanted to look like a princess or a diva on her big day. Leslie was a big help too, she had recommended the printer for the invitations, who gave them a great discount and she also gave her the name of a florist.

By the end of July, Parris had their invitation printed and mailed out. They were expecting one hundred and fifty guests. Shelly and Kenya started planning the bridal shower and decided to have it at Shelly's place. Parris emailed the list of names and addresses for them to invite and when Shelly saw Leslie's name she frowned.

"What's that face for?" Kenya asked as she addressed an envelope. "You look like you've got gas."

"Nothing really, I just don't like that Leslie chick. She's just a little too helpful and she rubs me the wrong way."

"I've never met her, but Parris talks about her all the time. Pass me another envelope."

"I know that's what bothers me." She said handing her the envelope. "She doesn't know her that well and the way they met is beyond strange. I mean, who in their right mind, picks up a stranger?"

"My sister. You know how she is. She seems to have a lot of connections and Parris said she hooked her up with the invitation guy and the florist."

"I know, but you'll see what I mean when you meet her." Shelly replied.

"Hopefully, she'll come." Kenya said counting the stack invitations.

"Oh, she'll be there, I'm sure she wouldn't miss it for the world."

Chapter

45

Photographs were scattered all over the bed, along with old birthday cards and some dried up rose petals. Candles illuminated the room and the flames seemed to dance to the beat, as Sade sang about a lost love. Leslie poured another glass of Scotch, as she sat on the edge of the bed, wearing her old wedding gown, staring at the pieces of her broken heart. She was holding a set of keys that she had taken from Victor's house. She thought it was funny how some people were such creatures of habit, Victor being one of them, and no matter how much time passed, old habits never die. Victor always kept an extra set of keys for every lock on one key ring. He hid the keys in an old sweat sock in his sock drawer. The car, house, New York apartment and safe deposit box keys were all on one ring and in her hand. Leslie decided that being an 'ex' had advantages that the 'soon-to-be' probably wasn't privy to yet. She even found the paperwork for the alarm system and hoped the password was still the same, just in case she needed to get into the house again. She had all the codes to contact them and have it reset, if necessary. She could not believe how easy he was making this for her, it almost took the fun out of it.

She got up from the bed and walked over to the dresser. More pictures of the two of them were taped to the mirror, some were from their wedding, others from a vacation in the islands. Leslie took a long drag from the cigarette and opened the top drawer. The .38 caliber gun was sitting on top of a pair of red satin panties. She held it with both hands and pointed it at her image in the mirror.

"Bang, bang." She said taking a sip of her drink. "Too hot in August, huh? Well, I've got some heat for your ass Mr. Baxter."

The telephone rang and she wasn't going to answer it, but changed her mind because it could be important.

"Hey baby, I'm just looking at some old pictures."(pause) We've been over this three times already! It's going to work, trust me. The password should be "VBESQ", if that doesn't work, try "ATTYVB"." (pause) Just make it sound realistic, but don't go overboard." (pause) "Okay, I'll see you tomorrow." She said and then hung up the phone.

Ironically, *Bullet Proof Soul*, was playing as she returned the gun to the drawer. She sang along with Sade, lying down in the center of the bed, wanting to drown in her memories.

"I came in like a lamb, but I intend to leave like a lion." She sang softly as the tears rolled down her face.

Chapter

46

Parris had a sneaky feeling that her bridal shower was today. It was two weeks before the wedding and no one had said a word about it. Shelly claimed to be hosting a jewelry demonstration this afternoon, but Parris knew it was a lie. She followed her regular Saturday routine at the salon, this way her hair and nails would be done, just in case they were waiting to surprise her when she got there. She begged Shelly to give her the date, but she refused. Either way, Parris was going to be ready.

Her mother called twice before she got in the shower. Kenya even called to chit-chat and that was a dead give away, because she never calls just to talk. Parris chuckled to herself at how silly they were acting, but had to admit she loved all the fuss they were making. She finished getting dressed and headed out the door for the salon. Victor got in late last night and went straight to his place. Parris decided to stop by his place on the way. She rang the doorbell, but there was no answer. She could hear music playing, so she was sure he was inside and decided to use her key to let herself in.

"Hello? Babe, where are you?" she yelled.

The stereo was blasting and the television was muted. Parris did not understand why he needed to have every electronic device he owned going at the same time. She walked over and turned down the music.

"Victor!" She yelled upstairs. "It's me."

"I'm in the shower!" he replied.

Victor usually took twenty minute showers, so she knew he would be a while. She wanted to sit down, but the sofa was covered with folders and papers. The living room was a mess, hundreds of file folders and newspapers were scattered around the room. Parris couldn't resist cleaning up and started by picking up his damp gym clothes. Her natural instinct was to smell them, luckily she didn't have to put her nose too close to get a good whiff of the funk.

"Damn." She said shaking her head.

She threw the wet clothes in the laundry room. Just as she began gathering the empty pizza box and beer bottles off of his desk, she heard the AOL mail message reminder coming from the laptop. *"You've got mail!"*

She continued to clean up, but her curiosity got the best of her, so she walked around the desk and sat down. She didn't even realize that he had another email account because he used his Blackberry for everything. Normally, she was not an advocate of spying on people, but she was getting married in two weeks and he wasn't people, he was her fiancé. There were a couple of unread messages, one from Sean and the rest looked like junk emails, except for the one that was just delivered. When Parris saw who it was from, she had a feeling it wasn't about business.

"I wonder why Cleo's sending him an email to his personal account." She whispered to herself. "Shit! I didn't even know he had a personal account."

Feeling nervous and pissed, she listened to see if Victor was still in the shower. The water was still running, but she had to read it quickly, because he would be done any minute. She clicked on the message and like she suspected, it wasn't work related.

Hi Victor:

The flowers are beautiful. I'm sorry. Let me make

it up to you, the right way this time. ☺

My album release party is in NY next weekend,

at The Point, see you then. Call me.

Much luv, Cleo

Parris closed the message and debated if she should mark it "unread". She was spying and that was wrong, but he may be cheating and that was worse, so she left it. She didn't know what to do or how she should react to the message. He sent her flowers and she wanted to make something up to him. Even though it didn't sound legit, she thought it could have a very simple explanation. Parris decided to wait and not jump to conclusions.

A cloud of steam hit her in the face when she opened the bathroom door. Victor was drying off.

"Hey Babe." He said wrapping the towel around his waist. "God, that shower felt great!"

"Hey."

"I would kiss you, but I didn't brush yet."

Parris stood in the doorway staring at him. She closed her eyes tight and started rubbing her temples when she heard the voice.

"He's playing you Parris, don't be a fool."

In between brushes, with toothpaste dripping from his mouth, he asked, "What's wrong P?"

"Nothing, I just have a headache."

"He doesn't really care about you, he wants Cleo."

"Do you want some aspirin?" he said wiping off the steamy mirror. "I think I have some Advil in here somewhere."

"No, I'll be alright. I'm going to the salon, then over Shelly's for a jewelry demonstration, but I think today's my shower, I'll talk to you later."

Parris turned to walk away, when he grabbed her arm and pulled her close.

"Now, I'm ready for that kiss." He said closing his eyes and puckering up.

She gave him a peck on the lips and turned to walk away again.

"Is that it? What's wrong with you?"

"I told you I have a headache and I'm late for my appointment. I'll talk to you later." She said as she headed down the stairs.

Victor stood at the top of the stairs wondering what had gotten into her. He assumed it was PMS or maybe she was just getting nervous about the wedding.

When she got in the car, the voice grew louder.

"You dumb bitch! Why didn't you ask him about the email?"

"Because I want to be sure." She said out loud.

"You are sure! Just take care of him before it goes any further!"

"Take care of him?"

"Just do it!"

The driver behind her honked the horn because the light had turned green and Parris had not moved.

"Sorry." She said waving her hand.

As quickly as it came, the voice had left, but Parris could not get the words, *"take care of him"* out of her mind. The last thing she wanted to do was hurt Victor.

Chapter

47

When Parris walked through the door, everyone yelled surprise. To their dismay, she wasn't surprised and she was barely smiling.

"Oh P, did you know?" Shelly asked when she gave her a hug.

"Sort of." She replied.

"Are you alright?" Shelly whispered in her ear.

"No, but I'll talk to you about it later."

Shelly's apartment was so beautifully decorated and they had prepared such a wonderful spread that Parris hated to put a damper on her special day, so she tried to clear her mind and put on a happy face. It looked like almost everyone they invited had shown up, even Victor's mother arrived early. This was the first time they were meeting face to face and Parris was a little nervous.

"Hello Parris darling, it's a pleasure to finally meet you and I must say, you are as lovely as Victor described." Lillian said with a genuine, soft tone.

"Why thank you Mrs. Baxter, the pleasure is all mine." Parris replied giving her a warm hug. "You look beautiful."

"Oh thanks, and please, call me Lillian."

She was a very sophisticated woman, who looked like she was accustomed to the finer things in life. Now, Parris knew where Victor acquired his sense of style. She was dressed in a pale yellow linen dress, with a floral scarf. Her yellow Prada shoes matched perfectly. Her hair was pulled back into a tight bun and her makeup was flawless. Victor looked just like her, with the exception of skin tone, she was much lighter.

"Are you getting nervous yet?" Lillian asked.

"A little. I'll just be glad when it's over. I had no idea how much planning was involved." Parris replied.

"That's why you pay a wedding coordinator, honey. You shouldn't be bothered with all of those details." Lillian replied. "You do have a coordinator, don't you?"

"No, I really wanted to do everything myself, so that it would be exactly how Victor and I envisioned."

"Well, no wonder you can't wait for it to all be over. I know wedding coordinators can be expensive, but if you get a good one, they're worth every penny, dear. I can't believe Victor didn't insist. That's not like him."

"Victor's been very busy, Lillian. He's about to make partner, you know."

"Oh yes, I'm well aware. I just can't believe it's taken him this long. Victor's an excellent attorney. He really takes the time to know his clients and that makes all the difference in the world." She replied.

"Oh yeah, I know all about that."

On that note, Parris excused herself and went into the kitchen. Kenya was in there helping her mother serve the food, while Shelly gave out ink pens and clothes pins for the games.

"What's wrong with P, she could at least *pretend* like she's excited after all the work we put this party." Kenya said to her mother not realizing that she was standing right behind her.

"I am excited and happy too Kenya. Thank you guys, everything looks and smells great."

"Oh, hey P, I didn't even know you were there." Kenya said.

"Well, you don't look happy. What's wrong? Are you feeling okay?" her mother asked. "Here, let me fix you a plate."

"Thanks Ma, I'm fine, you're right, I just need to eat something."

"You're not pregnant are you P?" Kenya asked.

"No!" Parris replied.

When the telephone rang, Shelly called Parris into the living room where her cousins, April and Dana were sitting talking with the other women.

"It's for you." Shelly said handing her the phone.

"Who is it?"

"The hitchhiker, I guess she couldn't bum another ride." Shelly replied covering the phone with her hand.

Kenya laughed out loud, which made Parris laugh as she rolled her eyes at Shelly and grabbed the phone.

"Hey girl, where are you?"

"I'm on my way to the hospital, my nephew broke his leg. I'm really sorry I won't be able to make it, Parris." Leslie replied.

"Oh that's okay, I understand. I hope everything's okay."

"Me too. I have a gift for you, I'll drop it off tomorrow or something." Leslie said.

"That's fine. Thanks for calling."

Leslie really did want to attend, but she couldn't risk running into Lillian, so she just sat in her car, outside Shelly's apartment complex, thinking about how happy she was the day of her shower.

Two hours later, after the gifts were opened and the games were played, Shelly cut the cake and guests began to filter out. When everyone was gone, including Kenya who didn't bother to help clean up, Helen specifically waited around to talk to Parris.

"Okay Pumpkin, are you ready to talk?" Helen asked.

"Yeah P, what happened?" Shelly asked.

Parris took a deep breath and sat down at the table.

"I don't think I can do this." She replied and began to cry.

"But why, what happened?" Shelly said sitting down across from her.

"Mom, remember when you told me to wait until I had enough evidence to confront him?"

"Oh Parris, Lord have mercy, don't tell me…" Helen said shaking her head.

"Yes. He got an email from one of his clients, you know the one Shell, Cleo."

"Oh God, I can only image what it said." Shelly replied.

"Who's Cleo?" Helen asked.

"She's the girl that sings that sickening song called 'Emotions'."

"Oh yeah, that pretty girl. I know who you mean. Your dad likes that video." Helen replied.

"Yes, Ma, the pretty one." Parris hated to admit. "First of all, I didn't even know he had an AOL account. Secondly, she sent him an email this morning apologizing for something and wants to make it up to him. And get this, she's the one apologizing, but he sent *her* flowers. Oh yeah, she's having an album release party in New York and he didn't ask me to go yet."

"So, what's wrong with that? And maybe he didn't get around to asking you yet." Shelly asked.

"Yeah baby, honestly, that doesn't so sound bad to me." Helen said.

"Flowers Mom? You guys don't see anything wrong with an engaged man sending another woman flowers?"

"Well, not really, she is a client, right? And maybe the office sent them as a courtesy." Shelly said.

"Okay, then what about the, "let me make it up to you the right way?" Parris said as her tone got louder.

"Oh, now that shit's a different story!" Helen exclaimed.

"Ma!" Shelly and Parris both said in unison.

"What? Well, it is." She insisted.

"Oh yeah, and she closed with "Much love, Cleo". Now, do you see why I'm so upset?"

"So, did you say something to him yet?" Shelly asked.

"No. I don't know what to say and the fact that I read his email is a whole other story."

"Well, you're gonna have to, you cannot get married under these conditions. It's too much." Helen replied. "You can't start off your marriage with secrets and lies, you just can't!"

"I just hope that Victor tells the truth. Maybe it was all innocent on his part; you know how these young girls are today. She probably has a crush and she's trying to entice him with words." Shelly said trying to keep hope alive.

"Maybe, but with the crank calls, panties, then the condoms and now this, I doubt it. I should have never let it go this far." Parris replied.

"Crank calls! Panties and condoms, what condoms? And whose panties? Girl, what is going on?" Helen asked.

"That's exactly what I intend to find out."

Chapter

48

Parris was on her way back to his house when he called. She was determined to get to the bottom of this tonight, but didn't want to discuss it over the phone. Her mother was right and she refused to go into a marriage knowing it might be full of lies and deception.

"Parris, I know you read the email and I can explain."

"I certainly hope so, I'll be there in a few minutes." She said and hung up.

When she got there, he opened the door before she even had a chance to knock. He stood in the doorway, wearing only a pair of beat-up sweats. Parris refused to let those broad shoulders and his smooth chest distract her from what she needed to do. She pushed him out of her way and walked into the den. To ensure there wouldn't be any other distractions, she immediately turned off the stereo and the television; she even turned off her cell phone.

"Look, before you say a word. Let me explain." Victor insisted.

"I'm listening." she said crossing her arms.

"I would have never had my secretary send those flowers to Cleo, if I thought she was going to take it the wrong way. I just thought it was a nice gesture since her album was being released."

"Did you use bad judgment in LA when you went back to her hotel room too?"

"Probably, but nothing happened."

"Oh, don't give me that shit Victor! What do you think, I'm stupid?"

"Of course not P. She's young and I guess she thought I would be down for something physical, but I straightened that out before anything transpired."

"Transpired, what exactly do you mean?"

Victor looked away trying to choose his words very carefully.

"Basically, she thought I was coming up to her room for more than just business and once I told her I was engaged, I left."

"See! See! I told you, but no, you said I was overreacting, remember? I know how these girls are, they make me sick!" Parris yelled.

"P, you don't have anything to worry about because nothing happened!"

"Well, from the sound of her email, she definitely wants another chance to try." Parris replied. "And how come you didn't tell me about your AOL account?"

"I forgot, and I hardly ever use it. You know I use my Blackberry for everything." He said giving her a hug. "Come on Parris, let's not argue anymore."

"I'm not finished Victor." She said trying to think of her next question.

"So, did you guys ever meet or did you miss my banquet for nothing?"

"Yes, we met downstairs in the lobby and unfortunately, I missed my flight, but it couldn't be helped." He said now pacing the floor. "I said I was sorry."

"What the hell does she need to make up to you? And why is she so damn sorry?"

"How the hell should I know! I guess because she was embarrassed that I turned her advances down. Look Parris, if I wanted to cheat on you, I certainly don't have to go all the way to California to do it."

"Oh really, then where do you have to go, or do you just do it right here in the house, running around in glow-in-the-dark condoms, chasing bitches in crotch-less panties!"

"See, now you're being ridiculous." He said as he sat down on the sofa and turned on the TV.

"Oh am I?"

"Yes." He replied staring at the screen.

"Well, you're an asshole!" She said and walked into the bathroom slamming the door as hard as she could.

Parris was so angry, she didn't know whether to leave, cry or just start breaking shit up. She stood at the sink and watched the tears roll down her cheek, she didn't know if he was telling the truth or if this was just more lies.

"He's a fucking liar and you know it!" the voice said.

The tears continued to flow.

"Please God, make it go away." She prayed.

"Take care of him!"

"Leave me alone." She whimpered. "What do you want from me, why, why are you saying these things?" she sobbed.

"Just do it, now!"

Victor knocked on the door.

"P, are you alright?"

"Ah yes, uh, I'll be out in a minute."

Parris wiped her face with a tissue and opened the door. Victor was standing right outside the door and hugged her tight before she could get away. His arms felt so strong and safe. She wished he could protect her from the voices. She couldn't understand why they were telling her to hurt the man whose touch made it all feel better. He lifted her head with both hands and fixed her hair, then he kisses her ever so gently on the lips and his tender touch made her cry again.

Chapter

49

The next morning Parris woke up feeling both comforted and confused, she was beginning to think she was really loosing her mind. She really wanted to believe Victor, but between the voices and the evidence presented, it was making for a very difficult case. She didn't know whether to listen to her heart or her head and at this point, neither one was proving to be a reliable source. She just wanted to get through the next couple of days without any drama. The week before the wedding flew by at work, even though Sean was in her office every ten minutes asking a thousand questions and talking trash.

"So, is it open bar all night or just a couple of hours?" he asked. "And are there going to be some fine, eligible women there or should I bring Brenda to be safe?"

"I thought you two were doing okay?" she said surprised.

"We are okay, but she's got some issues." He replied. "I just don't want to miss out on "Mrs. Right", if I've got "Miss Okay for Right Now" following me around."

"Sean, I don't believe you just said that." She said shaking her head. "I thought you were one of the nice guys."

"I am a nice guy, I'm just not a stupid one. There's a difference." Sean said confidently.

"No, *you*, like your fellow brethren, are just never satisfied. Brenda is attractive, smart and funny. What more do you want?" Parris asked.

"Come on Parris, you know, there's always going to be someone more attractive, smarter and funnier. You can't just settle for the first pretty face you meet." He continued. "You have to understand; smart men don't buy the first car they see, even though it looks goods and rides nice. We need to shop around and make sure we're getting the most bang for our buck!" he said with a chuckle. "Most of these shiny paint jobs and fancy rims are just lemons underneath and then it's too late and you're stuck."

"Stuck, huh?" she replied shaking her head.

"Stuck! Besides why should Victor be the only one who gets the girl of his dreams?"

"You've got a point."

"I mean what's he got that I don't?"

Parris hoped that was a rhetorical question, so she did not answer.

"Some dudes think all they gotta do is look good, spend money and have sex. Half of them don't even do that right."

It was clear he was getting ready to step up on a soap box and Parris wasn't sure if she should interrupt.

"I know how to really please a woman, you know what I mean? Kissing and cuddling and when it comes to sex, it's not about running all up in it. You gotta take your time and caress it. Foreplay is very important."

He was getting carried away now, so she stopped him in his tracks.

"You know what Sean, I'm getting married in a couple of days, and this is not the conversation I need to be having with my fiancé's best man." She said as she stood up from her desk.

"I'm sorry Parris, I'm trippin', my bad. Women just don't get it sometimes, especially when a good man is standing right in front of them."

"Well, I do Sean, I know Victor's a good man."

"Yeah, and he's not the *only* good man out here." He replied.

"Of course not."

"You should be glad you've got a man who knows what he wants and obviously, it's you. Hell, Victor always gets what he wants, he always has."

"Yeah well, don't try to change his mind by having a bunch of nasty, trifling hookers at the bachelor party."

"It ain't a real bachelor party if the hoochies don't show." He said laughing.

On that note, Sean left the office leaving her with something else to worry about, like she didn't have enough on her plate. She finished going over her schedule and agenda for the next two weeks with Maria, since she would be on vacation, then she headed out the door.

"Good luck Parris, I hope you have a wonderful day." Maria said.

"You're coming to the wedding, right?"

"I'm going to try, my son is sick again and I may not be able to get a sitter."

"Oh Maria, I'm sorry to hear that, I hope he feels better. Maybe your husband can stay home and you could at least come to the ceremony."

"That's a good idea. Hector should be able to handle it for a couple of hours. Oh yeah, what will your new last name be? I'll have your email account changed while you're on your honeymoon."

"Baxter. Mrs. Parris Baxter." She said with a smile.

The weekend was busy with making all the final arrangements. Victor still wasn't much help because he was working on a big case that was finally going to trial next week. He tried to postpone it because of the wedding, but the heavy metal bandleader was not sympathetic, it was a paternity case and it wasn't looking good for him. Victor wanted to send another attorney in his place, but the rocker insisted that he be present in court. Saturday afternoon, the girls met at the boutique for their final fitting. Parris' gown was gorgeous; she even tried on the tiara. Her mother started crying as soon as she came out of the fitting room.

"Oh, Pumpkin it's beautiful. You look like a princess!" Helen said wiping her eyes.

"It is, isn't it? I absolutely love it!" Parris replied twirling around in the mirror.

"Victor will be speechless when he sees you." Shelly added.

"Well, he better be able to say, I do." Kenya said.

"The way you look, he won't be able to get it out fast enough, now go take it off, before you get something on it." Helen replied.

Parris went back into the fitting room to change, while Kenya and Shelly tried their gowns on and even though they couldn't see each other, it didn't stop them from talking over the walls.

"P, why is Victor having his bachelor party all the way in New York?" Kenya asked.

"Because he's is trying to finish up a big case before next week and he's going to stay up there to make it easier, and I guess he thought it would be better to have the party up there too." Parris replied. "Oh yeah Shelly, where did you get that strapless bra with all the lace, I think I need to invest in one?"

"At Nordstrom's, it was on sale too. Are they having it at a club or at his apartment?" Shelly asked.

"I must be bloated because this is a little tight in the waist." Kenya said as she walked out of her room.

"Well, I don't think you should have it taken out, if it's just water weight. Parris said when she came out. "It's going to be at his place Shell, I told him that he really needs to keep it low-key, since he insisted on having it the night before."

"Well, they better be on time and better not be hung-over!" Helen said adamantly.

"I told Kevin, he better not have any naked women up in there." Shelly said.

"Come on now Shelly, be serious. It's a bachelor party for crying out loud. You know there will be plenty of chicks running around." Kenya said. "And why do you care, I thought you and Kev broke up?"

"We did." Shelly replied.

"You know Shelly continues to run her men, even *after* they've broken up." Parris said.

"That's right. You never know when you might need them, even if it's just for a bootie-call." Shelly said smiling.

"She's right. Shelly, keep your options open, because men certainly do." Helen said. "Although that Kevin fella is a good guy and I think he's good for you."

Laughing, Parris asked, "Ma, what do you know about options?"

Sophie, the designer, checked the hem on the girls' gowns and also suggested that Kenya not eat anything the morning of the wedding.

"I worked too hard on these gowns, girl, so starve yourself if you have to." Sophie joked.

"I really appreciate you doing these gowns for us Sophie. I know how busy you are." Parris said.

"Oh, it was no problem. Victor has saved me a lot of money over the years, it's the least I could do." She replied.

"They look beautiful, you've done a wonderful job." Helen said. "Shelly, are you wearing your hair up or down?"

"Up."

"Me too." Kenya said as she walked back into the fitting room.

While the girls where changing, Helen pulled Parris over to the side to talk privately.

"I take it, you and Victor have worked things out?"

"Yes, he told me that…"

"I don't need the details baby, I just wanted to know if you were okay." Helen said cutting her off. "This is one of the biggest steps you'll ever take and you need to be sure."

"But how are you ever *really* sure Mom?"

"A little voice inside will let you know." Helen replied and kissed her on the cheek.

Chapter

50

Monday morning, Victor packed for the week and went to New York, reassuring her of his love and devotion before he left. When she thought about his smile, she couldn't deny that she loved this man and he loved her too. She hoped that the few days they were apart, would make their hearts grow stronger.

Parris was going over the final seating arrangements when Leslie called.

"Oh hey girl, how are you?"

"I'm great, how are you? Are you nervous yet?"

"A little." Parris admitted. "No, I'm lying, a lot."

"Good, that's normal. I just wanted to drop off your shower gift, if you're not too busy?"

"I told you, you didn't have to get me anything Leslie."

"I'll be right over."

Twenty minutes later when Leslie arrived, she was carrying a large shopping bag up the driveway. She was struggling a little, so Parris ran out to help.

"Girl, what do you have in that bag? Let me help you."

"No thanks, I'm okay, but you can get the door for me." Leslie replied.

Leslie placed the bag down on the floor and sat down on the couch. Before Parris sat down to join her, Leslie removed the large gift-wrapped box from the bag. The paper was a beautiful silver and white foil with tiny wedding bells all over. The silver bow was also in the shape of a church bell.

"Oh my goodness, you *really* didn't have to do this." Parris said completed surprised by the size of the gift. Her imagination was running wild and she couldn't, for the life of her, imagine what was inside. She knew they both had similar taste, so she was sure she would like it.

"Parris, you know I had to get you something; my mother taught me better than that. Besides, you deserve it. I just wish I could do more, weddings just bring out the best in me." Leslie said pushing the gift closer to her.

"Thanks Leslie, I really appreciate it."

The box was somewhat heavy, so Parris got down on the floor to open it. She carefully peeled the pretty paper away from the box as her eyes danced with anticipation.

"Now, I know you're not trying to save that paper." Leslie teased.

"Yes I am, it's so pretty and I hate to ruin it."

"Girl, just open it!" Leslie insisted.

Parris ripped off the paper and to her surprise, what was inside was rather unique or maybe just odd for a bridal shower gift.

"Wow, a DVD player." Parris said sounding unsure.

"Look, I know it's not the typical shower gift, but I just thought that since Victor's got stolen, it might come in handy, especially if you're having the ceremony videoed, they can put it on a DVD instead of VHS." Leslie replied.

"That's sweet. Well, you're right about it not being typical, but it is very thoughtful. Thank you."

Parris got up from the floor and gave Leslie a hug. Their brief embrace was interrupted by the phone. Parris reached over the coffee table to answer it. Leslie started gathering up the wrapping paper.

"Hey love."

"Oh, hey baby."

"How are you?

"I'm fine, guess what?"

"What?"

"I just got one of the best shower gifts ever."

"Oh yeah, well if it wasn't me, in a box, butt naked with a big red bow, then it ain't the best." Victor replied.

"You're right, okay, the second best."

"That's better."

"Leslie gave me, I mean us, a new DVD player. Wasn't that sweet?"

"A what? And who's Leslie?"

"A DVD player, since yours got stolen, remember? And Leslie my friend, the one I gave a ride, she had car trouble, remember?"

"Oh yeah, that's cool, I guess." Victor replied obviously not impressed. "That's a weird gift, ain't it?"

Leslie put the paper in the kitchen trash can and returned to the sofa. She grabbed the remote and with Parris' permission, turned on the television.

"Look, the reason why I'm calling is to let you know that Sean and the guys moved the bachelor party to Thursday night, instead of Friday. They didn't want to be all drunk-up for the wedding and neither did I, so just in case you called and I don't answer, you know what's up."

"Oh good, that's better anyway, I don't know why they didn't have it on Thursday from the jump." Parris replied.

"You know how men are, they're just worried about drinking and..."

"And what? Huh? I can't hear you? I'm sorry what did you say, drinking and what? Strippers? Oh, I see. Okay." Parris teased.

"Ain't nobody having strippers, where did you get that from?" Victor teased back.

"Yeah, okay, I know better. You just be on your best behavior Mr. Baxter."

"Yes, ma'am Miss Reed." Victor laughed devilishly. "Well, let me get back to work, so I can finish up here. I love you Babe."

"I love you too. Bye."

Parris hung up the phone and apologized for the interruption. Leslie grabbed her handbag and stood up.

"Don't apologize Parris, I know how it is; I was in love once."

"I'm just so excited and nervous at the same time."

"I overheard you say something about strippers. They must be for the bachelor party, right?"

"Unfortunately, yes." Parris replied.

"Why do they always have to go there?"

"I don't know, but I can't wait until it's over. I'm just glad they moved it to Thursday, instead of Friday, that will give them time to sober up."

"That is good, they're gonna need that extra time." Leslie said looking at her watch. "I don't mean to rush out, but I've got some things I need to take care of."

"Okay, thank you again for the gift and I guess I'll see you on Saturday."

"Saturday it is and I will be there with bells on." Leslie said smiling.

Chapter

51

Thirty minutes later, Leslie signed the receipt and impatiently waited for the salesman to put the box in a bag.

"This is one of the best on the market. I think you'll be happy with the picture. A lot of parents buy this kind to keep an eye on their nannies. It's small enough that you can hide it just about anywhere and catch 'em red-handed." The older gentlemen said with a smile.

"Good, because that exactly what I plan to do."

"You know, you can even convert the tapes into picture images, I think they call them jpegs or jpets, something like that, anyway, you can send emails to your friends and family. I even heard of folk turning them into DVDs, just like real movies, it's amazing what they can do with technology these days."

"Amazing." Leslie replied unimpressed.

"Well now, enjoy and you have a nice day."

"Thanks, you too." She said as she walked out of the store.

She put the bag in the trunk and got in the car. But before she drove off, she made a phone call.

"Hey, I got it and if you're a good little boy, maybe I'll come over so we can practice making our own movie." She said checking her hair and makeup in the rearview mirror.

"You don't think he knows anything, do you?" she asked. "Good. I'll see you in a few."

Chapter

52

Thursday afternoon, Parris met with the florist to make a minor change to the table arrangements. The addition of yellow roses was going to cost an extra twenty-five dollar per table. Parris immediately wrote out a check for the full amount. With the wedding only two days away, she wasn't about to squabble over something so minor, after all, she was the one making the change.

She had one last stop to make before going home. A friend of her father's owns a store, on jeweler's row downtown and after much thought, she decided to give the Shelly and Kenya diamond earrings as a gift. She knew it was something neither of them owned and would really appreciate. Parris hated giving gifts, just for the sake of gift-giving. She wanted it to be special. As she drove across the bridge into the city, the golden rays from the sun were beaming through the windshield, practically blinding her. The warm air made her smile, and she prayed that the wonderful weather held up until Saturday.

Melvin's was rather crowded for a weekday, so when the door buzzed, she walked directly over to the earring counter, hoping she would get faster service if she acted like knew what she wanted.

The salesman was a cute, young brother, who obviously sensed her haste and quickly offered his assistance.

"Hello, I'm Michael, can I help you with something?" he asked with a smile.

"Yes, I'm looking for some diamond stud earrings."

"Okay, what size? Quarter, half or bigger?"

"Let's look at half a carat." Parris replied trying to look back in the office. "Is Melvin around?"

"Yes, he's in the back, would you like for me to get him." Michael replied looking a little disappointed.

"In a minute, you can help me out first."

He pulled out a small case with several sets of earrings and placed it on the counter top.

"Do you prefer round or the princess cut?" he said sitting each set of studs on a black velvet pad.

"Oh, they're not for me, this is going to be a gift for my maid-of-honor and bride's maid. But, to answer your question, I like the princess cut."

"That's a very nice gift, you've got expensive taste." He said handing her a pair of each. "But I see, judging from that rock on *your* finger, money's not an issue."

"Thankfully, it's not." Parris replied as she admired the earrings. "These are pretty, I'll take two pair."

"Okay, I'll be right back and I'll get Mr. Mel too."

Parris' cell phone rang, so she stepped outside into the sunshine to answer it.

"Hey girl."

"Hi Shell, what's up?"

"Not much, do you want to get together later for drinks or something? I figured we can do a little something, since the guys are getting their groove on tonight." Shelly replied.

"Sure, sounds good to me. I should be home in about an hour."

"Okay, just come over whenever you get ready and we can decide what to do from here."

Melvin was waiting behind the counter with two gift boxes in front of him, when she walked back into the store. Melvin Jackson had to be in his late sixties by now. His gray hair and beard made him look even older.

"Parris, how are you? I see you're looking prettier than ever." Melvin said sounding just like Barry White.

"I'm fine Mr. Mel, how are you?" Parris replied giving him a kiss on the cheek.

"I'm fine, just fine. Your mom and dad okay?"

"Everyone's fine, we're all just waiting for Saturday to get here." Parris replied.

"Yes, it ought to be quite an event, if your mother has anything to do with it." He said laughing. "She's one hell of a classy lady, that Helen." He said shaking his head.

"Mr. Mel, if I didn't know better, I'd think you had a crush on my mother."

"I did! And still do, but ol' Cole stole her from me." He said.

"What? I never heard that story before. I thought you guys all met in college or something."

"We did." He said writing out the sales receipt.

"So, what happened?" Parris asked curiously.

"It don't matter now, that was a long time ago. I just wish I would have fought harder to win your momma, that's all." He replied taking her credit card and processing it.

"Wow, ain't that something. You could have been my daddy!" Parris teased as she signed the receipt.

"Sho-nuff, coulda." He replied with a hint of disappointment in his eyes. "Here now, you takes these and get on out of here. Me and Ella will see you on Saturday."

As she drove home, she wondered what it must feel like to love someone and lose them to someone else. Judging by the look in Mr. Mel's eyes, Parris knew that it must be heartbreaking.

There was a message from Victor, letting her know that he and the guys were getting a head-start on the party. Parris tried to call him back, but got voicemail, so she left a message. The thought of the guys getting their groove on made her want to do the same, so she jumped in the shower and headed over to Shelly's place.

Of course, when she got there, she wasn't ready and didn't look like she would be any time soon. Parris plopped herself down into the bean bag chair in her bedroom while she waited.

"I can't believe you're not even half way ready."

"P, any other time you call when you're on your way, so don't get mad at me." Shelly said curling her hair with the curling iron. "There's some Kaluha, Vodka and wine in the cabinet by the fridge, go make us some drinks, so you can stop rolling your eyes at me."

"That's a good idea." She said struggling to get up out of the chair.

Parris mixed up two Vodka tonics and turned on the radio. Nelly's song, *"Hot in Here"* came on, which brought Shelly out of the bedroom dancing and her hair still not done. The two of them danced around the living room like they were on Soul Train.

Two hours later, Shelly hair was a mess and they were both drunk. Shelly had pulled out every CD, 45 and album she owned and they laughed and danced to every one of them as they reminisced.

"Hey P, remember when ugly Greg fell down the steps at Rhonda's party! Shelly said laughing hysterically.

"Yes, it was so funny and he was so embarrassed! And wasn't that the same night you met that cute guy, what was his name?"

"Reggie, and yes that was the same night. You think that was really funny, don't you?" Shelly said lying down on the sofa.

"Come on Shell, you know that shit was funny, when you laughed and your gum flew out and stuck to his shirt, I thought I was gonna die!"

"It was funny, but the best part, was that he didn't realize it was on there!" They both screamed with laughter. "And, I tried to hit it off, playing it off like it was a bug!"

They both laughed for another ten minutes straight. Then, like magic, the mood turned serious. Alcohol had a strange way of doing that to some people.

"P, I'm so happy for you."

"Thanks Shell." Parris said lying down on the floor.

"I hope our friendship doesn't change, just because you're getting married." Shelly said wiping her eyes. "I mean, I don't know what I'd do without you P."

Parris rolled over and sat up. She looked over at her best friend wanting to do more than verbally reassure her that their relationship would never change.

"Shelly, you are my best friend and I promise that nothing will ever change that, so stop crying before you make me cry too." Parris managed to get up and turn off the stereo. "Just because I'm getting married, doesn't mean I stop having friends. We'll still do things together, maybe not as often, but we'll work it out, you know what I mean?"

There was no answer. When Parris looked over at the sofa, Shelly was knocked out, mouth open and snoring.

"Oooh Miss Thang, this is definitely a Kodak moment." Parris said as she went to go look for the camera.

Chapter

53

In New York, the guys were finishing up their dinner at the Shark Bar. The waitress asked if they needed another round of drinks and the men declined and asked for the check.

"Yo! How many shots of Tequila did you have?"

"Four, I think." Victor replied. "How many did you do punk?"

"Two. You know I can't drink like that." Kevin said counting all the empty shot glasses on the table.

"She is fine and she was definitely checking you out Vic." Kevin said when waitress walked away.

"That ass looks good too." Sean added while turning his head all the way around to look. "Damn."

"No doubt, but I already got me a fine one." Victor agreed as he finished his drink.

"True, but you can never have too many can you, player?" Sean replied looking at Victor.

"Why are you looking at me?" Victor asked.

"You know why?" Sean replied.

"No, I don't." Victor insisted. "Talk to me."

"Never mind." Sean replied. "Let's go."

"Thank you! Let's get this party started." Kevin said "I'm ready to see some women."

"Let's do it." Victor said slamming his glass down.

When the waitress returned, Sean took the check and left cash on the table. The rest of the guys got up from the table and started heading for the door.

"Keep the change." Sean said winking at her.

"Thank you. You gentlemen have a good night." She said.

"You think I can get your number? Maybe I could take you out sometime?" Sean asked making note of her tongue ring.

"No, I don't think so, but you can give your friend over there my number." She said handing him a piece of paper with her number on it and pointing in Victor's direction.

"Sorry, but he's getting married tomorrow, so he'll be off the market. Don't sleep, I'm a good brother and I'll treat you right."

"Damn, that's a shame, cause he's fine. The wedding's tomorrow, huh?"

"Yeah, but you never know, anything could happen between now and then." Sean said putting her number in his pocket and walking away.

"Have fun at the bachelor party!" she said still looking at Victor.

"Oh, we will." Sean replied slyly.

Three black men trying to flag down a cab, in New York, at night, was quite a challenge, but four empty cabs later, one finally stopped.

When they got to the apartment, Victor's younger brother Vincent was there setting up, along with ten other men, who already started drinking.

"Yo, Boobe, what's up?" Vincent said embracing his brother.

"Nothing man, I didn't think you were going to make it. When I talked to Mom, she said she hadn't heard from your black ass. What's up with that?" Victor replied.

"Boobe? Who the fuck is Boobe?" Kevin asked.

"Oh, that's Victor's nickname, yall didn't know that?" Vincent said laughing. A couple of the guys listening, chimed in chanting Boo-be! Boo-be! Boo-be!

"Thanks, man." Victor said to his brother. "What's up with you? How's school?"

"Grad school is kicking my ass!" he replied. "But, come on now Vic, you know I couldn't miss this! Besides, you know how Mom likes to blow things out of proportion. I just talked to her last week."

"Yeah, well, you hang in there; those two letters in front of your name will make you a wealthy man one day. I don't' know a woman alive that can resist a good-looking doctor."

From across the room, Kenneth, Victor's colleague, yelled, "Look, yall need to stop bull-shittin' over there and bring on the tities! What time do the strippers arrive?"

"Calm down old dude, we know your wife doesn't let you out often." Someone else joked.

"Damn right! That's why I'm trying to get it in when I can." Kenneth replied. "You'll see. You just wait."

Checking his watch, Sean announced, "The tities and ass are due to arrive any minute."

Somebody turned up the music and handed Victor another drink, but before he could take a seat, Kevin opened the door and in walked five of the most beautiful black women they had ever seen. It was hard to believe they were strippers. A couple of the guys agreed, that whoever put up the dough, must have broken the bank because they were far from your ordinary strippers. They came in a range of rich skin tones, from vanilla to caramel and of course, chocolate, something for every man in the room. These ladies were guaranteed to satisfy a man's sweet tooth.

Each was dressed in different costumes, kind of like the Village People. There was a doctor, firefighter, police officer, construction worker, and businesswoman in a pin-striped suit. The suit and tie appeared to be running the show, as they all stood in a circle with their backs to each other, looking around the smoky, testosterone filled room.

"We have an appointment with a Mr. Victor Baxter, is he here?" The light-skinned sistah in the suit asked.

"Ah, yes ma'am, he's right over here." Sean said as he took her hand and led him over to where Victor was standing.

"My, my ladies, we've got ourselves a handsome one tonight." She said as she approached him. "And you know what that means, don't you Victor?"

"Uh, no. Why don't you tell me?" he grinned.

"That means, anything goes. Your wish is our command, one lady at a time or all at once." She replied.

All of the men cheered, barked and whistled. Kevin pulled a chair into the middle of the floor.

"Would you like to have a seat Mr. Baxter so we can begin?" she asked holding out her hand.

"Don't mind if I do." Victor replied as she led him to the chair. "Yo, somebody get me another drink and make it a double!" He yelled.

"So, what do you want to be when you grow up?" Vanilla asked pointing to the other ladies.

"Uh, I'm not sure." Victor replied scratching his chin.

"Well, how about we give you a little sample of each and maybe that will help you figure it out."

When he sat down, the music started and everyone started cheering them on. They each took turns, one-by-one, undressing down to their g-strings in front of him and each woman provided him with their own special lap dance. Victor was enjoying every minute. This was his last night as a single man and he wanted to savor every moment. The other men were going crazy; anxiously waiting their turns and wishing they were in his shoes. Once they were finished catering to the groom, they spread out and worked the room. But the sistah in the suit and tie focused all of her attention on Victor. Several drinks later, she led him to the bedroom for a private show. Sean was coming out of the bedroom as they were walking in.

"Yo man, don't do anything I wouldn't do." He said.

"Huh?" Victor replied. "What? I'm just chillin'. It's all good." He was obviously intoxicated and had a bottle of champagne in one hand and the stripper in the other, helping him walk.

"Yo, Sean!"

"What?"

"This is it!" Victor slurred holding up the bottle.

"Yeah man, it's over!" he replied laughing.

Chapter

54

Friday morning, Leslie had to drive into the city to meet someone and pick up something that was very important. She waited in her car for the woman to arrive. When she got in the car, Leslie didn't waste time with idle chit-chat.

"How did it go?" Leslie asked.

"Exactly as planned. His fiancé is one lucky bitch. I'd give all this shit up for a man like that."

Leslie ignored her and began counting out one hundred dollar bills. "You made it look natural didn't you? I mean you weren't looking at the camera were you?"

"Come on Leslie, I'm a professional I do this shit for a living, remember? I know enough not to look at the fuckin' camera, besides I do my best work on film." The light-skinned stripper said handing her the tiny spy camera. "He was so drunk, I don't think he even enjoyed it. I did, though, I had a ball, or should I say balls." She said laughing.

"This was more for my enjoyment than his." Leslie said handing her the last of the bills. "That should be it, three thousand, just like we agreed."

The stripper quickly recounted the money and put them back in the envelope. "It was nice doing business with you. Let me know if you ever need my services again."

"I doubt it."

"What are you gonna do, blackmail him?"

"Not exactly."

"You must really hate him, huh?"

It was starting to rain, Leslie started the car and turned on the windshield wipers.

"Hate's a strong word. It's more like sweet revenge."

"Damn. I'm glad I'm on your good side."

Chapter

55

The sound of the rain beating against the window, made Parris open her eyes, only to realize that her head was throbbing. She was a little disoriented for a minute and didn't realize where she was, until she glanced over at the clock and saw the picture of her and Shelly on the night table. She didn't remember lying down on the bed, but when she saw the camera by the pillow, it all came back.

She slowly got up from the bed and walked over to the window, it was almost ten-thirty and it looked like it was seven at night. The wind was blowing and the rain was relentless. She almost started crying when she saw all of the puddles forming in the street.

"But, yesterday was so beautiful." She whispered to herself.

"Ain't that some shit? How are we going to get our hair done in this crap?" Shelly said rubbing her eyes.

"I don't know." Parris replied. "I don't believe this."

"What time is our appointment anyway?"

"Not until four, maybe it'll stop by then."

"Maybe." Shelly said. "Or maybe we can just get them done tomorrow morning."

Parris sat on the bed and started putting on her shoes. Shelly crawled into bed and snuggled up under the covers.

"I've gotta call Mommy, she left me a message saying something about moving the rehearsal to seven-thirty or something."

"Oh yeah, that's right, I forgot all about rehearsal. Are the guys going to make it back in time?"

"They better. I'll call him when I get home." Parris replied as she looked in the mirror and tried to fix her hair.

"Alright, well, call me later. I'm going back to sleep, my head is killing me."

"Mine too. See ya later." Parris said walking out the bedroom.

"Hey P! Why is my camera in the bed?" Shelly asked.

"I don't know, but give it here, so I can get the film developed." Parris said with a smile.

When she got home, her mother had left three messages and Kenya left two, both of them asking questions about rehearsal. She quickly dialed her mother's number.

"Hi Ma."

"Girl, where have you been? Didn't you get my message? I left you three of them!" Helen yelled.

"I'm sorry. I just walked in, I spent the night over Shelly's and my cell phone was on vibrate." Parris explained as she opened the refrigerator looking for something to eat.

"Well, what time are we all supposed to be at the salon?"

"Four o'clock, but I don't know if we should even bother. Shelly said maybe I can call Shareetta and see if she can do us early tomorrow morning." She said drinking orange juice from the carton.

"That's a good idea because otherwise, it's just going to be a waste if this rain doesn't stop." Helen said disgusted. "You know how my hair frizzes up."

"I know Ma, I know."

"There was a mix up with the caterer, so they are bringing the food at quarter to eight. I figure we should be done rehearsing by then, if we move it up to seven. Kathy next door, is going to wait here at the house to let them in so they can set up." Helen said only pausing for a second to take a breath. "I've already called Pastor Williams and that's fine with him. You make sure you let Shelly and the guys know, okay?"

"I will."

"What's wrong with you chile?"

"My stomach's a little upset, I think I need to go to the bathroom." Parris replied.

"That ain't nothing but the jitters. Drink some ginger ale, that'll calm your stomach."

"Okay, I will, let me call you back after I talk to Shareetta."

When she came out of the bathroom, she stretched out across the bed and called Victor. She hoped he wasn't too hung over.

"Hello." He said sounding hung over.

"Hey, are you alright?"

"Yeah, I'm cool." He said removing the sheets. The fact that he was naked put him at a loss because he couldn't remember taking off his clothes.

"You sound horrible. I know you have a hangover, don't you?"

"Yes."

"Well, I wanted to let you know that rehearsal is at seven o'clock, Mommy moved it up. So, please tell Sean and Kevin not to be late."

"Alright." He said rubbing his temple.

"What time are you planning to get on the road?"

"What time is it now?"

"Twelve-fifteen."

"Probably in about an hour or so. It looks like Sean and Kev left early this morning. So, Vinny will ride back with me." He said walking into the living room.

"Oh good, Vincent made it. I can't wait to meet him. So, how was the party?"

"It was cool." He replied not wanting to say too much.

"Were they're any strippers?"

Looking at Vinny, who was laying on the floor, he replied, "Ah, no, but they did have one chick who did a little dance for us."

"She danced, but didn't take off her clothes?" Parris replied not sounding convinced. "That's a good one; I know she took something off."

"Yeah, hey P, Vinny wants to say hello." Victor said as he threw him the phone.

"Hello, soon to be sister-in-law."

"Hi Vincent, tell your brother I'm gonna smack him when he gets home."

Laughing, "Okay, well, I guess I'll see you when we get there." Vinny replied.

As soon as Vinny hung up the phone, Victor started yelling.

"Yo man, what the hell happened last night?"

"What do you mean? Don't tell me you don't remember Vic?"

"No man, I honestly don't. I mean, I remember the girls stripping and how can I forget the lap dances, but after that, I'm not sure what the hell happened, I must have passed out." Victor said genuinely.

"Aw man, stop lying! There ain't no way you don't remember that fine-ass trick, with the double-breasted, pinstriped suit or should I say "double D's". Vinny said making a gesture with his hands. "Once she finished giving you the lap dance of life, home-girl took you straight to the bedroom. But, I ain't mad, cause the police officer threw the handcuffs on and gave me a full body search!" he said laughing.

Victor stood in the middle of the room dumb-founded.

"Man, don't worry about it, whatever happened in there is your business, no one else ever has to know." Vinny said as he got up and went into the bathroom.

"Don't worry bro, I got your back!" he yelled once the door closed.

Victor sat down and tried desperately to remember what happened. He knew his brother wasn't lying and the fact that he was butt-ass naked when he woke up was a clear indication that something definitely happened.

Chapter

56

It was four o'clock, still raining and didn't look like it was going to let up any time soon. Shareetta gave Parris a dissertation about the last time she went on vacation and that no one was going to stop her from getting on that plane to Aruba tomorrow. Saturday morning was out, it was now or never, so they all met at the salon trying to dodge the rain drops.

"Hey P, I checked the weather channel before I left and they said it's supposed to clear up tonight." Kenya said as the girl filed her nails.

"I hope so." Parris replied as the shampoo girl washed her hair.

Two hours later, all four heads and eighty finger and toe nails were finished and looking great. It was their faces that needed a makeover; they were all frowning and dreading having to walk out into the rain.

"I'll meet you at the church. I have to stop home and get the programs, I forgot them." Parris said before she left. "If Victor's home, I'll just ride with him."

It was only 6:15, but dark enough for headlights. Before she reached the house, Victor called on her cell.

"Hey Babe, I'm home."

"Oh, good."

"I just dropped Vinny off at the barber shop."

"Will he be finished in time for rehearsal at seven?"

"Probably not, because Percy's good, but he talks too much. He'll be alright, he's walking with Shelly and she'll make sure he's on point. Don't worry. I told him call me if he thinks he'll be done by quarter of, if not, he can catch a cab over to the church."

"Does he have the address?" she asked.

"Yes, P. Don't worry, everything is going to be fine." Victor assured her.

Okay, I know. I'm getting nervous now. Are you?"

"No, not really. I can't wait to call you Mrs. Baxter." He replied.

"Not to be confused with the other Mrs. Baxter, of course."

Victor laughed, "Of course, but don't worry about Mom, she'll be fine."

"I hope so. I'm leaving the salon and on my way to the house to pick up of the programs." She replied.

"Cool. Come get me and we can ride over together." Victor said.

"That's exactly what I was planning to do. I'll see ya in a few."

Parris came in through the garage and remembered that she forgot to check the mail. When she opened the front door to go back outside, a small envelope fell on her feet. It was another mysterious delivery with no address, just her name. Inside was a CD with a note attached.

Watch it now before it's too late!

The words written in black magic marker made her stomach cramp. She glanced at the clock and it was almost six thirty. She was running short on time, but there was no way she could resist watching the DVD. She remembered that the DVD player Leslie gave them, it was still in the box.

"Shit!" she said as she quickly removed it and hooked it up to the television. Parris thanked God for small favors, because everything was color coded making the installation quick and simple. When she inserted the disc and pushed play, at first the screen was black, and then there was a picture of what looked like Victor's bedroom at the apartment in New York.

"Oh, my God." Parris said covering her mouth.

Then she heard loud music and laughter, as if the bedroom door opened, but there still wasn't anyone in the picture. About a minute later, this light-skinned woman, wearing only a thong came into the picture. She quickly glanced at the camera, and then went out of the picture again. The door closed and the music was muffled again. This time when she returned, she was holding a man's hand and leading him over to the bed his, back was to the camera. He staggered to the bed, obviously drunk. His shirt was off and his back was still to the camera, but Parris knew immediately it was Victor.

She started feeling faint, so she sat down on the coffee table in front of the TV to get herself together. But nothing could prepare her for what she was about to see next.

Chapter

57

The doorbell rang twice, as Victor got up from his desk to answer it, he looked at his watch. It was 6:45pm. He wondered by Parris wasn't using her key. To his surprise, it was Lisa, his ex-wife.

"Hello, Victor."

"Lisa. What are you doing here?" he asked looking totally stunned.

"Aren't you going to ask me in?"

"Um, sure. I have to leave in a few minutes, so you can't stay."

"Don't worry, this won't take long." She said as she walked passed him. "I can't believe you haven't replaced any of the furniture yet?"

"If you hadn't taken everything that wasn't nailed down, it wouldn't be an issue." He replied. "What do you want Lisa?"

Victor closed the door slowly, wondering what on earth brought her out the woodwork. He figured she must have heard about the wedding and maybe she was going to wish him well. In all honesty, he knew that was doubtful, because she hated him. When he walked into the living room, she was standing next to his desk, holding a framed picture of Parris. He walked over to the sofa and sat down.

"Well?"

"Is this your fiancé?"

"Yes."

"Pretty girl, you always did like the pretty ones, didn't you Vic?" she said throwing the picture in his direction and when it hit the floor, the glass shattered.

"Lisa! What are you doing? Are you crazy!" he yelled as he jumped up. "I don't believe you just did that!"

"Believe it. Crazy, maybe, but I thought you knew that already." She said smiling. "Now, sit down!" She yelled pulling the gun from the pocket of her black and white polka dot raincoat and pointing it at him.

"What the fuck are you doing?" Victor said looking at her in disbelief. "Is that thing loaded?"

"I need to get a few things off my chest." She said calmly. "I should have done this a long time ago, and yes, it's loaded."

The sound of the doorbell made Victor jump. Lisa walked closer to the sofa and told him to answer it. She followed close behind him, pointing the gun directly in his back. Victor knew she was a little off, but he never expected something as insane as this. He also knew that she was a good shot, because he took her to the shooting range several times while they were dating. They also attended a few karate classes together. He wanted her to know how to defend herself and she was very good. He figured now was not the time to be a hero, so he did what she said and answered the door.

"What's up, man?" Sean said. "Hey Lisa."

"What took you so fucking long?" Lisa asked.

"Can't you see it's raining like cats and dogs out there?" Sean replied kissing her on the lips.

Sean pushed Victor out of the way and walked into the living room. Victor looked at his best friend like he was a complete stranger as he walked passed.

"She ain't here yet?" Sean asked looking around.

"No. Did you give it to her?" Lisa replied as she pushed Victor back into the living room.

"She wasn't home, so I left it in the door." He said sitting down on the sofa.

"What if she doesn't see it Sean? Then what?" Lisa replied.

"She'll see it, don't worry." He replied.

"See what? What the fuck is going on, Sean? Is this some kind of joke? Cause if it is man, it ain't funny." Victor said trying to remain calm.

"Oh, it's no joke, my brother. This is for real." He replied as he put his feet on the coffee table, leaned back and crossed his legs. "I can't wait to see how you get your pretty-ass out of this one!" he said laughing.

"Out of what? Victor asked looking back in forth between them. "Well? Is someone going to answer me?"

Chapter

58

Parris barely stopped at stop signs and almost went through a red light on the way to Victor's. The rain was coming down so hard, she could barely see in front of her. The windshield wipers were going crazy, making that notorious, nerve-racking, scraping sound. The rain was coming down in buckets and visibility was poor. Parris was gripping the steering wheel so hard, her knuckles were aching. Between the tears and the rain, she could hardly see. Fighting her emotions like a boxer with his belt on the line, Parris replayed what had taken place over and over again in her head. How could he do this to her? This wasn't the way it was supposed to turn out, she thought.

She really didn't want an explanation, because there was none. He had sex with the stripper and she had seen it with her own eyes. She just wanted the satisfaction of slapping him across the face and telling him what a disgrace he is to all the "good" brothers out there. He had her fooled all this time. Even though she was crying, there were more tears falling in anger, than of sorrow.

"I told you he was a liar, but you didn't want to listen." The voice said. *"I told you to take care of him, are you going to listen this time?"*

Parris tried hard to ignore the voice. At this point, she was afraid of herself and the last thing she needed was coaxing from a voice inside her head. Her mind was playing a very dangerous game.

When she pulled up to the house, there was a car parked behind Victor's in the driveway, but she was so angry, she didn't notice that it looked just like Leslie's car. She got out the car, not bothering to use an umbrella and was unconcerned about her hair at this point. It didn't matter anyway, because as far as she was concerned, the wedding was off.

When she put the key in the door, she could hear talking inside. Sean quickly opened the door before she had the chance to turn the key.

"Oh, Sean, you scared me. What are you doing here? You're supposed to be at the church?" she asked walking into the living room. "Where's Victor? I really need to talk to him, so can you…"

When she saw Leslie standing next to Victor, she was totally confused and immediately started asking questions.

"What the hell are you doing here Leslie?"

"Leslie?" Victor said. "Her name isn't Leslie, it's Lisa."

"No, it's not, this is my friend Leslie or at least I thought she was my friend, the one I gave the ride to?" Parris insisted.

"It's Lisa, Parris, Lisa Baxter, this is Vic's ex-wife." Sean said. "Damn, I can't believe you really fell for it. I thought you were a lot smarter."

"Fell for what?" Parris exclaimed. "What the hell is going on?"

"Let me explain P, isn't that what they call you? My name is Lisa and yes I used to be married to this heartbreaker."

"So, what?" Are you fucking him too?" Parris asked.

"I wish, but I've been there and done that." Lisa replied. "So, did you get chance to look at the DVD?"

"What DVD?" Victor asked.

Lisa smiled, "You look like you've been crying, so I guess you did."

"That video needs to be on the internet. Shit, we could make a fortune. I mean, it was triple X material. Wasn't it Parris? Man, you were fucking that bitch's brains out last night." Sean replied laughing.

"Oh, my God, you didn't." Victor said covering his face with his hands. "Sean, man, how could you?"

"Don't you remember?" Sean asked.

Victor was embarrassed because he really didn't remember, but he obviously had done it because the look on Parris' face was that of disgust.

Her mind was racing, she didn't know who to question first.

"This is a nightmare." Parris asked. "Sean, you knew he was being video taped?"

"Who do you think set up the camera?" He replied.

"Mother-fucker, you set me up?" Victor yelled and started towards him.

Parris walked over, stepped in between them and slapped Victor across the face.

"He might have set you up, but he damn sure didn't *make* you fuck her!" Parris said rolling her eyes.

"Amen to that." Lisa added. "Now, sit down, bitch!"

"Who you calling a bitch? Bitch!" Parris said.

That's when Lisa showed her the gun. "You, now sit down!"

"Oh, shit! Leslie, I mean Lisa, why are you doing this? If you have a problem with me or Victor, I'm sure we can work it out, now please, put the gun away." Parris begged.

"It's not that simple Parris. I've been dealing with his shit since high school." Sean said. "And it's time to get this settled once and for all."

"High school? Man, what are you talking about?" Victor asked. "I know you aren't carrying some grudge or bullshit from high school!"

Sean walked around the sofa and stood directly in front of him. Then he removed a gun from the back of his pants.

"Oh, my God Sean don't!" Parris yelled.

"Oh, like you don't know? You are unbelievable Vic. First, it was Tanya Brown in the tenth grade, then Stephanie Willis in college, and let's not forget, lovely Lisa here." He said shaking his head. "Every time I met a fine sistah, you had to come bogartin' in with your good looks and fancy cars. I met Lisa first, remember?"

"But…" Victor said.

"But nothing, shut the fuck up and let me finish!" Sean said backhanding him across the face with the gun.

Victor moaned in agony as he wiped the blood from his lip.

Lisa started laughing, "That's right, let the man finish."

Parris' cell phone started to ring. Everyone looked at their phones to make sure it wasn't theirs.

"Don't answer it." Lisa demanded.

"Who introduced you to Parris? Me, mother-fucker! You knew I was digging her because I told you all about her, but you went and got her number anyway." He continued. "I'm tired of playin' second fiddle to you man! I'm tired."

"But Sean, we were just friends; I thought I made that clear." Parris said in Victor's defense.

"Yeah, and you didn't even give me a chance. You knew I was diggin' you." He said turning towards her. "What was wrong with me? Huh?"

"Sean, nothing. I just don't like to date men that I work with?" Parris said trying to sound sincere.

"Oh, don't hand me that shit Parris because if Vic worked at the job, you would have dated him anyway. You must think *I'm* stupid."

"No I don't Sean, please put the gun away before someone gets hurt." Parris pleaded.

"I'm not putting shit away and it don't matter cause I'ma make sure it don't happen again. He said wiping his brow. "I really tried to be happy for you guys and let that shit slide, *again,* but it's to the point where I just can't fake it anymore."

"That's where I come in." Lisa added moving closer to Sean. "When I ran into Sean a while back and asked about you, he said you were in love with a woman on his job that he was interested in, but you beat him to the punch once again. He even told me that back in college he had a crush on me and you knew it, and asked me out anyway. And after a few drinks, we decided that we were tired of getting the short end of the stick."

"What short end?" Victor said. "Lisa, we got married, it didn't work, so we got divorced. It happens everyday."

"It could have worked Victor." Lisa said with a sad look in her eyes. "We were good together. I loved you and I thought you loved me until you slept with one of your clients and broke my heart. Let's be clear, *that's* why it didn't work Victor."

"I never cheated on you, but you were so crazy and jealous that you convinced yourself otherwise and it's not true." Victor said.

"That's bullshit; you're a liar and a cheat!" Lisa snapped.

"So wait, me giving you a ride that night was no coincidence, was it?" Parris asked. "You set me up too?"

"Well actually, it *was* a coincidence. Funny thing is, I didn't know who you were until you mentioned Victor's name, then I put two and two together. But Parris, there's no such thing as coincidence, everything happens for a reason."

"This is insane. I can't believe this." Parris said looking at Sean in disbelief. "Sean, you knew about this the entire time?"

Sean did not respond.

"He wasn't involved in the beginning, but he was pissed at you too. How did you like the pretty Christmas panties I sent and the crank calls, clever, huh?" Lisa smirked.

"So, you were the one who broke in and stole the DVD player." Victor said.

"No, Sean did that, he also planted the condoms. But, at least I was kind enough to buy you another one. Someone needed to teach you a lesson and who better than me and Sean."

"Let's be reasonable. Why don't we all go our separate ways and call it even." Victor replied trying to rationalize the situation.

"He's right. Victor and I…" Parris began.

"There will be no Victor and I, you two are over Parris. If I can't have him, no one will." Lisa said cutting her off.

"Look, we've done enough talking and I don't want to hear anymore shit about Victor. Lisa and me are working things out and decided we should handle this together." Sean said. "Lisa we need to go."

Both Victor and Parris' phones were ringing now and they both looked at each other for a hint of what to do next.

"Don't answer it! We better get out of here before they send out a search party." Sean told Lisa. "Get up, let's go!"

"Go where?" Victor asked. "I'm not going anywhere."

Sean grabbed Parris by the arm and then he pushed her towards the door.

"Sean, get off of her!" Victor yelled.

"Sean wait, I thought we were friends, can't we talk about this like adults." Parris pleaded.

"Friends? Yeah right, fuck you! You took one look at me and barely gave me the time of day. Move bitch!" he said pushing her again, this time she tripped on the rug and fell to the floor.

"Sean, if you hurt her, I swear to God, I'll kill you!" Victor yelled.

"Not if I don't kill you first play boy." Lisa said putting the gun up to his temple. "Hey Sean, maybe I should take her and you get Victor, just in case he gets stupid." Lisa suggested.

"Good idea." Sean replied.

As she was getting up off the floor, Parris felt her keys in her coat pocket and remembered she had pepper spray on the key ring her father gave her. It was old and she never even tested it to see if it worked. She prayed it wasn't empty.

"Meet me at 30th Street Station in an hour and don't forget Sean, no witnesses." Lisa said as she forced Parris out the door.

Chapter

59

Helen Reed was beginning to panic, the bride and groom were late to their own rehearsal and neither of them was answering their cell phones. The sound of the heavy rain falling onto the roof of the church had everyone feeling uneasy.

"Oh, Cole where do you think they could be?" Helen said pacing in front of the church.

"I don't know honey, but try to calm yourself okay. I'm sure we'll hear from them soon." He replied patting her on the back.

"This is isn't like Parris, you know she's anal when it comes to being on time. Who talked to her last?" Kenya asked.

At first no one answered. They just looked around at each unsure of who had last spoken to the bride and groom.

"The last time I talked her she was going home to get the programs. I told her I would meet her here." Shelly said. "I'll try her cell again."

"Where's his brother Vincent? Does anyone have his number, maybe they're together." Coleman said. "And where's Sean? This is unbelievable, where is everyone?" he said throwing his hands up.

No one had Vincent's number, nor did they know of Sean's whereabouts. Helen sat down on the front pew and began to cry. Kenya sat to try to console her mother.

"It'll be alright Ma, they'll be here. It's probably just the rain slowing them down."

"Yeah, that's right. It's nasty out there, so I'd rather have them late than in an accident. Let's just be patient, they'll show." Coleman said.

When the doors to the sanctuary opened, everyone turned around hoping it was them. Instead, Vincent walked in wet and annoyed.

"I'm sorry I'm late, but traffic is a mess and as you can see, it's pouring out there." He said shaking his umbrella.

"Is Victor with you?" Shelly asked.

"No, why? He's not here yet?" Vincent asked in disbelief.

"No, we all thought he was with you." Shelly replied.

"Did you try his cell?" Vincent asked.

"Yes, but he's not answering, neither is Parris." Kenya replied.

"Well, what the hell is going on?" Vincent asked forgetting that he was in a church. No else seemed to remember either. "Maybe someone should take a ride over to Vic's, maybe something's happened."

"Good idea, let's go." Shelly said grabbing her handbag.

Reverend Williams came from out the back door of the church with his bible in hand. Coleman walked over to meet him and informed him that there was a problem and that Parris and Victor were very late and no one could reach them. He frowned and walked over to say something to Helen. She nodded and wiped the tears from her eyes.

The pastor held up the bible in his right hand and called after Shelly and Vincent as they were leaving. "Wait a minute, please, before you leave, I think we should have a moment of prayer."

Chapter

60

Lisa told Parris to drive the Benz and gave her the keys. She held the gun at Parris' side to make sure she didn't try to run.

"Where are we going, Lisa?" Parris asked.

"To Camden, so get on the expressway." Lisa replied.

The rain had finally stopped. Parris looked at the clock, it was 7:35pm.

"You're not going to get away with this. Everyone is worried by now and will come looking for us."

"We'll see about that, just shut-up and drive."

"We were supposed to be at the church for rehearsal at seven. They'll probably go to Victor's house since it's closer."

"Yeah, well, I don't think they'll be looking in Camden. Now, shut up and drive, damn it!" Lisa said as she poked her in the side with the gun. "Get off at the Federal Street exit."

Parris was racking her brain trying to think about how she was going to get out of this alive. She didn't know Camden very well, so she was driving very slowly, looking for landmarks, a cop or someone that could help. It was obvious that Lisa was crazy and serious about hurting her, otherwise she wouldn't have a gun. She had to think smart and quick, because time was running out. They turned down several dark streets and Parris had no idea where they were. It looked like they were driving towards the waterfront and she knew there was nothing down there but water.

"Look, Lisa, it's over between Victor and me now that I've seen the video, so you can have him and if you let me out right here, I promise, I won't tell anyone."

Lisa started laughing, "This ain't let's make a deal, besides I don't want him anymore than you do, I just want to get even."

"Well, this is a little *more* than even, don't you think?"

"Maybe." Lisa replied. "Turn down that alley."

Parris was really scared now, all she had to defend herself was the pepper spray in her pocket and it was so old she didn't even know if it still worked. She wished she had taken that self defense class with Shelly months back. The end of the alley was dark and empty except for a trash dumpster.

"Turn off the car and get out." Lisa demanded as she opened her door.

"Wait Lisa, before we get out; can I ask you a question?"

Lisa hesitated and looked at her watch. "What? You've got one minute." She said closing the door.

Parris took a deep breath hoping that the conversation would buy her some time.

"Do you really think that killing me is going to make you feel better? You don't want to go to jail. Please, think about what you're doing."

Lisa stared silently out her window into the darkness.

"I know you're hurt and Victor may have been the cause, but killing him or me isn't going to ease the pain. He'll be dead and you'll be rotting in some jail still hurting." Parris said hoping she was convincing her to rethink her next steps.

Lisa continued to sit in silence and then wiped her eyes. She appeared to be crying.

"You know Parris, you're probably right, but it's the only way. Don't you see? He's hurt you too and he'll just keep doing it. It has to stop and I have to stop it."

"Lisa you're right, but killing us? You're not a murderer. I know that deep down inside you're a nice person and unfortunately bad things happen to nice people. Even though it might have been part of your plan, you were so nice to me and so helpful when it came to my wedding. You didn't have to do that, but you did and I really appreciated it. Now, let's just drive somewhere and talk okay?"

"Parris we're not going anywhere and that's enough talk. Your minute is up, now get out the car." She said calmly.

Parris reluctantly did as she was told, but before she opened the car door, she put her hand in her pocket and held onto the pepper spray, trying to make sure the nozzle was facing the right way.

"Don't get out." The voice said.

Lisa got out and walked around the front of the car, pointing the gun at her.

"I said, get out the car! Come on Parris, don't make this harder than it has to be."

"Don't move." The voice said again.

Lisa was standing directly in front of her door now.

"Get out!" she said as she fired a shot off into the air.

The sound of the shot fired was loud and Parris was scared and prayed to God that someone heard it. She opened the car door slowly, putting her index finger on the top of the tiny sprayer. Lisa grabbed the handle and swung open the door.

"I'm not fucking up my car and I'm not playing, get out!"

Parris counted to three and hoped her reflexes and aim would be accurate.

"Now!" The voice said.

She stepped out of the car, pulled her hand out of her pocket and started spraying.

The liquid stream landed directly in Lisa's eyes and she immediately dropped the gun and grabbed her face screaming in agony. Parris quickly reached down and grabbed the gun while Lisa was temporarily blinded. Parris kept her eyes and the gun on her as she stumbled around in the dark.

"You bitch! My eyes are burning! Oh my God, my eyes!" she screamed.

Wasting no time, she used her cell phone to dial 911. Lisa continued to cry and complain about her burning eyes. Parris felt bad, but wasn't going to give her another opportunity to get the upper hand, so she told her get on the ground, face down.

"Fuck you!" I'm not laying down on the ground, it's wet!" she said rubbing her eyes.

"Lisa, get on the ground!"

Lisa ignored her and leaned up against the car, trying to regain her sight. Parris didn't know what to do next and the police were taking too long, but in the meantime, she had to maintain control of the situation. She had never used a gun before and certainly didn't want to start today. Camden, New Jersey is a mostly black, high crime city and the chance of the police showing up in a timely manner was slim. Parris kept the gun held in front of her, pointed in Lisa's direction.

"You can relax with the gun Parris. As a matter of fact, you need to put it down before you hurt yourself." Lisa said laughing.

"You think this is funny?"

"Actually, yes." She replied blinking several times trying to focus.

"Well, you've got a sick sense of humor Lisa." Parris replied looking over her shoulder. "You didn't really think you could get away with murder, did you?"

"I almost did."

"Yeah, well almost doesn't count."

The two women stood in the dark with only the headlights illuminating the dark alley. They could hear the sirens approaching.

"You know, I just want what every woman wants. I wanted the fairytale. A black prince that sweeps me off my feet and makes me feel beautiful and sexy. I want a man that loves me unconditionally and faithful, a good provider, father and hopefully a good lover. I want two kids, a girl and a boy named after his father." Lisa said looking at Parris. "I know it sounds crazy, right? But I almost had the fairytale. I had a good man, I just didn't know how to deal with him because I never had one before, I guess. The assholes I dated in the past were all losers; the druggie, the baby-daddy, the lazy, the insecure, the thinks he looks better than you, the sexually confused, and the big dummy. You name it, I dated him. Then, when I finally got a good one, I let all of my insecurities and baggage from those past relationships, influence the only good relationship I ever had."

Maybe Lisa wasn't crazy as after all, Parris thought.

"Lisa, you aren't alone. I think we've all dated one or two of those losers and messed up a couple of good relationships. It's definitely not all you fault, but you can't hold grudges and try to get revenge. You've gotta move on and try to learn from your mistakes." Parris said lowering the gun.

Two patrol cars with flashing lights, pulled up behind the car. The officer told them to drop their weapons and put their hands up. The women did as they were told. Lisa was immediately handcuffed. Before she got in the car, she said something to the officer and walked over to Parris with her head down and Parris gave her a hug and told her to keep her head up. Lisa began to cry. The officer grabbed her by the arm and told her it was time to go.

"I'm sorry Parris. Do me a favor, marry Victor. He's not perfect, but he's a good man and he loves you. Maybe one of us can learn from my mistakes and live happily ever after."

Chapter

61

Victor refused to move from the couch, even after Sean threatened to shoot him if he didn't. He could tell this was Sean's first time handling a gun because he was nervous and starting to sweat. Time was ticking away and he was behind schedule. Victor knew he didn't really want to kill him, mainly because he wasn't violent by nature and secondly because he was petrified of going to jail. After one of their high school buddies was released from prison for armed robbery, the stories he told were enough to make the rest of the guys think twice before breaking the law.

"Sean, put the gun down before someone gets hurt?" Victor advised.

"The only one that's gonna get hurt is you, my friend. Now, let's go!" He sensed Victor wasn't taking him seriously, so he walked around to the back of the couch.

"Let's go." Sean said poking him with the gun.

Victor was beginning to get nervous because Sean was behind him and he couldn't see. "Sean, I can't believe you are willing to go to jail over something like this and you let crazy-ass Lisa, of all people, talk you into it!"

The reality of what Victor said was beginning to set in because Sean sounded like he was starting to panic.

"Get up!" he yelled.

Victor slowly stood up, but before he reach an upright position, he quickly reached back and grabbed Sean's wrist, twisting his arm and flipped him over the couch, sending him crashing into the glass coffee table. The force and pressure made the glass top shatter into a thousand pieces. The gun flew out of his hand and slid over by the desk. The two men scrambled and fought to get to the gun first. Victor was bigger and stronger, making the struggle much tougher for Sean. But, Victor knew that adrenaline and fear can never be underestimated, no matter what size the man happens to be. They struggled some more, punching and pushing each other. Then Victor caught a break, reached out and grabbed the gun. In an instant, the tables were turned and he was pointing the gun at Sean.

Sean got to his feet and swiftly grabbed a pointy letter opener from the desk. Then he slowly walked towards Victor as if the gun never existed. Victor instinctively started backing up.

"Okay counselor, let's see if *you* have the balls to shoot." Sean said as he continued to move forward. "I believe that jail-time will apply to your ass too."

Victor lowered the gun to his side and wiped the sweat from his forehead. He felt less threatened especially now that his weapon was a letter opener.

"Sean, it's over." Victor said hoping he would stop. "We go back a long way, don't do this shit man. Come on."

Sean kept coming ignoring is best friend.

"Sean, I don't want to hurt you! Stop!" Victor yelled.

Sean stopped, but never took his eyes off of him. Victor felt for his cell phone to call the police, but the clip was empty. He scanned the floor, but saw nothing but broken glass and pieces of the table.

"Look man, I'm calling the police. We're gonna get you some help. Okay?" Victor said walking towards the phone in the kitchen. As soon as he turned away Sean came after him.

He lunged forward and Victor turned around firing twice, hitting him in the chest and stomach. Sean stumbled backwards and fell to the floor; he was dead.

Victor stood over his friend and silently asked God for forgiveness. The doorbell rang, he figured it was the police, but it was Shelly and Vincent. When they came in side and saw what had happened, Victor explained that they had to save Parris. He grabbed his keys, jumped in the car and headed for the city. He prayed Parris was still alive and he wasn't too late to save her. Shelly and Vincent stayed behind to explain the unbelievably tragic story to the police.

Chapter

62

30th Street Station was unusually busy, people running to catch their train, others waiting to be picked up. Voices echoed off of the high cathedral ceilings.

Lisa never said exactly where they were supposed to meet, but Victor remembered how much she loved the old coffee shop in there, so he hoped she would meet Sean there. Before heading to the coffee shop, he checked the train schedules to see when and where the next departing trains' were going. A train was leaving in twenty minutes to New York another was leaving for Washington DC. Victor figured Lisa would go to New York before DC, since she was more familiar with that city. He continued to look frantically in every gift shop and eatery to see if she was there waiting for Sean. He even checked the ladies room, just to be sure. Two elderly women were washing their hands and yelled for security as soon as they saw him. He tried to assure them he was looking for someone, but they weren't buying it and continued to fuss.

The coffee shop was on the other side of the station. Victor ran through the crowds, dodging people with loads of luggage, as well as restless children playing in the aisles. He accidentally knocked down a young boy who was playing with a GameBoy system. The small hand-held game went flying across the floor, and batteries scattered when the boy fell to the floor. Victor apologized profusely and bent down to help the boy back to his feet. That's when the boy saw the gun in Victor's pants.

"I'm really sorry kid, I'll buy you a new one. I promise."

"Wow! Are you a cop?" The excited child asked.

By that time the child's parents came running over to see if he was alright, Victor apologized again and took off running.

When he finally reached the coffee shop, he stopped and adjusted his shirt. He didn't want to risk anyone else seeing the gun. He thought about calling the police, but knew that by the time he explained what was going on it might be too late. He knew that it all sounded unbelievable because he couldn't believe it himself. The coffee shop was crowded. People were reading, working on laptops and simply enjoying the hot java. Victor looked around the shop for Lisa. Towards the back, there was a woman sitting alone; she was wearing the same black and white polka dot raincoat that Lisa had on. There was no sign of Parris, which could only mean one thing. He felt nauseous. He looked around for Sean, but didn't see him anywhere. Victor proceeded over to her table. A young woman, not looking where she was going, accidentally bumped into him and spilled coffee on his pants. Unfazed, Victor brushed away the hot liquid and continued towards the table. Once he was directly behind her, he reached out and touched her shoulder. Two undercover cops, sitting at the table next to her, immediately jumped up, grabbed his arms and held him at gunpoint.

"Don't move! Sean Edwards, you're under arrest. You have the right to remain silent. If you give up this right, you…." The officer said directly in his ear as he twisted his arm further behind his back.

Parris quickly turned around, only to find that the man they had apprehended wasn't Sean.

"Officers wait! That's not Sean! Stop!" she yelled removing the raincoat.

Within minutes, two additional officers had joined them and a crowd had begun to form. Victor was trying to explain who he was, but they weren't listening. When they found the gun, they slammed him up against the wall and put the handcuffs on him.

"Stop it! Please! You've got the wrong guy, this is my fiancé!" She said. "He's not Sean!"

"But, I don't understand. You said the suspect was supposed to meet Mrs. Baxter here." One officer said as he eased his grip on Victor's arm. "That's the only reason we were willing to use you as a decoy. Otherwise, we would have never put your life in danger Ms. Reed." He replied.

"I know, I know." Parris said pushing past the policeman. "Victor, are you alright?"

"Yeah, I'm fine." He said as the other officer unlocked the cuffs. "Where's Lisa?"

"She's in custody." Parris replied kissing him on the lips. "Where's Sean?"

Victor took a deep breath, "Sean's dead."

The crowd had grown twice its size and everyone was whispering trying to find out what was happening. The other officers were trying to disburse the crowd.

"Oh my God, Victor, what happened?" She asked in disbelief.

"It was self defense, an accident; he came after me and…." Victor replied looking directly at the officer in charge. "And I shot him."

"Is this the weapon that was used?" The officer asked holding up the gun.

"Yes." Victor said reaching for Parris' hand.

"Do you have any witnesses to corroborate your story?"

"No." Victor replied lowering his head.

"Sir, we're going to need you to come down to the station so that we can get a statement."

"No problem officer."

Chapter

63

The police did not finish questioning Victor until midnight. He suggested that she spend the night at her parents and promised to call as soon as he finished.

"Hello, are you awake?"

"Uh, yeah, are you okay?" she replied. "I dozed off for a second I guess."

"I thought they'd never finish. I must have answered every question at least twice and they still weren't satisfied. They were trying to get me to admit to premeditated murder."

"Premeditated? It was clearly self defense."

"Well, it wasn't that clear. Apparently, when Sean or Lisa broke into my house, one of them logged onto my laptop and sent several threatening emails to Sean's email account."

"What? How'd they do that?" Parris asked.

"It's really my fault. When we broke up, I never thought to change my email password on the AOL account or anything else for that matter and Lisa had access to all my stuff. Once we divorced, I never thought twice about it. Besides, I use my Blackberry most of the time."

"Damn. You still should have changed your password. How did they get hold of your laptop?"

"Lisa, she was the mastermind behind the emails because Sean wasn't slick enough to think of something so devious. Anyway, my house is a crime scene, so anything in it is considered evidence, laptop included. Now people are committing crimes and leaving evidence in their email and that's one of the first places the cops look because there's always a paper trail."

"So what did the emails say?"

"The first email was from Sean to me telling me about this fine sistah he met and saying how much he liked her. Then Lisa would reply from my account sounding jealous and shit. Then, a couple of emails later, I told him I could take his girl if I wanted and some other ridiculous nonsense that made me sound like a damn lunatic."

"What? You mean he turned the whole thing around?"

"Yes."

"That is so deep. I had no idea." She replied.

"But P, the kicker was the final message that said I was having an affair with his girl, we were in love. Then Sean wrote something about getting her back and my response said I'd kill him if he came near her. Thus, the threat, which proves premeditation. Lisa made sure she mentioned the gun and some other nonsense. So, this was far from being clear-cut, self defense. It could have really been ugly."

"Well, how did they finally figure out that it was Sean and Lisa trying to kill us?"

"Lisa confessed and there were cell phone records between the two of them, plus a receipt that was found in Lisa's car for the hidden video camera."

Chapter

64

Saturday, September 20th, Victor arrived at the Reed's home at 6:30am and everyone was still sleeping. Coleman answered the door in his silk pajamas scratching where men like to scratch.

"Victor, is everything alright?" he said yawning.

"I'm good. How's Parris?"

"She'll be okay; she's been through a lot. But she's going to need a strong man to help her get through this one. Do you think you can handle it?"

"I know I can Sir. I love your daughter and I promise, as God's my witness, I will never do anything to hurt her." Victor replied. "And Mr. Reed, for the record, I need a strong woman."

"Alright then son, go on and get your bride!" Coleman said patting him on the back. "Her room is the second door on the left. She's probably still sleeping, like I should be right now."

Victor walked quietly up the steps and down the hall. The door still had an old sticker that read, "PARRIS'S ROOM – ENTER AT YOUR OWN RISK!" Victor smiled at the irony of the message because when they hung up last night, neither of them mentioned the wedding, which was scheduled to take place in a few hours. He walked over to the bed and knelt down beside her, he thought she looked like an angel sleeping peacefully. He watched her for a few minutes and then leaned over and kissed her gently on the lips. She stirred a little and then opened her eyes.

"Hey baby." He said.

"What are you doing here? What time is it?" she said rubbing her eyes.

"It's only six-fifteen. It's still early."

"Oh."

Parris sat up in the bed and Victor remained on his knees. They remained silent for about a minute and then both began to speak at the same time.

"You go first."

"No, you go first."

"Okay, I'll go." Victor said. "The last twenty-four hours turned out to be the worse day of my life. I can't begin to tell you how sorry I am, for everything Parris."

"I know, me too."

"We're supposed to get married in a few hours and if you tell me you don't want to anymore, I understand. I mean, hell, the video is real and unfortunately it's me, but I wish it was R. Kelly." he said laughing.

Parris laughed too. "Good one."

He grabbed her hands and looked into her eyes.

"Please forgive me. I was very drunk and didn't use good judgment. I know it's going to be hard as hell for you to forget, but if you could find it in your heart to forgive me, even if we don't get married, it would mean a lot to me."

"I forgive you Victor."

"You do?" he said excited. "I mean, thank you." He said kissing the back of her hand. "I love you P."

"I love you too. Now, what do you mean, *even if we don't get married?*"

"Well, after that shit, most women would have kicked my ass to the curb."

"I'm *not* most women."

"You certainly are not. So, do you still want to marry me?" he asked still unsure of the answer.

Parris got out of bed and walked over to look out the window. The sun was coming up past the trees and the sky was crystal clear, not a cloud in the sky. The storm had passed. She closed her eyes and silently thanked God for such a beautiful day, when she opened them, she noticed a pretty Blue Jay sitting on a branch of the tree directly across from her window. Parris turn around and looked at Victor.

"A wise woman once told me to learn from her mistakes and thankfully, I have." Then she walked over and opened the bedroom door.

"Daddy! Come get Victor because he's not supposed to see the bride before the wedding!"

Chapter

65

The church was full of guests patiently waiting for the nuptials to take place; most of them were completely unaware of how close this event had come to being cancelled.

Victor walked out with Reverend Williams and stood proudly at the alter awaiting his bride. His black tuxedo fit like a glove and he was, in fact, a handsome black prince. When the music started, everyone turned around anxiously with cameras ready to snap the first pictures.

Kenya and Kevin were first. The Maid of Honor and best man were next. Shelly and Vincent walked arm in arm looking relaxed and smiling from ear to ear. Everyone stood when the traditional wedding march began. Coleman Reed, standing proudly, wrapped his eldest daughter's arm around his and proceeded to walk her down the long, aisle lined with rose petals. Parris was a vision to behold. Her gown was exquisite and she could hear everyone quietly ooohing and aaahing as she strolled down the aisle.

Helen sat silently weeping in her seat, this time they were tears of joy. She was so proud of her daughter, not many women could endure the tragedies that occurred during the past few hours and manage to look so beautiful. Victor's mother, Lillian, sat calmly on the opposite side of the aisle fanning with an ivory colored lace fan.

Victor, was awestruck when he saw her and he eagerly waited, for what seemed like a lifetime, for his bride to meet him at the alter. When Coleman handed her off, they couldn't take their eyes off of each other. It was almost as if they were standing alone, just the two of them, together.

After they recited their vowels, Reverend Williams gave the groom permission to kiss his bride. Victor took a deep breathe, he lifted her veil and looked deep into her eyes.

"My world is empty without you, Parris. I love you."

Parris closed her eyes holding back tears and feeling thankful that the voices she once feared were silent.

Five Years Later

The nurse instructed Parris to push when she felt another contraction. She had been in labor for the past twelve hours; this pregnancy was definitely a lot harder than the first. Parris had gained fifty pounds with this one, compared to the twenty-five pounds she gained and lost immediately with Ebony. Victor held her hand, helping her breathe through the pain. This one was going to be a boy, if he ever decided to grace them with his presence. He would be a junior and Victor couldn't be happier.

Helen, Coleman and Shelly waited patiently in the waiting room trying to entertain Ebony while she played with her dolls and asked a thousand questions about her little brother.

Kevin was on his way to the hospital and now that he and Shelly were engaged, he couldn't wait to start working on a child of their own.

"I wonder how she's making out." Helen said anxiously. "This boy has given her the dickens from day one."

"He sure has, I think she threw up every day for the first three months. I pray I don't have to go through that mess." Shelly replied.

"Mom-mom, what are dickens?" Ebony asked.

Everyone laughed as Helen tried to explain. The doctor came out and let everyone know that Parris was fine and that she had a health baby boy, weighing 8lbs, 10ozs.

"He's a big boy!" Coleman said proudly.

"We knew he was going to be big because Parris was big as a house." Shelly said laughing.

"I wouldn't laugh too loud, chile. You'll be next and with those healthy hips of yours, you're likely to be twice her size." Helen replied.

"Not in this life time, I won't." Shelly insisted.

"Okay, we'll see."

"When can I see my brother?" Ebony asked jumping up and down. "I wanna see little Victor!"

"I'll send a nurse out to get you. It'll be just a few minutes. Congratulations!" the doctor said and then walked away.

Victor came out about five minutes later with an unlit cigar in his mouth. His chest was poked out and he was grinning from ear to ear.

Ebony went running across the room and jumped up into her daddy's arms.

"Hey, Pumpkin! You're gonna be a big sister!" he said kissing her on the forehead.

"Where's he at? I wanna see him." She replied.

"He's with Mommy. Come on yall, let's go see my beautiful new son."

Victor handed Coleman and Kevin a cigar as they walked into the room. Parris was holding their new bundle of joy. Ebony carefully climbed up on the bed and sat next to her mother giggling and trying to touch his pudgy face.

"Can I hold him Mommy? Please." She begged.

"Sure, you can baby, now, be careful and hold on tight." Parris replied placing the baby gently in her arms.

"He looks just like one of my dollies, except he's a boy. His hair is so curly. Can I comb it Mommy?"

"Not right now honey, he's sleeping, just let him sleep okay?"

"Okay, I'll comb it later." Ebony replied looking very happy to finally be a big sister.

Coleman was snapping pictures left and right, while Victor and Kevin talked about all the big plans Victor had in store for Victor Jr., from Sixers basketball camp to military school. Shelly sat on the other side of the bed, while Helen placed another delivery of flowers on the window sill.

"Well girl, you did it again." Shelly said.

"I sure did, but, you best believe that will be the last time. God, that was the worse pain I've ever felt. I had to get ten stitches!"

"Ouch." Shelly said making a face.

"Oh yeah, my behind is going to be hurting for a minute."

"Make sure they give you some Tucks pads, P, and as soon as you get home you take a Sitz bath. That'll help with the pain." Helen assured her.

"What's a Sitz bath, Mommy? Can I take one too?" Ebony interjected. "And can little Victor take one with me?"

"No, baby you don't need to take one, just me okay? Parris replied adjusting the baby in her daughter's arms. "Where's Kenya? Did anyone call her?"

"She called and said she would see you tomorrow. She's hosting a fundraising event for the Mayor and can't get away tonight." Helen said.

"The Mayor? I'm impressed." Parris replied.

"Her event planning business is really doing well, she told me about a couple of her most recent clients and they're pretty impressive." Shelly said.

"She's finally maturing and I pray she sticks with this event planning thing because she's really good at it. Helen added. "Lord knows, anything is better than her flittin' and flyin' from this to that like a young jitterbug."

"I'm just glad that girl is finally putting all that schooling and money I spent to good use. Now, maybe she can start paying me back some of the money she owes me." Coleman said.

"Don't count on it Daddy. That money is history." Parris replied laughing. "Kenya's changed, but she hasn't changed that much!"

Chapter

66

Now that Victor made partner and his name was on the door of Franklin, Brown and Baxter, he was able to spend more time working from home and his commute to New York was reduced significantly. After the wedding, Parris immediately sold her house and moved into Victor's because it was bigger. She was a little apprehensive about moving into the home that Victor once shared with Lisa, but he reassured her that it would only be for a short time until they found another house. He held true to his word and within six months, his house was sold and they were moved into a house they had built, not too far from where her parents lived.

The neighborhood was quiet and they had become very friendly with their next door neighbors, Kathy and Jonathan Steinberg. Jonathan was also an attorney at a firm in Philadelphia and Kathy was a nurse at the nearby hospital. The Steinberg's moved into their home about a week after Parris and Victor. They also had a little girl, named Sarah, who was four years old. Ebony and Sarah hit it off immediately. Parris liked to joke and call them Ebony and Ivory because they were always together.

Parris was enjoying her extended maternity leave by helping Shelly plan her reception. Kevin wanted to get married on Valentine's Day and she could not refuse him because she managed to get him to agree to a whole lot more. Shelly didn't want a big wedding ceremony, she simply wanted to go down to City Hall and get it over with. She did, however, insist on having reception at a hotel. Kevin was such a sweetheart because he was willing to go along with her wishes, even though he had a big family and they wanted a big church wedding with all the trimmings. Shelly wanted a band and a DJ and was willing to pay for a four hour open bar. "Parris, I want everyone to have a great time with good food and plenty to drink. Kevin's cousin works at the hotel and was able to get us a good deal." Shelly said as she reviewed the menu options.

"That's great. Do you want a sit down dinner or buffet?" Parris asked.

"The per plate prices are outrageous, so I think buffet will be my best bet." Shelly replied.

Ebony and Sarah came running through the kitchen yelling and screaming as they played tag. Their cocker spaniel, Cookie, followed behind barking and chasing after them.

"Ebony! Stop running before you get hurt and wake up your brother!" Parris yelled. "Are you girls ready for lunch?"

They both answered yes in unison.

"Can I have peanut butter and jelly Mommy?" Ebony asked sitting down at the kitchen table.

"You sure can. Would you like one too, Sarah?" Parris said grabbing the loaf of bread.

"I would like a tuna fish sandwich on wheat bread, please." Sarah answered politely.

Shelly couldn't help but laugh at the little girl's very specific lunch request. Parris chuckled too because every time Sarah came over, she asked for the same thing and every time, Parris told her no. No one in their house liked tuna fish, so she didn't buy it.

"Sarah, I don't have any tuna fish, honey. How about a peanut butter and jelly sandwich?" Parris asked.

"If that's all you have, I guess that's okay." Sarah replied sitting down next to Ebony.

"Sarah, we *never* have tuna fish, so why do you keep asking my mom to make it?" Ebony said.

"Because I was hoping your mom would buy some." Sarah replied.

"Not just for you, dummy!" Ebony said.

"Ebony! We do not call people names. Apologize to Sarah." Parris said to her daughter.

"Sorry Sarah." Ebony reluctantly muttered.

Shelly didn't want Ebony to see her laughing, so she went upstairs. "P, you're gonna have your hands full with that one. I'll be right back; I'm going to check on little man."

"Girl, who are you tellin'?" Parris said placing the sandwiches in front of the girls. "Do you want chocolate or strawberry milk?"

"Strawberry!" they both replied.

The telephone rang and Parris walked into the den so she could sit down.

"Hey babe, how ya feelin'?" Victor asked.

"I'm fine, my breasts are leaking, my butt hurts and I don't know which end to take care of first." She replied.

Victor thought that was hysterical. "Oh P, I don't mean to laugh, but I can picture you squeezing your boobs and holding your butt at the same time! It's quite a sight. You gotta admit that's funny!" he said still laughing.

"Well, we'll see how funny you think it is when I don't wake up when Victor starts crying at three in the morning."

"Okay, I'm sorry. I apologize. Seriously."

"Yeah, that's what I thought." Parris replied turning the channel to 'The View'.

"How is my little guy doing?"

"Oh, here he is now, Shelly went and got him. He's fine and I'm sure he's hungry."

Shelly kissed him on both of his fat cheeks and then handed him to Parris and sat down in the recliner to hear what Star Jones was saying about her wedding. Parris continued talking and began breast feeding. She could hear Ebony and Sarah arguing and asked Victor to be quiet for a second while she listened. They usually got along famously, but the last few times they've been together it's been different. Ebony was beginning to get very bossy and started name calling. Parris initially contributed it to having a new baby around and the lack of attention focused on her, but now she was beginning to think it might be something else.

"My friend says your hair is ugly!" Ebony said.

"No its not, my mom says I have hair just like her and she has pretty hair!" Sarah replied.

"It's ugly and you only have one ponytail! My friend said two ponies is better, like mine!" Ebony said sticking her tongue out.

By this time, Parris had told Victor she would call him back and she was peeking behind the wall to see what was going on. Sarah looked like she was going to cry and Ebony was still teasing her. Ebony looked exactly like Victor, except she was Parris' chocolate brown complexion. She had long, thick black hair that she hated to have combed. Every day was a medieval torture session and tears were inevitable, but twice a week Parris took her to the salon so they could deal with it. She didn't seem to cry as much when there were other people watching. Now, she was swinging her thick ponytails back in forth like a spoiled brat.

"Ebony!" Parris yelled while still feeding little Victor.

She scared the crap out of both of them and Ebony froze, wide-eyed looking like the cat that ate the canary.

"What is wrong with you? I have had enough of you for one day! Go to your room."

Ebony got up from her chair and headed for the stairs.

"And apologize, *again,* to Sarah."

"Sorry." She said as she slowly walked way.

"I'm sorry Sarah; I don't know what's gotten into her lately. Come on sweetie, I'll walk you home. I think you girls need a little break."

Chapter

67

Later that night, while Victor was giving the baby a bath, Parris decided to go talk to her daughter to see what was bothering her. Ebony was sitting on her bed in her pink Dora the Explorer pajamas reading her Dora the Explorer book. Parris went in and sat down beside her.

"Hi Mommy."

"Hi Pumpkin. What are you reading?"

"Dora the Explorer. Mommy, Dora has to find the missing key, so she can free Boots from the magic castle." She replied.

"Oh, wow, I hope she finds it." Parris said.

"She will Mommy, Dora's smart."

"Ebony, I want to talk about what happened this afternoon. Why were you treating Sarah so mean, I thought she was your best friend?"

"She was but, I've got a new best friend." Ebony replied still looking at her book.

"Who? Did you meet her at day care?"

"Yes."

"What's her name?"

"I don't know." She said shrugging her shoulders.

"Well, what does she look like?"

"I don't know."

"Ebony, how is she your friend, if you don't know her name and you don't even know what she looks like?"

"I don't know Mommy; I guess I'm just being silly. Can you read the rest of Dora to me?"

"I want you to stop being silly and mean to Sarah or she's not going to be your friend anymore, okay?"

"Okay, Mommy. I love you."

"I love you too. I think you need to go to bed now, I'll finish reading Dora tomorrow night."

"Good night, Mommy."

"Sleep tight baby." Parris said as she tucked her in and kissed her good night.

Parris turned on the night-light and left the bedroom door ajar. When she got to the master bedroom, Victor had managed to bathe, feed and put little Victor down for the night. Victor was also bathed, fed and eagerly waiting for his wife to come to bed.

"Thanks Babe, for dealing with the baby, I can't believe he actually went to sleep so early tonight." She said as she took off her robe and climbed into bed.

"See, what you don't understand is that my son and I have an understanding. He said kissing her neck. "I told him, when Daddy needs playtime with Mommy, he needs to cooperate and go to sleep for at least two hours."

Parris started to giggle because he was kissing her all over now, from her fingers tips to her ear lobes.

"And he agreed to this little playtime arrangement?"

"Of course, why wouldn't he, I'm his father?"

"Maybe, because I'm his *mother* and I can't get him to sleep long enough for me to even take a bath."

"That's because you don't have the touch." He replied as he rolled her on top. "See how I did that? It's all in the touch."

"Oh yeah, you're good alright, but you know I can't do anything yet, right?"

"I know, but I thought maybe you could hook a brother up while he waits." He said smiling.

"You got the magic touch, right, hook it up yourself." Parris teased as she rolled off and back onto her side of the bed.

"Awl P, good one. Are you serious?" Victor asked sitting up.

"No, I'll hook you up, but first I want to talk to you about Ebony. She was acting a fool today with Sarah. She called her a dummy and was teasing her about her ponytails."

"You know how kids are at her age; she's just going through some changes now that Victor's here. It'll pass."

"I hope so because she's gonna make me break her little neck if it doesn't. You should have heard her; she was being mean and nasty."

"All right now Mommy, why don't you come over here and be nasty for me?"

Chapter

68

Two weeks went by and Ebony was on her best behavior, no more name calling and Ebony and Ivory were best friends again. It was time for Parris to go back to work and her mother volunteered to watch the kids twice a week. The other three days Parris enrolled them in a new daycare center at her job. Everyone was raving about Kids Close By. It was clean and appeared to be a safe and nurturing environment for children. The daily rates were a little more expensive, but the convenience made up for the price. Having your children right down stairs was a life and time saver and gave every mother working in the building at least eight hours of not worrying about their children, so they could concentrate on their jobs. Maria enrolled her kids as well and she and Parris took turns checking on them.

When she dropped the kids off, she admitted to Victor that she felt bad about leaving Victor since he was only two and a half months old. Victor tried to reassure her, but told her if she wasn't ready, she should take some more time off. She had the plenty of vacation time and her boss even offered her an extended leave of absence if she really needed it. Mr. Clancy had five kids of his own and even though they were all grown, he still remembered what it was like to have a newborn.

Ann Harrison was the manager at Kids Close By. She was wonderful with the kids and Ebony liked her right away. Once Ann showed her the collection of Dora the Explorer books, toys and games, she was in heaven and barely said good-bye. Victor Jr. was asleep in his portable crib when Parris finished giving instructions, double-checking the baby bag and finally left.

Maria had already dropped her kids off when Parris got to the office. She had a stack of messages, a pile of mail and a ton of emails to return. It was a little overwhelming, but she started right in and slowly but surely worked through it. Gladys retired last year and Paul moved to another department, so they were a little short-handed. Hiring a new person was one of the first things on her list of things to do.

By lunch time, Parris was exhausted and needed a caffeine boost to tackle the second half of the day. She walked into the break room and immediately thought of Sean. She had not thought about him in a long time and they rarely spoke his name after that fatal night. She refilled her Gemini mug and added three spoonfuls of sugar. As she was walking back to her office, her cell phone rang and she didn't recognize the number.

"Hello, Mrs. Baxter?"

"Yes, this is Mrs. Baxter."

"This is Ann Harrison from Kids Close By. We've had a little incident and would like for you to stop down." She said calmly.

"Oh my God, is everything alright? Is Victor okay?"

"Oh, yes, he's fine. It's Ebony. If you could stop by my office that would be great."

"I'll be right there."

Parris left her coffee mug on top of a file cabinet and headed for the elevators. Her mind was racing on the way down; she couldn't imagine what the problem was with Ebony and she hoped she wasn't starting to act out again. When she walked through the doors, she could see Ebony sitting in Ann's office; Ann got up immediately to greet her at the door.

"Mrs. Baxter, thank you for coming down so quickly. We hate to bother the parents unless absolutely necessary, but in this case, I thought you should be contacted.

"Thanks, and please, call me Parris."

Ann and Parris walked in the office and Ebony was sitting in the chair swinging her legs. She was wearing one of Parris' favorite outfits today, a red cable knit sweater with a puffy white snowman on the front, along with a pair of Baby Gap jeans. Red bows were tied in each ponytail. She didn't look upset or like she had been crying, she was actually smiling.

"Hi Mommy."

"Hello Ebony, why has Ms. Harrison called me down here?"

"I don't know. I didn't do anything." Ebony replied innocently.

"Ebony, that's not exactly true, now is it?" Ann asked. "You hit Brittney in the head with the block, didn't you?"

Ebony did not answer; she just kept swinging her legs happily in the chair.

"Ebony! Answer Ms. Harrison. Did you hit Brittney?"

Ebony adjusted herself in the chair and folded her hands lacing her small fingers together.

"Brittney took my book and she wouldn't give it back. Mommy, she hid it so I couldn't find it!" Ebony said.

"That's not a reason to hit someone. What did I tell you about keeping your hands to yourself?" Parris said.

"Not to." Ebony replied.

"But Mommy, my friend told me Brittney was playing a trick on me and I had to get my Dora book back!" Ebony said on the verge of tears.

"What friend Ebony? Who are you talking about?" Parris said raising her voice.

"She's not here right now." Ebony replied. "Never mind."

"Ebony, we do not tolerate hitting, so I hope that we won't have this problem again. Is that understood?" Ann said.

"Yes." Ebony said.

"Yes, what?" Parris interjected.

"Yes Ms. Harrison."

When her daughter was excused, Parris explained to Ann that she thought her behavior was a result of little Victor coming into the picture. Ann agreed that having a new addition in the family can have a big impact on the other children. She said she completely understood and recommended that Parris plan something special for just the two of them, a 'girls' day out. Parris thought that was a great idea and thanked Ann for her understanding and assistance. Ms. Harrison also promised to contact her immediately if there were any other problems.

Chapter

69

When the weekend came, Parris took Ann's advice and made arrangements to spend the entire day with Ebony. Victor kept the baby and was looking forward to spending some father and son time alone.

Parris made an appointment at the salon for the both of them, followed by lunch at Chucky Cheese and a trip to the Please Touch Museum in Philly. If they had enough time, she promised to take her to the movies too. When Ebony heard what she had planned for the day, she did not appear to be very enthused, but once she told her it was going to be just the two of them, she was delighted.

Ebony was a perfect angel for the first half of the day. She even managed to control the tears while she was getting her hair done. The afternoon was a different story. At the Please Touch Museum, there was a small altercation with a little boy who jumped in front of Ebony while she was in line to see the butterfly exhibit. Parris wasn't sure who started it because she was chatting with another parent, but by the time she realized what was happening, Ebony had pushed the little boy and the little boy pushed her back, except he wasn't that little. He was around seven and big for his age. The mother wasn't apologetic and didn't seem too concerned. Parris gave her a piece of her mind anyway and advised her son to keep his hands to himself. She responded nonchalantly and went on her way. But not before saying she didn't want to hear crap from a mother whose little girl uses words like "jerk". Ebony did call the boy a jerk and Parris wasn't happy about it, but it was true. Usually, dummy or stupid was her insult of choice, but today, she expanded her vocabulary with another bad word. In the car, Ebony sat in the car seat quietly and listened to a lecture about naming calling.

Parris was tired and annoyed, so the movie was out. She picked up some Chinese food on the way home and couldn't wait to tell Victor what happened. Victor was like silly putty when it came to Ebony, especially if those big brown eyes filled with tears. She looked exactly like him and sometimes acted like him too. Before Parris could close the front door, Ebony was in his arms, explaining what happened, talking a mile a minute. Needless to say, Victor was ready to go back to the museum and find the woman.

"P, I know you got wit her?"

"Of course, but she had the nerve to act like she it wasn't a big deal."

"She better be glad I wasn't there because I would have grabbed her like this and made her beg for mercy!" He replied tickling and kissing Ebony until she screamed for him to stop.

Parris went into kitchen and started setting the table.

"We're using paper plates. I'm not washing dishes tonight. Ebony, go wash your hands, so we can eat." Parris said. "Victor, is the baby asleep?"

"No, he's not here. Your mom came and got him for a little while."

"Oh, okay, did she say what time she would bring him back?"

"No, you should give her a call."

Parris walked into the den, where Victor was sitting in his recliner, working on his laptop. Cookie was sleeping at his feet.

"So, since you didn't have to watch your son, what did you do all day Mr. Baxter?"

"Jon and I played a round of gulf and I kicked his butt." Victor bragged. "Do you think your day alone with Ebony helped?"

Parris threw the dish towel over her shoulder and shrugged. "I hope so. She seems to react so negatively to anything that doesn't go her way or makes her mad."

"Like mother, like daughter." Victor replied.

"What? I'm not like that, am I?"

"P, you sorta are, you just don't physically lash out, but verbally you can hold your own."

"I can't believe you just said that."

"I'm just being honest babe. You have to be patient; hopefully she'll out grow it."

Ebony came prancing back into the den and sat down in front of the television. "Daddy, can I turn it on Nickelodeon?"

"Yes Pumpkin."

"That's the real problem right there." Parris whispered to Victor. "You spoil her." She said and walked back into the kitchen.

Parris decided to call her mom, she missed and wanted to see little Victor. Twenty minutes later, Helen showed up with the baby and another stuffed animal. She felt compelled to buy a new toy every time she saw him; his nursery was overflowing with furry, stuffed animals. She did not stay long because she had a pie in the oven and couldn't count on her father to take it out in time.

Parris spent the rest of the evening thinking about what her husband said. She hoped and prayed that she did not pass her unappealing traits down to her daughter.

Chapter

70

When Parris woke up Sunday morning, it was very cold and the temperature had dropped during the night down to twenty-eight degrees. She got out of bed and immediately went to check the thermostat. Victor was going to fuss about the gas bill at the end of the month, but she didn't care, it was freezing outside and chilly in the house. Everyone was still sleeping and the house was quiet. Parris took the opportunity to read the Sunday paper and enjoy a cup of green tea in peace.

Little Victor's baptism ceremony was scheduled during the church service today. Shelly was his Godmother and she picked out the cutest double-breasted white suit with matching patent leather shoes for him to wear. Helen picked out a pink and white lace dress for Ebony. Parris thought she paid too much for the dress, but Helen insisted she needed to have something special to wear so she wouldn't feel left out.

Within an hour, every member of the Baxter household woke up one by one. Victor was first and he was in the mood to cook a big breakfast, so Parris allowed him to proceed uninterrupted. Ebony was next. She wasn't a morning person, so she sat quietly in front of the television until breakfast was ready. Finally, little Victor woke up crying at the top of his lungs. He must have had a bad dream because he was irritable and normally woke up in a good mood. Parris had been expressing her milk and putting it in bottles for convenience, but he obviously craved her breast, because as soon as she sat down in her grandmother's old rocking chair and put her nipple to his mouth, he began sucking contently.

Kevin and Shelly came by the house before going to the church to see the kids beforehand and take pictures.

Kevin was Victor's Godfather and had a video camera in hand to capture every moment.

"Is everyone ready? Come on, we're going to be late!" Parris yelled up the stairs, as she finished packing the baby bag.

"I'm coming, everyone's ready." Victor replied as the came down the steps. "Come on Ebony, baby, let's go. Mommy's ready."

"Okay Daddy, I'm coming." Ebony replied.

Ebony came happily bouncing down the stairs, looking like a little princess in her lace dress. She begged to wear her hair out like a big girl today, so Parris tied a pink ribbon around her head and the thick curls were bouncing and behaving as she walked down the stairs.

Everyone piled into the SUV and headed to the church. Kenya and her parents were already seated and holding seats for everyone. After the announcements, Reverend Williams called the family up to the altar for the baptism. Victor Jr. slept through the entire ceremony; he didn't even wake up when Reverend Williams dripped the holy water on his forehead.

Parris invited everyone back to the house after church for brunch. She had it catered and they were already set up when the got back to the house. Lillian and Vincent also flew in for the weekend to attend the ceremony; they were staying at an Embassy Suites nearby. Victor wanted them to stay at the house, but Lillian insisted she would be more comfortable at the hotel. The house was full of family and friends, little Victor was being passed around from person to person and had become irritable, so Parris took him out of his misery and put him down for a nap. Ebony was playing Candy Land with Sarah and her other cousins, so far, everyone was getting along.

Kenya had a new male friend and invited him over. His name was Cleveland and yes, he looked like a Cleveland. He was very conservative, neatly dressed and well spoken. He even wore a bow tie. He was the complete opposite of every man she had dated in the past. She was obviously maturing in more ways than one. Coleman instantly took a liking to him because he was an avid golfer. He was also an accountant.

"Kenya, where did you find Poindexter?" Shelly asked once the women were all alone. "He seems nice."

"We met at the Mayor's event I did a couple of weeks ago. He's actually very nice and not as corny as he looks." Kenya replied.

"Really? That bow tie looks like its going to choke him, go loosen it up for him." Parris said laughing.

"See, I knew you guys were gonna to try to clown me, but I don't care, he treats me good and fucks like a stallion!" Kenya said confidently. "So, don't be fooled by the bow tie, ladies."

"I heard that." Shelly said. "Maybe I need to buy a bow tie for Kevin."

The women continued chatting in the kitchen while the men talked in the den. Ebony and the other children were playing in her room. It was turning out to be a wonderful day, despite the bitter cold weather. After dinner, Helen served her famous homemade apple pie and vanilla ice cream.

"Mom, you know this is the last thing I need to be eating right now." Parris said. "I've still got ten pounds to lose."

"Don't worry P, I love you just the way you are." Victor said giving her a kiss.

"Thank you baby." She replied. "See yall, my husband loves me fat and all!"

Everyone laughed and continued talking about their weight and the affects of old age. Ebony interrupted the adult's conversation when she yelled downstairs at the top of her lungs.

"Moooommmmmeeee! Victor's crying!"

Parris jumped and ran up the steps quickly, Ebony made it sound like something was wrong, but when she reached his nursery, everything was fine. He might have been crying, but now he had found his thumb and was sucking contently. His diaper was wet, so Parris changed him. Ebony came into the room and stood beside the changing table.

"What's wrong with him Mommy? Why is he making all that noise?"

"What noise? He's quiet now, his diaper was wet, so maybe that's why he woke up crying." Parris replied.

"He makes too much noise and why does he pee so much?" she said with an attitude.

"What are you talking about Ebony, he's a baby, and he can't help it."

It was almost like he heard her and wanted to prove her right, because he started crying again.

"See, Mommy, make him stop!" Ebony said holding her hands over her ears. "He makes to much noise!"

Parris finished putting on his new diaper and picked him up hoping he would stop crying.

"Ebony, why don't you hush and go back to your room. You're making too much noise now." She said patting his back.

"I don't like him anymore." She muttered as she walked out of the room, but Parris didn't hear her.

Chapter

71

After a busy weekend with the children, Parris was happy to get back to work and deal with adults. Victor had another big case and would probably be staying in New York for a night or two. Helen volunteered to help out if Parris ran into a jam. Parris felt pretty confident that she could handle the two kids on her own with no problems. Fortunately, she only had two meetings and a couple of phone calls to return, other than that, the day was light. Shelly was getting married on Friday and the reception was going to be on Saturday. Parris agreed to meet her downtown at lunch time to go look at a few dresses. Shelly couldn't decide between a winter white wool suit or a dress. They went in a few stores and finally found the perfect suit in Bloomingdales.

"Oh, Shelly, that looks great, I love the rhinestone buttons." Parris said.

"I think I'll wear my diamond studs with this and maybe get a simple necklace to match, what do you think?" Shelly replied turning around to see the back in the mirror.

"That'll be sharp. As a matter of fact, I have a diamond necklace that Victor got me on our honeymoon that would look good. That can be what you borrow. Now, all you need is something blue."

"I've already got that covered. I found a very pretty pale blue bra and thong from Victoria's Secret the other day. So, I'm all set." Shelly replied. "Thanks P for coming with me."

"Girl, you know that's no problem. I can't believe you're really getting married."

"I know, me either."

"Who would have thought that five years ago, we would have both met two great guys, who were already friends, fallen in love and married them."

Shelly laughed, "It is special, ain't it? And between you and me P, I'm *really* nervous; I hope I can do this whole wife and kids thing."

"Don't worry, you'll be fine and I will be right here to help you through it." Parris said giving her a hug.

When five o'clock rolled around, Parris rolled out the door. She wanted to get the kids home, fed and in the bed, so that she could watch a movie that was coming on HBO. Ms. Harrison said that both children had a good day and Ebony was her helper today.

"Ms. Harrison said you were a good helper today." Parris said putting little Victor in the car seat.

"I was and I got to help hand out the snacks too." Ebony said smiling.

"You are getting to be such a big girl, I am so proud of you."

"Thank you Mommy."

"When we get home, I may need you to help me out since Daddy's not going to be home, okay?"

"Where's he at?"

"He's got a lot of work to do, so he's going to stay in New York tonight."

"Aw, man. I wanted to tell him I was a good helper today."

"How about if we call him after you get your bath and you can tell him then."

"Oh, goodie."

After a quick dinner of chicken nuggets, mashed potatoes and broccoli, Parris gave Ebony a bath and helped her get into her pajamas. She wanted to take a quick shower herself before the movie, so she prepared a bottle for Victor and asked her little helper to watch him until she got out. Ebony was more than happy to help and Parris made sure they were both sitting in the middle of her bed. She even turned the television on Nickelodeon so that Ebony wouldn't move and propped Victor up between some pillows while his big sister held the bottle.

Parris undressed and got in the shower, but did not close the door. She yelled out over the water to make sure everything was okay.

"I'm okay, Mommy, he's still drinking!" Ebony yelled back. "He's really thirsty!"

Parris checked her underarms and she needed to shave. She figured another minute or so, wouldn't hurt. She called Ebony's name just to keep contact with her, but this time she did not answer.

"Ebony!"

Parris turned off the shower, "Ebony baby, are you okay?"

Dead silence. Parris started to panic. She dropped the razor and with soap running down the side of her body, she stepped out of the shower and grabbed a towel. When she walked into the master bedroom, where she left her four year old little helper for no more than a few minutes, she could not believe her eyes.

"Ebony! What are you doing?" She screamed.

Before she could answer, Parris ran over to the bed, pushing her daughter out of the way and quickly removing the pillow that she was holding over little Victor's face.

"Oh, my God!, Oh, my God! What were you doing! Oh, my God, please, no!" she said picking him up to see if he was still breathing, and he was, but it was very faint. "Ebony get the phone and dial 911! Hurry!"

When the ambulance arrived, Parris sent Ebony next door to the Steinberg's, it was Kathy's day off, but she called ahead to the emergency room to give her colleagues a heads up. The paramedics were truly lifesavers and were able to get his breathing back to a normal rate. When all was said and done, little Victor was going to be okay, but he would have to stay a day or two for observation.

Parris caught a cab back home around eleven-thirty and called Victor, Shelly and her mother to tell them what had happened. Victor tried to calm her down as best he could and promised to catch the next train home.

Chapter

72

When the alarm when off at 7:15am, Victor pressed the snooze button for the second time. He didn't get home until after midnight and neither one of them could go to sleep. They finally drifted off sometime after three. Parris called out sick and they headed back to the hospital to check on Victor.

Last night, when she picked Ebony up from the Steinberg's, she was sound asleep; she didn't bother to wake her. She figured Ebony would be in a better frame of mind to talk in the morning. Parris didn't know where to begin or what questions to ask first, but she knew her eyes had not deceived her, she just couldn't believe what they had witnessed. Her four year old daughter was trying to suffocate her infant son and she had no idea why. Victor asked her to wait until the baby was back at home, so they could have the discussion together as a family, Parris agreed.

Helen and Coleman came over to the house to watch Ebony while they went back to the hospital. Little Victor was hooked up to a couple of monitors and appeared to be doing fine. By late afternoon, his pediatrician was satisfied with his results and was ready to release him. They were told to keep an eye on him and more importantly to keep an eye on Ebony. He even recommended a therapist for Ebony in order to deal with the underlying issues behind her bazaar behavior.

Later, after her parents left, Parris went upstairs to check on Ebony, her mother said she was playing in her room. As Parris walked down the hallway, she could hear her daughter talking to someone and to her knowledge, she was alone, but the closer she got to her room, she knew who she was talking to. Parris bit her lip to hold back the tears as she listened more closely to Ebony's conversation.

"No, I don't want to! Why do you keep telling me to do those mean things?"

Parris stood in the doorway and watched what she knew was her worst nightmare. She was afraid to ask, but knew she had to.

"Ebony, baby, who are you talking to?"

Ebony turned around, looked at her mother and said, "The voices Mommy, can't you hear them?"

www.ingramcontent.com/pod-product-compliance
Lightning Source LLC
Chambersburg PA
CBHW030708190726
48286CB00001B/228